FOREVER

BETROTHED #7

PENELOPE SKY

Hartwick Publishing

Forever

ONE

ANNABELLA

I was asleep in bed when my phone vibrated on the nightstand. It kept making an obnoxious sound against the wooden surface with every ring. I had no idea what time it was, but it was past midnight.

Who the hell was calling me?

When the phone stopped vibrating, I was awake enough to wipe the sleep from my eyes and sit up in bed. My eyes were still closed because they were too tired to open.

My phone vibrated again, this time with a text message.

I leaned over to grab it, my fingers fumbling in the dark until I finally got it in my grasp. I pulled it to me and blinked a couple times until my vision returned. The missed call was from Damien. And he'd also sent a text.

Liam knows.

I was half asleep, so it took me a few seconds to understand his meaning, the full significance.

The three dots popped up before he sent another message. *He's probably on his way over there now.*

I let those words sink in before I called him.

He answered right away. "Annabella—"

"What happened?" My voice was hoarse because I was still so tired.

"He had a fight tonight. Hades and I were there. Then he went to the bar, and I joined him."

"And you just blurted it out?" I asked incredulously, agitated that my precious sleep had been interrupted.

"No. I think seeing me at the bar jogged his memory, reminded him that I'd been there the night he fucked around, and he figured out that I must have told you what he did. And he also figured out why I told you..." There was no remorse or concern in his voice, as if Liam knowing the truth was completely inconsequential.

"Then what?" Knowing Liam, he tried to kill Damien on the spot.

"We had words...and I left."

"He didn't fight you?" I asked in surprise.

"He was too drunk. But he threatened to kill me later..."

I knew my life had just become complicated. Liam had been easier to deal with when he had no idea who my mysterious lover was. But now that he knew...our lives were about to change.

"He's probably on his way over there—"

Heavy fists immediately beat on the door, making a noise so loud that Damien heard it over the phone.

Liam continued to bang like an angry gorilla. "Open this fucking door, or I'll break it down."

Damien stayed calm. "I'm just down the street. I'll be there—"

"I can handle him." I kicked the sheets back and got out of bed.

"He's been drinking—"

"I'm gonna have to deal with him, regardless, Damien. He's not the kind of man to let anything go." I pulled on my sweatpants and turned on the lamp. "Go home. I'll call you when he leaves."

"Annabella—"

I hung up and put the phone on do not disturb.

Liam had started to slam his body into the door in an attempt to break it down.

"Jesus..." I jogged to the front door. "Liam!"

He stopped trying to bulldoze it. "Open this fucking door—"

"Geez, give me a second. I was asleep." I undid the chain and the locks and opened it. There was already a crack in the wood where he'd smashed his shoulder into it. I sighed in annoyance and looked at him, not afraid of the ring of fire in each eye. He looked like a psychopath that had shown up on my doorstep to kill me, like something out of a scene from a horror movie.

He stared at me with so many emotions, from rage to sadness and everything in between. He breathed so hard that his heavy breaths were louder than a siren. Now I wasn't the woman he loved. I was the person who'd played him for a fool, stabbed him in the back. He entered my apartment and forced me back before he slammed the door shut behind me.

I crossed my arms over my chest, not giving in to the intimidation. "Yes?"

He took another deep breath. "Looks like Loverboy got to you before I did." He stepped forward again, pushing me farther back just because he could. "What the fuck, Anna?" He was growling, acting like the predator about to break the neck of its prey. "You let me deal with that guy every fucking day? You let me do business with him while he was fucking my wife?"

"Ex-wife," I snapped. "I'm not the cheater, Liam." I shoved my forefinger hard into his chest. "That's you."

He grabbed my wrist and threw it aside. "I'm the cheater?" He stepped forward again, forcing me back once more. When my ass hit the back of the couch, I couldn't move any farther. I was stuck. He placed his large hands on the top of the couch, boxing me in like a prison guard. "You were spending all that time with him, every single fucking day." Atomic bombs exploded in his gaze. "I was your rebound because he didn't want you, and we were dining with him, drinking with him, and forming a friendship, while you all laughed at me." He leaned down so his face was right in front of mine. "And you have the balls to say I'm the reason this marriage failed?" His nostrils flared, and he glared. "Fuck you, Anna." Spit sprayed from his lips onto my face. "Fuck. You." He dropped his arms and stepped back. "You used me. You betrayed me. And you're the cancer that killed us. You act like I'm a piece of shit, when you're the biggest cunt in the whole fucking world."

I remained steady, with my arms across my chest, staying calm despite the profanities and the threats. He was drunk, so he probably wouldn't have said half of the things sober he was saying now. But his anger was completely real...and valid.

"You're lucky I don't hit women...because I'd do to you what I'm about to do to him."

I took a deep breath in fear, but I hid it as much as I could. I refused to give in to his threats because that would give him all the power in the situation. That would give him more adrenaline, more energy to feed off of.

His chest continued to rise and fall deeply, while the vein down his forehead bulged. The red tint to his face didn't disappear, so dark it showed all the blood that bubbled directly underneath the surface, right below his skin. "I'll see you soon." He turned back toward the door after he dismissed the conversation.

I'd expected this to go on all night because he was so anxious to break down the door and get to me. Now it was jarring, as if I'd missed something. "What's that supposed to mean?" If he had his way, there was no reason to speak at all.

He opened the slightly cracked door and stepped into the hallway. He turned back to me, staring at me with a menacing gaze. Heartbeats passed, and his thoughts were a mystery, as if he already had a detailed plot hidden up his sleeve. "You'll see."

WHEN HE WAS GONE, I called Damien.

It rang a couple times before voice mail picked up. I knew I was paranoid to fear Liam had already gotten to Damien, which was simply impossible. Then I heard the front door open and close.

I turned back around and lowered the phone.

Damien was inspecting the back side of the door, indicating he'd noticed the crack when he approached the entryway. He tested the locks to make sure they worked before he turned back to me, a mix of concern and anger in his eyes. A shadow was on his jawline, and his thick arms stretched the sleeves of his black t-shirt. His jeans were also black, along with his boots. His eyes quickly roamed over my face, neck, and arms, making sure there were no signs of abuse.

"I'm fine." I set the phone on the end table and crossed my arms over my chest. I had furniture in my apartment now, and that was all new to him. The one time he'd been there, the place had been empty except for my sad mattress on the floor.

"I was around the corner just in case." He examined the room like a detective looking for clues, trying to paint a picture of what had happened in here. He no longer looked at me like I was the only woman in the room, like he couldn't take his eyes off me. Now, he was on the job, acting like the criminal mastermind that he was. "What happened?"

"He yelled at me for a bit. That was it."

One hand slid into his pocket as he shifted his weight to one leg, bending the other knee. He was calm despite the predicament we were in. But that was a sign of a strong man. Not panicking when everything went to shit. He turned quiet, pragmatic.

"Said our marriage failed because of me...not him."

His eyes studied my face.

"I don't think he's completely wrong about that."

He kept his opinion to himself.

"But then he said some other things...and I didn't feel so bad about it anymore."

"Did he threaten you?" His deep voice reverberated against the walls.

"I'm not sure. But he did threaten you..."

He didn't give any reaction.

"Said I should consider myself lucky that he doesn't hit women, because he would do to me what he's about to do to you."

His eyes showed a slight reaction, but still very minimal. "If he really said that to you, you shouldn't feel bad at all."

Liam probably wouldn't have said that if he weren't drunk, but it was still a shitty thing to say. "Said he would see me soon, but he didn't give any details."

"Then you should stay with me."

My arms tightened over my chest. "Stay with the man who's on the top of his kill list?"

"He doesn't know who he's dealing with."

I didn't want to stay with him, though. That would only make Liam angrier. "I'm fine here."

"Then stay with Hades and Sofia."

I would never burden them when this wasn't their fight. "They have nothing to do with this. Don't involve them."

"Hades is my best friend, and you're the woman I love." He stood near the back of my couch, his frame outlined in shadow, and he studied me with those watchful eyes, like a falcon that could spot its prey a mile away. "So, he's already involved."

I held his gaze as I listened to his confession, feeling a distinct warmth move down my throat and into my tummy. When we were lovers, I would have burst into tears if he said those words. I yearned to hear them even after we broke up, fantasizing about the moment he would step through my front door and say he couldn't live without me. Now, he said it often, unafraid, and he looked me in the eye as if he was marking me as his property. He seemed like a man too rough to feel something like love, too cold to feel something that warm. I stayed quiet because I felt so much, all at the same time. I was newly divorced and still hurt by my husband's betrayal, and I felt like

I was still involved with Liam even after he'd broken down my front door. I didn't feel like I could love someone else right now...way too much baggage.

Damien's eyes didn't shine in disappointment at my silence, as if my rejection didn't sting. He looked at me a while longer before he turned away, his eyes glancing out the windows of the living room.

"If he was going to hurt me, he would have done it already." Liam had been drunk and livid, but the only thing he'd destroyed was my door. He didn't grab me by the neck or blacken one of my eyes. That was the test—and he passed.

Damien slowly turned back to me.

"You're the one he wants."

He slid his other hand into his pocket. "Then he can come get me."

I knew Damien was strong and confident, but I was surprised he wasn't the least bit concerned that a champion fighter had put him on a hit list. I'd seen Liam kill men with his bare hands, seen him crush skulls with his powerful knuckles.

"There's only one thing I'm worried about."

"What?" I whispered.

He bowed his head and stared at the floor for a while as he considered his response. His green eyes were open and focused, staring at one of the pieces of wood that comprised the floor. "You." He lifted his gaze and met my look head on. "Will you forgive me if I kill him?"

My voice became weak and escaped as a whisper. "That's what you're worried about?"

"You're the only thing I worry about."

It felt almost too intimate to stare at him right now, to have this heated conversation in my apartment in the middle of the night. When Liam had confronted me, it was uncomfortable, but this...this was far more intense.

"I don't have a lot of options. He'll continue to come after me until I put him in the ground. It doesn't matter how many times I defeat him, how many times I grant him mercy, he'll continue to pursue me until I'm dead. His vendetta can't be assuaged rationally."

He was absolutely right. "I'll talk to him..."

He shook his head. "I don't want you near him."

"Well, I don't want you guys to kill each other."

"Annabella, you don't understand the underworld. This will not end peacefully. One man lives and one dies."

I wish I'd had handled this better, had told Liam who my old lover was—or had the strength to stay away from Damien or something... I didn't know what.

"I'm asking for your permission to kill him."

Liam had hurt me so much, I wasn't sure I could recover a second time. Then he'd barged in here and spoke to me like I meant nothing to him. He wasn't the husband he promised to be, didn't give me everything I deserved. But, no...I didn't want him dead. "And you expect me to say yes?"

"I need you to say yes." He tilted his head slightly as his eyes burned into my face. His hands remained in his pockets, and his strong physique remained relaxed, not hostile the way Liam's had been. "Otherwise, he'll kill me."

TWO

DAMIEN

"It's four in the goddamn morning." Hades shut the bedroom door behind himself and walked beside me down the hallway. He was quiet as he passed Andrew's bedroom, making sure his sleeping family didn't wake up to this intrusion. "What the fuck is so important?" He took the stairs to the next landing so our voices wouldn't be overheard.

"He knows." I hadn't slept much in days because the shit had hit the fan all at once.

He stood in his sweatpants, his bare chest rising and falling with aggressive energy. His muscular shoulders were rigid and tense, ready for a fight with an unknown foe. "Who knows what?"

"Liam knows it's me."

His anger diminished. "How did that happen?"

"I joined him at the bar, and he just figured it out. Seeing me there probably made him remember that night. That I was there...that I was the only person who knew what he did besides you. And of course...my name."

"Took him long enough." He turned away and headed down the next flight of stairs until he entered the kitchen. He opened a couple cabinets until he found what he was looking for—a giant bottle of scotch.

I grabbed it out of his hand. "Hades, come on."

His eyes narrowed. "I think this situation warrants a drink." He snatched it back.

I pushed him until he fell back and then grabbed the bottle from his weakened grip.

"What the fuck—"

I opened the cap and poured it into the sink.

He righted himself, giving me a distinct look of rage. "It's like that?"

When the bottle was empty, I shook it to dispel the last few drops. "Yeah. It's like that." I left the bottle in the sink. "You've got a family to think about, Hades. And I'm not just talking about Sofia, Andrew, and the baby." I came back to him. "I'm your family too, and I'm not letting you poison yourself more—regardless of the circumstances." I leaned against the counter beside him and held his gaze.

His rage slowly faded away, but there was a baseline that was constantly present. "What happened next?"

"What you'd expect. Threatened to kill me...blah, blah."

He raised an eyebrow. "And you aren't concerned about that? That's a pretty credible threat."

"No. I'm concerned about Annabella."

"You think he'd hurt her?"

I shook my head. "No. He already confronted her. Nothing happened."

"Then what do you mean?" He leaned against the counter and crossed his arms over his chest.

It was a problem with no solution, a situation so complicated, there was no answer. "I can't kill him. If I do..."

He caught up. "It'll ruin your relationship with Anna."

Now I wish I still had that scotch. "Yeah."

"So, he can kill you, but you can't kill him?"

"He already lost her, so he doesn't have that problem."

He sighed loudly. "That's fucking annoying."

"Yeah."

"She must understand you don't have a choice, right?"

"I'm sure she does, but she doesn't want Liam to die. And even if it's necessary and I have no choice, we'll never recover from that. I'll always be the man who murdered the man she was married to. The man she wanted to have a family with. The man she loved."

"You lose, no matter what."

"Yes."

"Then maybe we could get someone else to kill him."

The thought had already crossed my mind. "Even if I pay a hit man, she's gonna know it's me."

"What if I do it?" It was a testament to our relationship that he would offer after he'd made it abundantly clear he'd wiped his hands clean and walked away from that life.

"No."

"We could make it look like an accident—"

"No. Because if she ever asks me, I can't lie."

"Alright..." He gripped the edge of the counter while he leaned back against it. "Then I don't see a solution, Damien."

"Neither do I."

"Unless she can convince him to let this go."

"I don't want her to have any interaction with him at all." Liam had had his chance, he blew it, and now he needed to walk away. She didn't see me as her man, but she was my woman as far as I was concerned.

"I'm sorry, man." His look of sympathy was bright in his dark eyes. "But it's the only option you have."

HER DOOR WAS OPEN, so I entered her office without knocking.

She sat behind her desk and typed on her laptop. Her hair and makeup were done, but that usual spark wasn't in her eyes. She looked tired, as if she hadn't slept much the night before. Or maybe she was just miserable, upset that all of her bad decisions had led to this terrible moment.

I sank into the white armchair that faced her desk. Her office was decorated in her style, a small vase of fresh flowers on the corner of her desk, a painting of wildflowers on the wall behind her, along with the brightly colored accents that made the office feel like perpetual spring.

When she heard my weight sink into the chair, she looked up. A spark of surprise moved over her features, but it was quickly replaced by stoicism once more. She didn't fill the room with heat the way she used to when she saw me. All that desire that erupted between us was gone, masked by all the shit that happened.

I fucking hated it.

It was unrealistic to expect her to jump into my arms right away, but it was also unrealistic to expect me not to want her.

She shut her laptop so there was no barrier between us. "Hi..."

I didn't return her words.

"Is everything alright?"

"No." My hands rested on the padded armrests, and my fingers hung over the edge. "I've been thinking about this for a few days, and I've come to realize there's no real solution."

Her eyes fell in sadness.

"Every time I don't kill him, it gives him another chance to kill me."

She took a deep breath as if just the thought made her feel sick to her stomach.

"And you can live with that? I know what he meant to you, but he's your past. I'm your future. If you have to choose, I think the answer is obvious. And if it's not obvious to you, then I'm concerned."

She lifted her gaze again. "It's not about choosing, Damien. I don't want him to kill you as much as I don't want you to kill him. Death and violence are not the solution I want. I want Liam to let this go, to fade into the background, to find happiness in whichever way he chooses. And I obviously want the same for you. The idea of him hurting you...makes me so sick."

I wanted Liam to disappear too... And I wished I could make

him disappear with my fists. I wanted to kill him for what he did to her, for hurting her so many goddamn times. It wasn't hard to be a good man to a good woman. I'd never even done it, and I still knew it would be a walk in the goddamn park.

"Let me talk to him. He's had a few days to decompress."

I didn't want them to be in a room alone together, but this was the only solution she was willing to accept. "Alright."

Her eyes shifted back and forth in surprise, taken aback by my agreement.

"Do it somewhere public."

She cocked an eyebrow. "What's that supposed to mean?"

"It's pretty clear what I mean. If you're alone together in a soundproof house, you won't be able to scream for help if you need it."

She must have thought my suggestion meant something else entirely. "He wouldn't hurt me, but fair enough."

My fingers lightly tapped against the armrests as I stared at her, wanting to say more. But I was out of bullets. A part of me wanted to ask her to lunch, but with this cloud over our heads, asking her out seemed pointless. "Let me know how it goes." I rose from the chair and headed to the door.

"Damien."

I turned around, hoping for something substantial to escape her lips.

She stared at me for a while, as if she was searching for the right words to make this situation better. But when nothing came out, she gave up. "I'll call him when I get home."

❄

WHEN I LEFT the bank at the end of the day, I walked out of the double doors and headed to the parking lot. My ride was parked in the back, in a reserved section so no one could park anywhere near our expensive vehicles.

I stopped halfway when I noticed the man leaning up against the hood of my car.

My expensive-as-fuck car.

Liam had his arms crossed over his chest, wearing a t-shirt and sweatpants like he intended to fight me right then and there. He might have a weapon on him, hidden in the back of his pants. His body was so large that it would be impossible to tell. His eyes were focused on me with deadly intensity.

I slid my hands into the pockets of my slacks.

He raised his hand then beckoned me toward him with his fingers.

The right thing to do would be to turn around and walk away. He wouldn't die, and neither would I. But I wasn't going to turn into a pussy and walk away from a fight for a woman. I wouldn't change the man I was for any woman—not even Annabella.

I started to walk forward again.

He grinned in victory.

My pulse stayed extremely slow even while the adrenaline dumped into my blood. A part of me wanted this to happen, for me to beat him so badly that he died as a result of his injuries and maybe Annabella wouldn't directly blame me.

I stopped when I was just feet away. "In the parking lot in broad daylight. Seems like you're scared." I kept my hands in the pockets of my slacks and remained aloof. Other men quivered in fear at the sight of him. Not me.

He continued to grin. "No. I just want to watch you run." He rose off the car, the vehicle lifting once his heavy weight wasn't making it sink. "Like the little bitch you are." He massaged his knuckles as he stared at me, ready to swing.

"I can't kill you, Liam."

"At least you're honest about it."

"No." I pulled my hands out of my pockets. "Annabella doesn't want me to. So, I won't."

His eyes narrowed.

"And the only reason I'll honor her request is because I love her."

His face immediately turned red once I confessed my feelings for the first time, when I declared my love for the woman he also loved. He slammed his fist into his palm and grunted like an animal.

"I know you won't honor the same request—because you don't love her the way I do."

He lunged at me.

I was ready for it, so I dodged out of the way.

He moved with such momentum that he tripped forward and lost his footing. He underestimated my speed and experience, thinking my reaction wouldn't be quick enough for a professional.

"I'm not gonna kill you, Liam. So, this isn't a fair fight."

He recovered himself and turned around, even more livid that I'd nearly made him trip on his face. "I don't want a fair fight. I want to kill you, so I'll get my chance—a real chance."

I stood in a relaxed position, but my eyes took in his movements, the way he crept toward me so he could get me again. This time, he would be smarter about it now that he knew what I was capable of. "Dead or alive, she'll never take you back."

"She doesn't need to."

I kept the same expression even though I didn't know what that meant.

"With you gone, nothing will stand in my way."

"Annabella will always stand in your way—because she doesn't want you."

He jumped on me again.

But I knew he was going to pounce when I spoke, because he would think that meant a part of my brain was distracted. I stepped out of the way then bent over to avoid that powerful fist that was meant for my throat. I dodged the hit then grabbed him by the arm to spin him around. I kicked his knees out from under him then shoved him forward until his heavy body thudded against the pavement.

He didn't stay down for long. He rolled and was back on his feet, ready to lunge at me again.

The gun was already pulled from my belt, and I aimed it right at his head, my finger on the trigger with the safety off.

He stilled as he stared down the barrel. "You refused to kill me. So, I'm not afraid of your little toy. You didn't think that through, asshole."

"I won't kill you." I adjust the aim of the gun to his arm. "Doesn't mean I won't shoot you." The pull of the trigger was followed by the loud bang from the gun.

He screamed as the bullet pierced his skin and spilled blood everywhere. He gripped the wound and fell to his knees. "Coward. You're a fucking coward. Fight me like a man. I could have walked up to you and shot you. Not a fair fight."

I slid the gun into the back of my pants. "I can't kill you. So, it was never a fair fight."

THREE

ANNABELLA

Liam was already sitting at a table when I walked inside.

Large, muscular, and brooding, he was inherently intimidating. A drink was in front of him, pure liquor with no ice. He stared at a picture on the wall, his gaze emotionless. But then he seemed to notice I was there because his eyes turned in my direction.

And locked on me.

I believed Liam wouldn't hurt me, but that didn't stop me from being afraid of him. I walked across the restaurant and felt his gaze burning into me, felt the hostility fill the entire room. I slid into the seat across from him and sensed that intensity grow.

He stared at me with a rigid posture, examining me like an opponent rather than an innocent person. He was in a blue t-shirt that made his eyes burn a little brighter than usual.

That was when I noticed the gauze wrapped around his bicep. "What happened?"

"Your boyfriend shot me."

"He's not my boyfriend, Liam."

His eyes still hadn't blinked.

"And why would he do that?" This was all news to me. Damien hadn't called me and told me about this interaction.

"Because I was waiting by his car at the bank."

I closed my eyes in dread.

"I tried to fight him like a man, but he chose to be a pussy instead."

I opened my eyes and glared at him. "I asked him not to kill you."

"Why?" He cocked his head slightly.

"I hope that answer is obvious, Liam."

"Nothing is obvious to me anymore, Anna. Damien should have been obvious to me a long time ago, but I trusted you blindly. Learned my lesson." He was so spiteful, so venomous.

"Because the last thing I want is for you to be dead. I still care about you... I'll always love you."

"Yeah?" he whispered. "Didn't love me enough to be honest with me. Didn't love me enough to give me a real chance."

"I did give you a real chance, Liam. I had many opportunities to be with Damien, but I told him I was committed to you. When he told me he loved me, I said I was determined to make this marriage work. I was willing to move to London for you—"

"Say what you want, Anna. You're wrong."

I shut my mouth and felt the burn of his gaze. "Please drop this."

All he did was shake his head.

"Liam—"

"He's the reason I lost you. None of that shit would have happened if he hadn't been a problem—"

"Please," I whispered. "I understand you're angry. I understand you feel betrayed. But please don't kill him."

There was no sympathy whatsoever. "I'm gonna break every bone, break every inch of his skin until he's fucking inside out."

The mental image flooded my brain, and I actually felt sick. "If you love me—"

"If I love you?" he snapped. "Bitch, if you loved me—"

"Call me that again, and I'll shoot you myself."

He turned quiet, but a subtle smile spread across his lips. "That's the woman I married..."

"I'm asking you to do this for me, Liam. After everything you've put me through, you should do this for me."

"Everything I put *you* through?"

"We wouldn't have gotten divorced in the first place if you hadn't ruined it. Our lives would be completely different right now. The butterfly effect started with you, and you devastated me so much. Let's not rewrite history."

He wore a bored look, like what I said meant nothing to him.

"Please."

He moved his arms to the table and rested them there as his eyes drilled into me. His bright blue eyes stared into mine as he took his time. He massaged the knuckles on his left hand as if he'd punched something hard earlier that day. "I'll make a deal with you..."

I didn't want to compromise, but I would if it meant I could save Damien's life.

"You take me back. We move to London. Start over."

That was a ridiculous demand.

"I won't touch your boyfriend."

"That's not a deal. You're blackmailing me into doing what you want."

"That's my price." He shrugged even though that was a completely inappropriate response. "I want that asshole dead more than anything, so you need to offer me something I want more. You."

"You would really want to be with a woman who doesn't want to be with you? Who's only there because she has to be?"

"Yes...because it's you." His sincerity was so bright, it was unmistakable. It was like a shooting star.

It was the first time I'd ever been truly disturbed by Liam. His desperation was so potent, so unmistakable. I wanted to keep Damien safe, but if I agreed to this, I would never get a chance to be with him...to see if things were as good as I remembered. That reality was terrifying to me, to leave everything behind... including the man I'd wanted for so long. "Liam, I want you to know nothing is going on between Damien and me. I told him I need time to get over this because I'm not ready to be with someone else. I don't want you to think I'm jumping into bed with another man because that's not what's happening."

His voice was so cold. "You think I'll believe anything you say?"

"I've never lied to you, Liam. I confessed everything that ever happened. I just didn't tell you who he—"

"Spin it however you want. You made me look like a fucking idiot, giving my money to those guys, while they thought I was the biggest dumbass on the planet. Say what you want, but you're wrong and you know it."

"I'm sorry I didn't tell you—"

"Then we're even. I forgive you for your lies, and you forgive me for my infidelity."

"They aren't—"

"One wouldn't have happened without the other." He held up two fingers. "If I'd had all the information, it would have changed everything. We would have moved and started over. You took that away from me."

I dropped my gaze.

"You want me to know how sorry you are? Prove it. Say yes."

A part of me felt guilty for the way I'd handled things. If the situation were reversed, I would be livid if I'd spent so much time with his former lover and had no idea. I wasn't completely innocent in all of this. But I also didn't want to give up my chance to be with the man I'd fallen in love with. "Liam—"

"Give me your answer." He wasn't the gentle giant he used to be. Now, he was treating me like he owned me...like I wasn't a person.

"You are one hell of a man, Liam. You can have any woman you want—"

"I want you." His eyes narrowed. "You're the only woman I want underneath me for the rest of my life. You're the only woman I give a shit about. You're the woman of my dreams, the future mother of my children, and I'm having you one way or another." He'd changed from a man into a maniac, turning psychopathic once he knew Damien's identity. He couldn't think clearly, his rage dictating everything. "It's gonna happen, no matter what. In one scenario, you can save his life. And in the other...he'll die, and I'll still have you."

"I would never take you back if you did that."

"Doesn't mean I won't take *you*." He leaned back against the chair and stared. "When I thought I fucked up, I was willing to step aside and let you go. But now that I know the game was rigged, that I never had a chance, I want a redo. And you're giving it to me."

My heart started to slam into the walls of my chest because I was actually afraid. "You're scaring me."

"Good. That means you understand how serious I am."

I pulled my hands off the table, my pulse so strong I felt my entire body vibrate with the feeling of drums. Everything felt different, as if my mind understood that I was in danger, that I should run before it was too late.

"Your answer."

I was afraid to say it out loud. "No..."

He stared at me for a long time, his body as rigid as a pile of rocks, his heartbeats stalled. His eyes were so pretty, but right now, they were sinister, terrifying. "I was hoping you would say that."

FOUR

ANNABELLA

I SAT IN MY LONELY APARTMENT AND WATCHED THE SUN disappear over the horizon until my living room went dark. The TV wasn't on to cast an intermediate glow across every corner. Dinner should be in my stomach by now. But I was too distressed to think about everyday life.

What the fuck just happened with Liam?

A knock sounded on my door. It was subtle, like he knew I was sitting right by the door and didn't need a loud and obnoxious announcement of his presence.

It couldn't be Liam because he'd never been so gentle. I turned on the lamp beside me then navigated through the living room furniture to the front door. Without checking the peephole, I opened the door.

Damien was dressed in black head to toe, his usual watch gone. He had a large wooden door leaning against the wall, already detailed with my address. He hardly looked at me before he got to work. He pulled a screwdriver from his back pocket and worked on the hinges that held my cracked door in place.

I crossed my arms over my chest and watched him work.

As if he'd been a contractor in a previous life, he worked step by step, knowing exactly what to do next without even checking. He got the door off the frame and then leaned it against the wall across the hall.

"Do you need help?"

He pulled the door closer and got to work. "No." He lined up the door then attached it with screws and tools. It only took him fifteen minutes to change the doors and move my locks, being far more efficient than my super would have been. When he was finished, he tested the swing, making sure it was perfectly level with the floor. "Shut the door and lock it."

I did as he asked and bolted everything.

He twisted the knob and tested it from the outside. Then he kicked it for good measure.

I jerked back at the loud sound.

He knocked when he was finished.

I unlocked all the locks again and opened it.

"Good." He left the other door across the hall then entered my apartment.

Watching him take care of me like that was touching, especially since I didn't ask. I could have asked the manager of the building to do it, but Damien would rather do it himself. He didn't even pay someone to do it; he did it with his bare hands. "Thank you..."

He stopped in front of me and stared, his green eyes searching my gaze for something. Maybe he saw my sincerity. Maybe he saw how much the simple gesture meant to me. The softness in his eyes quickly disappeared. "What happened with Liam?"

Our nice moment was destroyed. "Nothing good."

He flicked on the lights because he probably thought it felt like a cave. "Be more specific." He stood in front of me with his arms crossed over his chest, not extending any kind of affection. He used to touch me whenever he could, find any excuse to make that happen. But once I went through the heartbreak of Liam's betrayal, Damien gave me more space than he ever had.

"He'll only drop his vendetta if I take him back."

Damien's eyes immediately narrowed at the request, as if he hadn't anticipated something so absurd.

"Says he was never given a fair chance. I lied to him about your identity, and if he'd had that information, everything would have been different. He would have made other choices to make this marriage work."

Damien continued to show the same coldness. "Don't say yes, especially not on my account."

"I didn't."

"Good." He dropped his arms and leaned against the back of the couch. He stared at the opposite wall for a while before he turned his head in my direction. "You tried. That gives us one other option—and you know what it is."

He was asking for permission to kill my ex-husband—again. "And I'm just supposed to say yes?"

Devoid of all emotion, he stared at me with empty eyes.

"I can't just condone that."

"Well, if you don't, he's gonna kill me." His voice rose. "You prefer that?"

"Of course not."

"Then give me your blessing."

I dropped my chin to my chest and tucked my hair behind my ear, feeling the blood completely drain to my feet. "You don't understand, Damien. I was married to him—"

"I understand you don't want him killed. But he's making you choose—not me."

I positioned myself directly across from him, my back against the wall. My hands crossed over my chest and gripped each of my arms, feeling defeated by a battle I'd never fought. "He was different today."

His eyes were steady as he held my gaze.

"He was...malicious, maniacal, crazy..."

"What did he say to you?"

"That regardless of my choice, the outcome would be the same. He would take me."

His eyes narrowed, emitting a sudden change of energy. Now he was the one who was a little maniacal.

"But in this scenario, he would also kill you...which he prefers."

"Annabella." Without raising his voice, he conveyed the seriousness of this situation, the fear that gripped him by the chest. "I'm not afraid of him, but I'm afraid of what he'll do. That's a serious threat, and we need to have a serious response."

"I don't know... Would he really take me? What does that mean?"

"I don't want to know." He pushed off the couch and straightened. "Pack your things. You're staying with me."

I looked up to meet his gaze, shocked by what he'd just said. "That will only make it worse—"

"You can't stay here alone anymore. If he meant what he said, you're in serious danger."

"He wouldn't hurt me—"

"But he might take you away and lock you in a tower somewhere."

Oh my god...would Liam really do that? He wasn't himself at lunch. He was delirious with rage, his eyes so cold they were frozen.

"And there's nowhere safer in this world than with me."

"If Liam knows I'm staying with you, he'll assume—"

"I don't give a shit what he assumes. He already wants to kill me, so what difference does it make?"

I didn't have an argument against any of that, but I was still afraid to stay with Damien. We'd never had that kind of proximity, constantly being together, living under the same roof. Our time together had been so brief. This was more intimate than it ever had been before. "Then he really will kill you."

"He can try."

All of this was my fault. If I'd left my job and removed myself from Damien's life, none of this would have happened. Now, Damien's life was in danger, and his opponent was the strongest man I'd ever known. "Maybe I should just say yes—"

"No."

"I don't want anything to happen to you—"

"Then let me kill him." He stepped closer to me, his eyes

watching mine closely. "If you want to keep me safe, let me get rid of the problem." He pleaded as he looked into my gaze, wanting my blessing to end the life of someone I'd once loved.

The blood would be on my hands if I said yes.

"Annabella."

I closed my eyes. "Let me try to talk to him again—"

"No." He pressed me into the wall, cornering me like I was fleeing prey. "If you think I'm letting you anywhere near him again..."

I couldn't give Damien my blessing. I just couldn't do it. How could I live with myself if I allowed that to happen? I could call Liam. I could plead with him. There had to be a better solution.

Damien's expression filled with disappointment as he stepped away from me. But no, it was more than just disappointment; it was deeper than that. It was chronic resentment, subtle rage. His demeanor was packed with betrayal, as if I'd stabbed him in the back with a dirty knife. "Get your things." With his gaze on the floor, he slid his hands into his pockets.

"Damien—"

"I told you to get your things." He refused to look at me.

"Please look at me..."

He couldn't resist the plea in my voice and raised his head. "My not wanting you to kill him has nothing to do with my feelings for you."

"Those are just words, Annabella. Actions are what matter to people like me."

"Liam was unfaithful. That doesn't mean he deserves to die."

"But he's threatening to kill the man you love. So, he does."

After taking a painful breath, I returned my gaze to the floor. The brilliance of his eyes was too much to watch.

He dropped the conversation. "Pack your things. Or I'll do it for you."

FIVE

DAMIEN

IT WAS A LONG AND SILENT DRIVE TO MY PLACE. SHE WAS quiet in the passenger seat, her suitcase in my trunk, along with a couple extra bags of the essentials she needed. Everything that had been left behind were things she could live without...because who knew when she would return.

When we arrived at the house, I carried all of her things up the stairs to the top floor. She tried to carry her own shit, but I didn't let her touch anything. I still hadn't forgotten her scent on my sheets, and I wanted to carry everything into my bedroom so I could inhale that smell once again, to feel her presence all over the place.

But I carried her things into the bedroom next door. She had plenty of space in the suite. A king bed, a large fireplace, a small living room where she could watch TV, and a private bathroom. I could have put her farther down the hall, but I wanted her close enough to reach at a moment's notice.

I placed her stuff inside the empty closet.

She looked around at the bedroom, her shoulders visibly relaxed once she knew she had her own quarters. Her eyes lingered on the white bedspread before she looked at the matching furniture in the living room. A fire was already in the hearth because I'd asked Patricia to prepare it before I returned.

"If you need anything, I'm right next door. And you already know Patricia." It'd been a long time since we were together, but it felt strange to be alone in a bedroom with her without gliding my hands through her hair. Without making her mine. When she was married, I didn't cross the line after my mishap on the balcony, but now that she was available again, it was hard to respect that invisible barrier.

I wanted her to have her space to move on from her marriage. I didn't want to share her heart with anyone else. Liam had agreed to that condition, but I certainly wouldn't. But now that we would be sleeping just a few feet apart, it was hard not to rush. There were times when I forgot about the dilemma we faced. They were quick moments, more like instances, when I looked at her and just forgot...like now.

"Thanks...it's beautiful." She turned back to me, her arms across her chest.

I wanted to linger, but I knew I should give her some privacy. "I need to work on a few things." I dismissed myself and headed to the door. "Knock on my door if you need me." With my hand on the knob, I turned back to look at her, hoping she would say something.

Her eyes were locked with mine and she was rigid, like she wanted to say something but didn't have the words.

Neither did I.

HADES SAT across from me at the table in my bedroom. He'd

recovered from the moment when I'd tossed out his scotch and denied him the kick he needed, bouncing back as if that never happened. "You don't have to not drink because of me."

"Yes, I do." Now we drank water...like fucking pussies. "It's fine."

He cocked his head slightly. "Give me more credit than that."

"No."

His eyes narrowed.

"You were gonna drink that whole bottle of scotch by yourself."

"I wasn't, asshole. Just wanted a glass. Goddamn." His fingers interlocked behind his head. "Sometimes, I wonder if you're more loyal to Sofia than you are to me."

"Definitely her."

He smiled slightly. "So, you shot him?"

I nodded.

"And got blood on my car?"

"Sorry about that."

"You could have at least cleaned it up."

"After you told me to never fucking touch your car?" I countered.

He smiled again. "Fine...you win."

This was what I missed most about our relationship, how easy it was to talk back and forth, to know each other so well we could talk shit like it was nothing.

"And she won't let you kill him?"

I shook my head. "He gave her an ultimatum. He'll drop the feud if she takes him back."

He rolled his eyes. "That's romantic...forcing your woman to stay with you when you constantly cheat on her."

"She said no."

"I'd judge her if she didn't."

"But she won't let me kill him..."

"Okay, I judge her for that." He took a drink of his water and cringed slightly, as if he'd subconsciously been expecting scotch. The heated liquor would normally burn his throat, but once that heat was gone, it made him cringe.

"She's in the bedroom next door."

That made him do a double take, both of his eyebrows rising in surprise.

"She couldn't stay alone anymore. I suspect Liam will try to take her."

"Take her how?"

"Abduct her. Literally."

He pulled his fingers off the cold glass.

"Take her to another country, keep her as a prisoner until she's successful brainwashed or gives in out of exhaustion."

"You really think he'd do something like that?"

"He basically told her he would."

"Fuck, this guy is a nutcase."

It'd always been obvious to me. The way he was so easily baited into violence, the way his emotions would rise and fall without warning, the way he would love Annabella fiercely but then cheat on her a moment later. Now that he knew I'd fucked his wife, he'd flipped again...and this time, he wasn't going to un-flip. "Yeah."

"So, you have no plan right now?"

"Not really. I would just hunt him down and kill him, but she still won't allow it. What else am I supposed to do?"

"Seems unfair since you're the one protecting her right now."

"Yeah..." It made me angry if I thought about it too long.

"I get why it's a difficult decision to make, but since she loves you, I don't see why the decision is that difficult."

I shrugged. "Maybe she'll change her mind...eventually."

"Not eventually. Soon."

I wasn't gonna let Liam take my life, so I'd kill him if I absolutely had no choice...even if that meant losing her forever.

"How long has she been here?"

"Couple days."

"Anything happen? You know what I mean..."

"No." I took a drink from my glass and automatically cringed too, unable to believe I was drinking something so bland.

The corner of his mouth rose in a smile. "I said you can just drink the scotch."

"It's fine."

"Fine. Enjoy your horse piss." He clinked his glass against mine.

"She's stayed in her room most of the time. I think she wants space."

"So, you just sleep in here...alone?"

"There's no one else, if that's what you're asking."

"That's rough. If I had to sleep next door to Sofia and do nothing..." He shook his head. "I wouldn't last long."

"If Liam would just go away, it would speed up the process..."

"And that's not gonna happen."

"Unfortunately."

He finished his water then pushed it away. "We need to think of something. We can't just let you be a sitting duck."

That was exactly how I felt.

"Maybe I could entice him into a death match..."

"He wants nothing to do with you, Hades." Liam felt betrayed by Hades as much as me.

"Yeah...but I could ask someone else to do it."

"And then what?"

"Hope one of his opponents beats him."

"He's undefeated."

"Yeah, but I could slip him something before a fight."

I lifted my gaze from the glass and stared at him. "We can't do that."

"But I could do it."

"No. Because I'd have to carry that secret, and I refuse."

He sighed in annoyance.

"Would you wanna keep a secret like that from Sofia?"

"No. But she'd get over it. Come on, that woman is obsessed with me."

"Well, Annabella wouldn't get over this."

He stared at me blankly. "Then I can roll the dice and hope for the best."

"Yeah, but I still have a feeling it won't go anywhere. He's got rage on his side right now."

"Yeah." He interlocked his fingers behind his head again and stared out the window. "How's work?"

"You mean the drug empire?"

"Yeah. You don't talk about it much."

"Not much going on. I've replaced Maddox pretty easily."

"And Heath?" he asked.

"Still want to kill him, but I've gotta take care of this first."

"You didn't want to be with Anna because of that business. Now you've changed your mind?"

It was more complicated than that. "No. I just fell in love with her."

"Does that mean you'll walk away from the business?"

"I don't know. I haven't thought that far ahead."

He continued to watch me, reading all my subtle expressions.

"Annabella and I aren't even together. Not sure if or when that's gonna happen..."

"Yeah, I get it," he said. "I just know that it was the right decision for me. I wish I'd made it sooner. Because once you love someone, when they suffer...you suffer more. And trust me—you never want your woman to suffer."

I didn't need further explanation because I knew exactly what he was saying, exactly what he was referring to. And if someone like that happened to Annabella...I wouldn't recover.

Never.

PATRICIA PLACED my dinner on the table and poured me a glass of wine to pair with it. She even set a small vase of flowers beside it, as if I needed the decorative touch. Then she walked out and left me to eat alone.

I sat at the table with the flames from the fire against my back and opened my laptop. I usually worked while I ate. Otherwise, I stared ahead blankly, with no entertainment whatsoever. Annabella hadn't knocked on my door since she'd moved in. She hardly ever texted me either, only if she needed an answer to something.

I didn't encourage her to have dinner with me or watch a movie in my bedroom. If she wanted to see me, she knew where to find me.

I took a bite of my food just as someone knocked on the door.

I knew it wasn't Patricia because she would just come back in if she forgot something. My pulse quickened a bit because my heart was sensitive to Annabella's presence. When confronted with life-threatening danger, I had the heart rate of someone in deep sleep. But she affected me in a way no one else could. "It's open."

She pushed the door open and held a tray in her hands. Patricia made her the same dinner, serving it to her in her quarters so she could eat alone. She held the tray as she stared at me timidly, like the expressionless look on my face meant I wanted to be alone. "Can I join you?"

Did she even need to ask?

"I understand if you want to be alone—"

I kicked the chair under the table so it slid back. "Sit."

She set the tray down then sat across from me, wearing skintight yoga pants and a loose sweater she liked to wear around the house. Her hair framed her face perfectly with smooth strands, and she didn't wear makeup because she probably expected to go to sleep soon.

But I still thought she was stunning. Maybe it was because I hadn't seen her in so long that I'd forgotten how beautiful she was, how much I wanted her, how lonely I felt being next door to the woman I loved.

I poured her a glass of wine.

She mouthed "Thank you" and pulled the glass closer to her.

Now I didn't have an appetite. All I could do was focus on the woman across from me. My heart palpitated with a distinct rush. My fingertips felt numb. My breathing changed. Maybe on the outside, I looked completely calm, but underneath, I felt a hailstorm of sensations.

"What are you working on?" She glanced at my laptop.

I closed it and pushed it to the side. "Bank stuff."

"I remember you used to work from home a lot."

"I'm a workaholic."

"With two jobs, that's not surprising." She cut into her meat and took a few bites. Her eyes were downcast most of the time, and her posture was relaxed even though it'd been days since we'd seen each other.

I grabbed my fork and continued to eat, elbows on the table

because I didn't give a shit. Patricia had picked a subtle white wine to go with the chicken, creating another delicious meal that I took for granted...like all other things.

"Where did you find Patricia?" she asked. "She's the best chef ever."

"She went to culinary school in Paris. She worked in a bakery for a few years in Greece, but then her husband died."

"She didn't want to stay?"

I shrugged. "No. She said the memories were too painful."

"Oh...that's too bad."

"I think she sees me a son—or something like that. She picks up all my laundry off the floor, makes my bed, cooks my meals... I think she enjoys it."

She chuckled. "No woman enjoys picking up your underwear off the floor."

I paused before I took a bite, smiling slightly at her joke. "That's not what she tells me."

"Because you pay her."

"Touché." I grabbed a piece of asparagus and bit it the tip off the stem. "How are you? I haven't seen you much." I expected Liam to confront me at the bank every day, but he never showed his face. Hitting me at the same place twice was stupid because I was expecting it. Or maybe he assumed I would assume that...so I wouldn't expect it. In this game, you had to anticipate everything.

She turned melancholy at the question. "I've been spending most of my time in my room. There's a nice tub in there, and Patricia always has the fire going the second I get home from work. The food is great, way better than room service at the

Tuscan Rose..." She suddenly looked embarrassed. "Don't tell Sofia I said that. And the space is really comfortable. So, I've been fine."

"I didn't ask how you're enjoying your stay at Hotel Damien. I asked how *you* are doing."

She started to push her food around with her fork, her eyes downcast for a moment. "I'm stressed, to be honest."

"Has he called you?"

"No. That's why I'm worried."

"Maybe he's cooled off."

She gave a sarcastic chuckle. "That man never cools off. Does that mean you haven't heard from him?"

I gave a slight shake of my head. "Maybe his injury has forced him to recuperate."

She gave a slight nod. "Yeah... He told me you shot him." We'd never actually discussed the event.

"I had no other choice. He took my car hostage so I couldn't get out of there."

"I know. I'm not upset about it."

"Because if I wanted to shoot to kill, my aim would have been different." I shot him in a fleshy part of his arm, away from the bones, away from the arteries, barely grazing his flesh.

She pulled her gaze away. "I know, Damien." Her silverware slightly cut into the plate, the gentle tapping of metal against china. She cut her food into small bites because she had a petite mouth, but she could fit my big cock in there, so she could take bigger bites if she wanted to.

I ate in silence, watching her while she avoided my gaze. We had a meal together like two friends, even though we'd never felt like friends. "I've been thinking about this..."

She looked up as she sliced off a piece of meat.

"You shouldn't go into the Tuscan Rose anymore."

The knife made a squeaky sound against the plate as she lost control of the utensil. "What?"

"That's the perfect place to grab you."

"In a public place?" she asked incredulously. "When there are people around? Security? Cameras?"

"That's not gonna stop him. It wouldn't stop me."

"Well, I think—"

"All he has to do is point a gun at Sofia, and you'll cooperate."

Her argument diminished from her gaze instantly. "So, I have to quit my job? That I love?"

"No. I'm sure Sofia will let you work from home."

"That's still a lot to ask. I haven't even been working there a year..."

"She'll understand."

"I don't want to take advantage of her generosity."

"That's not how she'll see it," I said gently.

"And what am I going to do here?"

I shrugged. "You can pick up my underwear."

That made her burst with a chuckle.

I liked seeing that carefree expression, seeing that glow in her eyes. It reminded me of old times, when it was just the two of us and we were free. "You could hang out with my father."

"Oh yeah. I forgot he lived here. I haven't seen him."

"He stays in his room."

"And I've stayed in mine..."

"I know you don't want to be cooped up, but I don't see a way around it."

"Yeah."

"But every time I see Liam, you're putting me at a huge disadvantage. I'm fighting to disarm, not kill, but that's not the case for him. And while I'm strong, I'm not Batman."

The light left her gaze as she dropped her eyes.

"And if it really comes down to it—and I have no choice—I'm not going to let him take my life. I love you and want us to be together, but losing my life so he could take you away isn't worth it to me."

"I understand."

At least we were on the same page.

I returned to eating my dinner, out of ammunition to keep the conversation going.

She didn't have anything to say either, probably because this problem hung over her like a cloud.

It hung heavy over me too. "I hope you stop barricading yourself in your bedroom...because I would like to see you."

She turned back to me, affection in her gaze. "That was lonely, so I don't think I'll do that anymore."

SIX

ANNABELLA

Spring was in full force, bringing a distinct warmth that melted the frost on all the sidewalks. But since I was inside most of the time, I sat in front of the fire while I worked on my laptop. My bedroom didn't have a balcony, and I assumed Damien had put me in there for that very reason.

My phone rang on the cushion beside me, and I grabbed it with the assumption it was Damien or Sofia.

But it was Liam.

I'd been here for a week without seeing his name on my screen. I knew my time of peace was limited and this call was unavoidable. Instead of ignoring it, I accepted the call, knowing it would be worse if I brushed him off. I answered wordlessly, not sure what to say after our last conversation.

He didn't raise his voice, but his tone was so menacing, so frightening. "You're living with him now?"

So, he was watching me, deducing my whereabouts by stalking. "It's not what you think—"

"I'm sure it's exactly what I think, Anna." His voice was frostbitten.

"What did you expect me to do? You threatened to take me... whatever that means."

"I expected you to have more class than fucking Loverboy right away."

"You mean the kind of class when you fucked someone else while we were married? *Twice*?" I was sick of him twisting the story, using my relationship with Damien to justify every bad decision he'd made. Fuck no, I wasn't putting up with that shit. "I'm staying in a different guest room. Sometimes we share dinner together, but for the most part, I don't see him."

"You expect me to believe that when you're a fucking liar?"

"We're never getting back together, so why would I care about sparing your feelings?" I asked. "I'm telling you the truth because I have no reason to lie. I'm not going to jump into bed with someone else when I'm still hurt by what you did. That's not fair to him."

"So, it sounds like you care more about Loverboy's feelings than mine."

"He's the one protecting me, so I guess so."

"Protecting you?" he asked, his voice rising.

"Yes. From whatever you plan to do."

"My plan is to get my wife back."

"Well, I'm not your wife, and I don't want to be with you. So, that sounds like a pretty scary threat."

He was quiet as he breathed over the phone, his rage audible in the silence. "You think you're safe in there?"

"Yes. Otherwise, you would have gotten to me by now." I felt stupid provoking him like that, but I was tired of this torment. It made me understand that Damien had a valid point, that this wasn't going to end until one of them was dead—and it shouldn't be Damien...whose only crime was loving me.

He breathed heavily for a while longer. "I want to kill him first."

"You'll never have me if you kill him."

"It's pretty easy to force a woman to do whatever I want..."

"Then I'll kill myself."

Now he was dead silent.

"I would rather be dead than be forced. You kill Damien, then I'll kill myself. That's the deal."

He clearly didn't know what to say because he was quiet for so long.

Maybe I'd finally found a solution to this.

"I'm calling your bluff, Anna."

Suicide had never crossed my mind, even in the darkest of times. I didn't really mean it now; that was true. But if Damien was really dead on the floor and Liam was about to make me his prisoner, what would I have to live for? "It's not a bluff, Liam. If you kill the man I love, then I have no reason to live."

"And if he kills me, you'll be just fine?"

"No. That's why I asked him not to. Liam, you've had your chances with me, and you blew them both. If you love me, let me go. Let me be happy."

He was silenced again, breathing quietly over the line.

I hoped I'd said the right thing to fix this, to manage this crisis.

But then he hung up.

PATRICIA KNOCKED on my door before she opened it. "Miss Anna?"

"Hey, Patricia." I turned around on the sofa to look at her standing by the door.

"I was going to bring up your lunch, but Miss Catalina is here having lunch with her father. Would you like to join them?"

"Uh...who's Catalina?"

"Damien's sister."

"Oh..." He'd mentioned her before, but not by name. "Oh, I don't want to intrude."

"She asked me to extend the invitation. She's very lovely."

Having lunch with them was better than sitting here alone. "Sure. What's his father's name?"

"Richard." She started to close the door. "I'll let them know you'll be joining."

I ENTERED THE DINING ROOM, where cathedral-style windows took up the west side of the wall. Sunlight flooded the dining table, where tall white candles and various flower arrangements were placed across the surface. A young brunette sat there, thin and in a bright pink dress. She spoke quietly with her father, an older man who contained subtle hints of Damien's handsomeness.

Now I felt nervous, felt my heart drop into my stomach,

because I was meeting his family for the first time. "Thanks for inviting me to lunch." I walked to the dining table and watched them both turn to look at me. "Ooh...everything looks good." I glanced at the tea sandwiches and individual salads, full of juicy slices of tomatoes, thick pecans, and other delicious toppings.

Catalina halted her conversation with her father and turned to me, unintimidating despite her ridiculous beauty. Her pink dress had ruffles along the straps and down the back of the shoulders on each side. She wore thick mascara, smoky eye makeup, and painted lips. "So, you do exist?" She rose to her feet and greeted me with a hug that practically crushed me. "Damien doesn't tell us anything." She pulled away. "He didn't tell us you were hot. He didn't tell us you were cooped up in this castle like a princess. He mentioned you in passing this morning like it wasn't a big deal. Jackass." She rolled her eyes then patted me on the shoulder. "So sorry about that."

I liked her already. "He mentioned you were a ballet dancer."

"Yes. My feet are killing me as we speak." She turned to her father. "Daddy, this is Anna."

I came around the table so I could extend a hand. "Nice to meet you, sir. You look a lot like your son."

He started to rise from his chair.

"Oh, don't worry about standing..."

He gave me an affectionate smile then wrapped his arms around me to hug me. He patted me on the back despite his obvious frailty. Then he pulled away, his eyes much younger than the rest of his appearance. "You're going to give me grandchildren. So, damn right, I'm gonna stand."

My eyes widened in surprise. "Uh..."

Catalina patted me on the shoulder. "Don't freak out. Daddy is just—"

"You're the first woman of his I've ever seen," his father continued. "And you're living here...so let this old man have hope. I've told Damien so many times that he's getting old and he needs to have children. It's more important than money, drugs, and all that other shit he does." He gripped the sides of the chair and slowly lowered himself back into the seated position. "And you're beautiful, so that makes me more thrilled about it."

Damien was the quiet type, but the rest of his family certainly wasn't. I had no idea what Damien had said about me to his family, and I was still unsure. I moved around the table and took the seat across from his father, his sister at the head of the table.

Richard stabbed his fork into his salad. "I was older when I had my children, and that's something I regret. I won't have as much time with them as I wish I could."

"Daddy, don't talk like that." Catalina patted his arm. "You're still here."

"But your mother isn't," he said after he chewed his bite. "And she could have had more time with you too if I weren't so stubborn..."

"Mama is still here, Dad." Catalina turned back to me. "Anyway, I'm sorry that we freaked you out. My father is just very candid—and I'm even more candid."

"It's okay," I said with a chuckle. "It's refreshing."

"Because Damien looks like an old statue?" Catalina made a sour face, looking like an old woman with nothing left to do besides complain. "Like he's constantly pissed about something?"

Her impression was dead-on, so I laughed. "He usually is pissed about something."

"Oh, I know," she said with a laugh. "Like, pull that stick out of your ass."

Richard didn't seem to care about the mocking at his son's expense.

I would never have expected his family to be so easygoing, especially when Damien was subtly hostile all the time. I spread my napkin in my lap and placed a cucumber sandwich on my plate before I poured the dressing over my salad.

Catalina immediately spoke to me like a girlfriend, as if we'd known each other forever. "So, I went out with this guy the other night..." She told me the details about her date, what she ordered, and how she knew the guy, not caring if it made her father uncomfortable.

And it was as if that conversation with Liam had never happened.

I KNEW Damien was home because his footsteps were distinct down the hallway. He had a specific gait, moving like a man deep in youth, but with a purposeful stride that echoed his determination with every single step.

Then I heard his door open and close.

I closed my laptop, set it aside, and entered his bedroom. "Hey." I shut the door behind me then searched for him, but he was nowhere to be seen.

Then he stepped out of his walk-in closet. He must have just shed his suit because he was in only his black boxers, the material hugging his powerful thighs. His physique was as chiseled as I remembered, so cut that every single muscle was outlined as if it were carved out of marble. Confident as always, he didn't seem to care that I'd walked in on his semi-nakedness. He strolled over to his dresser and opened the top drawer so he could grab a clean pair of sweatpants.

Embarrassed, I wanted to look away and apologize...but I really didn't. "Sorry..."

"Don't be." He pulled on his bottoms then walked toward me, his powerful shoulders tight with strength. The way he carried himself, the muscles all worked together to propel him, contracting and relaxing repeatedly because they were all so tense and powerful. "I've got nothing to hide." His eyes shifted back and forth as he looked into mine, his thick arms resting by his sides. He waited for me to say something, probably noticing the blush of my cheeks and enjoying every second of my distress.

"I had lunch with your family today."

"And how was that?" He turned away and headed to his living room. A fire was already going, and Patricia had a decanter of scotch waiting for him. He poured himself a glass and took a seat on the sofa, both of his hands together and cupping his drink.

I took a seat in the armchair, still uncomfortable with his near nakedness. His muscular chest and chiseled abs had always been objects of my affection when he was on top of me. I used to feel him everywhere, touching those strong muscles. He was lean and slender, like an athlete, and I liked that too. Liam had much fairer skin, but I preferred the olive complexion of Damien's darker body. "Good. They're really nice."

"Nice?" He brought his glass to his lips and took a drink. "You must have met someone else, because my family isn't nice."

I knew he was teasing, so I rolled my eyes. "Your sister was really easy to talk to. She hugged me and talked to me like...she already knew me. She's really interesting and outgoing..."

"Are we talking about the same person?"

"Oh, come on," I said. "You know she's lovely. And she's beautiful."

"That's why she's nice?" he asked incredulously.

"Of course not. But she's really cool."

He whispered under his breath. "My sister is cool?"

"And your dad is sweet."

"I assume they made idiots out of themselves and me."

I didn't tell him about the grandchildren comment because he would probably get angry with his father. "Catalina is going to come over tomorrow for dinner. We're gonna watch a movie and drink some wine."

"You guys are friends now?"

"Yeah...is that okay?"

He shrugged. "I guess it's fine."

"It's nice to have a friend...since I can't leave the house."

He stared into his glass, becoming lost in thought.

"What did you tell them about me?"

"That you're staying with me for a while."

"But that's it...?"

He looked up once more, his finger tapping against the glass. "I don't discuss the details of my personal life with them."

"Sure, but knowing some woman is living with you must sound odd."

"They know what kind of business I run. I doubt they're that perplexed."

His father seemed to assume we were romantically involved, but I didn't tell Damien that. "Anyway, I really liked them—and I'm not just saying that."

He turned his attention on me, disregarding the drink in his hand and the flames in the hearth.

"I don't have a family of my own, so it's nice to be around one again."

"My family isn't as perfect as it seems. When my mother passed away, everything changed."

"Yeah...that came up. You're all broken, but you're broken together. And I think that's special."

He took a drink of his scotch until the glass was empty before setting it on the table.

"I understand why you're so protective of your father, and having him live here was probably the best idea. He seems to be really enamored of your sister."

"As is everyone else."

"Me included. And I suspect you are too."

He stared at the fire instead of me. "Anything else interesting happen to you today?"

"Uh...Liam called."

"Oh good," he said sarcastically. "I was beginning to worry..."

"Nothing has changed. But I did threaten to kill myself if he hurt you."

He turned back to me, but his gaze was darker than before. "I hope you didn't mean that."

"I'm not sure. If he really did kill you and then forced me...I think I would rather be dead."

"There's another solution besides suicide."

"But that involves his death."

His look suddenly turned cold. "You need to think about yourself, Annabella. Not him."

We'd promised to love and protect each other for the rest of our lives. It was hard to snap out of that, even after what he did, even after the threats he made. "How was your day?"

He grabbed the decanter and refilled his glass.

"That bad?" I teased.

"I constantly have to look over my shoulder, Annabella."

"Don't you do that already?"

He narrowed his eyes on my face. "No. Because most men know it's pointless to try to kill me." He took a drink then set the glass on the table. "I had a bunch of shit to do with clients, and tonight I have to take care of a few things."

I never asked him for specifics. It seemed like the less I knew, the better. "Damien?"

His gaze focused on my face further.

I thought about asking if he would leave his line of work, because his occupation had been the reason he wouldn't commit to me in the first place. But that seemed like a premature conversation when I didn't really know what we were right now. "Never mind..."

He stared at me for a while before he rose and grabbed another glass out of the cabinet. "Want a drink?"

"I can't drink scotch the way you do."

He left the glass on the table and didn't fill it. "That's unfortunate. Now I have no one to drink with."

"You always have Hades."

He shook his head. "He's given it up."

"Really?" I asked blankly. "Hades? We're talking about the same person?"

"It was a shock to me too. But yes."

"Sofia doesn't seem like a woman who cares about how much he drinks."

"True. But then he went to the doctor and found out his liver is damaged and he has high blood pressure because of it."

"Oh wow."

"It's just me now."

"Have you been to the doctor lately?"

He shook his head and leaned back into the cushions of the couch, staring at the fire. "Men like me don't go to the doctor."

"Maybe you should."

He grew quiet.

"Because maybe you're in just as bad shape as he is..." I was starting to worry, to grow concerned over his health.

He slowly turned his head back to me, still intimidating me. "When you're the woman in my bed, you get to worry about all that shit. But until you are, my health isn't your concern." He turned back to the fire.

I wasn't sure if that was his way of pressuring me. "Are you implying someone else is currently in your bed?" I hadn't seen him much, so I really had no idea. Women could come and go down the hallway, and I'd have no idea. These walls were thick. I never heard him in his bedroom, and I doubt he heard me in mine.

He leaned forward slightly, his arms resting on his thighs so his fingertips could touch. "Is that answer not obvious to you?"

The longer I held his gaze, the warmer my cheeks felt. I could feel the blood rise to the surface, innately aroused by the possessive way he stared at me. He'd told me he loved me and it floored me, but I'd never imagined a life with his fidelity, his commitment, even when he got nothing from me. It was the kind of loyalty I'd never received from Liam. The moment things weren't picture-perfect, he lost sight of his values. "You just said I had no right to have an opinion about your health."

"No. You don't have the right to nag. Men put up with that because they're getting laid. When I'm getting laid, you can give me shit all you want." He stared at me for several heart-beats before he turned away.

Sex and intimacy had been the last things on my mind for the past few weeks, but now that I was alone with him, watching his hard chest while he was shirtless, I craved those things more. Jumping into bed with someone else would seem too soon after a serious relationship, but since I was in love with this man...it was different.

"No." He kept his eyes on the fire. "I'm not seeing anyone else."

I was relieved I wouldn't have to see that supermodel ever again...with her double-zero waist and her legs for days. I was like most women, with a stomach and an ass.

"That seems pointless to me when there's only one woman I want." He grabbed the glass off the table and took another drink, as if he hadn't just said something deeply romantic.

I wanted to sit right next to him on that couch, to have my legs lying across his, my fingers in his hair. That had been one of our favorite places to make love in the heart of winter. It was hard not to think of those memories...especially when I could recreate them whenever I wanted.

SEVEN

DAMIEN

I walked down the hallway and headed down the stairs to the main dining room. It was early morning, and I needed to be in the office in an hour. When I reached the bottom floor, I saw the sunlight flooding in from every window, bringing the heat of springtime, the images of blooming flowers and vibrancy bright in my mind.

My father was already at the table, reading the paper while he enjoyed his morning coffee.

Sometimes I joined him. Sometimes I didn't have time. I took a seat and poured a steaming cup of coffee.

He finished the paragraph before he folded the paper and set it to the side. "'Bout time you showed your face."

The corner of my mouth rose in a smile. "Good morning to you too."

"It's been over a week since I've seen you."

"Well, I have a job. You don't."

He gave me an exasperated look before he drank from his coffee.

Patricia gave me a plate of egg whites with veggies and a piece of wheat toast. She gave my father a completely different meal —pancakes, bacon, and eggs.

He bathed everything in syrup before he started to eat.

I noticed my father had gained at least ten pounds since he'd moved in a few months ago. "Maybe you should have a light breakfast and have a bigger lunch."

"What's that supposed to mean?" He sliced into his pancakes and placed a large piece into his mouth, the syrup dripping.

"It means you're getting fat, Dad. I had you move in here to have a better life. But if you keep eating like this, you're gonna have a lot of other problems."

Just to be ridiculous, he took another enormous bite. "I'm a grown man, and I can eat what I want."

Even if I wanted to kick him out, he wouldn't leave. He loved his new life in my house. He loved having Patricia to wait on him, to make meals he couldn't get enough of. "Just giving you some friendly advice."

"Well, it wasn't very friendly."

"Tough love never is." I took a few bites and stared out the open windows.

"Catalina is fond of your lady friend."

"Annabella told me the feeling is mutual."

"Is this serious?"

I chewed the rest of my food as I considered my response. "You've never asked me stuff like that before, so don't ask now. You're living with me, so I can't hide those things like I used to."

His pancakes were devoured, so he picked up a slice of bacon and took a bite, the crunch audible. "I know you've had women come and go here, but I've never asked. The reason why I ask now is because she joined us for lunch. That's the first time I've ever seen you acknowledge a woman in your life at all."

That was a solid argument, and I couldn't counter it.

"And she's beautiful...lovely...interesting." He took another bite and continued to chew. He was aggravated minutes ago, but now he seemed involved, like this conversation was interesting rather than frustrating. "You have to think about your legacy, Damien. You're getting old."

"I'm not a woman, Dad."

"But you don't want to be an old man when your kids are finally grown."

I might not even live long enough to grow old. "You're still here, aren't you?"

"And you'll be the first one to say I'm an old-ass man."

I chuckled. "Dad, you're fine."

He shrugged. "You don't want me to live alone, you think I'm fat..."

"That's not what I said—"

"That's what I heard, and that's all that matters."

I rolled my eyes because it wasn't possible to argue with my old man.

"So, can I ask about this woman?"

I considered the request for a long time before I gave in. "I guess."

"Is it serious?"

My dad and I had never had this kind of conversation before, and it was almost weird. His fatherly duties faded away once I became a man, and he respected me as an adult and didn't pry into my life...unlike my mother. But he switched back into the role almost effortlessly. "Yes."

There was a powerful look of joy in his eyes, but it was also incredibly subtle, as if he did his best to hide how happy that made him. It was a softer expression, a great contradiction to the hardness he usually wore. "Is it the first time this has happened to you?"

"Yes."

"I wished I'd known that sooner...I would have made a better impression."

"She said you were both lovely—although I'm not sure why she thinks that."

He smiled slightly. "Then you two are living together."

"No. She's just staying here until we get a few things figured out."

"If it's serious, why doesn't she just stay here permanently?"

I wasn't going to share every single detail. "We haven't known each other long. She's recently divorced, so there's no rush."

He didn't make any protestations about her marital situation, when my mother definitely would have. "Did she leave him for you?"

"No. But we were together before she got married. Her marriage didn't last long..."

"She chose him over you?" he asked in surprise.

"No. She told me she loved me, and I said I didn't feel the same way."

As if he understood exactly what I meant, he nodded. "Once she was gone, you realized what she really meant to you."

"Sort of. We still saw each other a lot, and I slowly started to feel that way."

"Does she want children?"

I wasn't sure if she could have them at all. "Let's not jump ahead. This is all new to me."

"Fair enough." He returned to eating his food. "Wish you the best."

"Thanks, Dad." I went back to my meal, and we fell into comfortable silence.

WE SPENT OUR EVENINGS TOGETHER, but nothing physical had happened yet. She sat on a different couch, always drawing an invisible barrier between us. I could tell she was purposely holding back from me because the ease of our conversation hadn't returned. A part of her still felt guilty for being with me, for having a relationship with a man so quickly after her divorce.

It was frustrating as fuck.

But I was patient...because I had no choice. Unlike Liam, I was loyal through the bad and the good, and I wasn't going to pick up a piece of ass just because the woman I loved was unavailable.

I came home later than usual because I had a lot of stuff on my plate. I made it to the top of the stairs and loosened my tie as I maneuvered down the hallway. Suits weren't my thing. I'd work in sweatpants if it weren't tacky.

When I passed Annabella's door, I heard a loud sound... followed quickly by a second.

I halted in front of the door, listening closely.

It sounded like two women laughing.

I opened the door and peeked my head inside.

Catalina and Annabella were on the couch in front of the TV, laughing their asses off even though the movie they were watching looked like a drama. There were empty bottles of wine on the table in front of them, along with a cheese board and a stash of baguettes.

"Having a good time?" I asked sarcastically.

Catalina looked up, her cheeks flushed from the booze. "Aw, it's my big brother."

Yep, she was super drunk. "I'll leave you to it."

"Wait, wait." Catalina stumbled to her feet and headed toward me.

"Nope." I shut the door and walked to my bedroom, not wanting to deal with my drunk-ass sister, who was even more annoying than usual. I dropped my jacket on the edge of the bed and pulled the tie from around my neck.

She didn't respect boundaries, so she walked inside. "Damien, you've gotta help me."

I rolled my eyes as my back was turned to her. "Help with what?"

She grabbed the back of my arm for balance and then started laughing for no apparent reason.

I shrugged her off and walked to a chair so I could sit and slip off my dress shoes.

"Can you hook us up with more wine?" She followed me to the chair. "Patricia says she's out, but I don't buy that shit."

"Whoa...very ladylike."

She grabbed one of my shoes and threw it at me.

I let it bounce off my arm. "I'm sure she cut you off on purpose."

"Well, I'm sure you've got something stashed in here—"

"No."

She started to whine. "Come on, big brother. Please, please, pretty please..."

I walked to my liquor cabinet.

"Yes!"

I pulled out a bottle of water that was disguised as a bottle of vodka. "Here." I came back and handed it to her.

"Ooh...got any caviar?"

She really was drunk if she actually thought straight vodka sounded good after all that wine and cheese. All I did was give her a cold stare.

She rolled her eyes. "Party pooper." She started to walk back, barefoot and somewhat stumbling. "Want to join us?"

"Not even a little."

"Oh, come on." She got the door open and turned back around. "Anna is a super-cool chick. She's sooo hot too."

"I'm aware."

"Oh my god, you love her!" She walked out the door and shut it behind her, her loud voice audible behind her. "Anna, my brother wants to sex you up." The other door slammed behind her, and then their laughter was concealed in Annabella's bedroom.

I dragged my hand down my face, relieved that interaction hadn't lasted any longer than necessary. I'd just walked in the door, hadn't showered, and hadn't even had a goddamn drink. But I suspected Catalina wouldn't bother me again because she was fighting the clock after all that booze. She would collapse on the bed within the hour.

Problem solved.

I FACED the mirror as I adjusted my tie. I was in a gray suit, ready to head to the bank and complete another day's worth of bullshit. It was another sunny day, another warm kiss of spring.

The door opened without a knock.

Catalina stepped inside in the same pink dress she'd worn the night before, makeup gone from her face and her hair messy from sleeping off her intoxication. She dragged her fingers down the side of her face, getting the sleep from her eyes as she groaned.

"Don't expect me to feel bad for you."

She yawned and then came farther into the room. "You have aspirin or something?"

"I have everything, Catalina."

"Then give me the good shit." She fell into a chair at my table, sitting directly in the sunlight.

I opened my nightstand and pulled out a few tablets and then poured her a mug of coffee. I put the pills and beverage in front of her. "Caffeine will help your headache."

She swallowed the pills dry and then sipped her coffee.

I pulled on my shoes then sat in the chair across from her, feeling too guilty to leave her alone. I should pull on my jacket and head to work, but my DNA was programmed to care for this woman even when I didn't want to. I stared at her in the sunlight, seeing the bits of dust floating in the air around her. The heat was warm on the fabric of my clothes, and it made her brown hair have a distinct red cast to it because she dyed her hair. She was a beautiful woman, inheriting our mother's looks to where she looked like her sister rather than her daughter. "You're gonna feel like shit the rest of the day. But drink lots of water, and you'll be as good as new tomorrow."

"Damien, this isn't my first hangover." She took a sip of her coffee then rubbed her left eye, like that was the area where her migraine was the most prominent. "I've probably had more of them than you."

"Because I don't get hangovers, no matter how much I drink."

"Congratulations," she said sarcastically. "Your body is seventy percent booze. Not seventy percent water." She drank more of her coffee, the steam rising above her face and drifting to the ceiling.

"Seemed like you guys had fun."

"Oh, we did. Just can't totally remember how much fun we had…"

"How was the vodka I gave you?"

"Don't remember that either."

"Then it's a good thing the bottle actually had water in it."

She chuckled before she took another drink. "Geez, I was stupid drunk."

I nodded. "Yes."

"When I woke up, Anna was still passed out. I think she drank more than I did."

And I couldn't even take advantage of her. "Sounds like you two have become good friends."

"Definitely." Her painted nails rested against the white mug, and she gently tapped the ceramic surface before she lifted her gaze to look at me. "So, what's the story with you and her?"

"She didn't tell you?" Isn't that what women did? Shared every little detail?

"She told me she was recently divorced and she shouldn't have married him in the first place. She's staying with you now for protection. But she didn't say much about you, specifically. I thought I would just ask you."

"I don't ask about your boyfriends."

"So, she's your girlfriend, then?" she asked, a victorious look on her face.

I'd walked right into that, hadn't I? "She's not my girlfriend. I don't like that term."

"Then what is she?"

I shrugged. "Not sure."

"Why does she sleep in a different room?"

Catalina wasn't going to let this go until she dragged everything out. I would ignore her interrogation, but if they were going to be friends, it was bound to come up anyway. "She just got divorced. She doesn't want to rush into anything."

"But you two are kinda together?"

I gave a nod.

"Ooh…my brother is in love."

"I never said I was."

"My manwhore brother is trying to get with a divorced woman. I don't see why you would be patient for someone unless she was important to you. And if she's important to you…then there must be something there." She reached for the packets of sugar and added them to the black coffee, her eyebrows high in an obnoxious, know-it-all way.

"We were together before she got married."

"Ooh…now that she's available, you want her again."

I'd wanted her long before she was available. "You're nosy."

"This is the first time my brother has ever been seen with a woman. It's a big fucking deal. You've got a girlfriend."

"She's not my girlfriend," I repeated.

"Are you seeing anyone else?"

My response was a cold look.

"Then she's your girlfriend," she said simply. "You don't want a put a label on it? Fine. But that's what she is." She added more sugar and stirred the mug. Her tanned skin had a distinct glow in the sunlight, becoming more bronzed right before my eyes. "She's a really sweet girl, so you picked well."

"You're fine with the fact that she's been divorced? Aren't you supposed to be protective? Judgmental?"

Both of her eyebrows rose high. "Uh, no." She placed her hand across her chest. "I'm the least judgmental person on the planet. You're the judgmental one. I don't care that she's been married. The guy was a dick who cheated on her. It wasn't her fault. And from what I've seen of her with my own eyes, she's a lovely person. She's kind, compassionate, funny...hot. What else are you looking for?"

I hadn't expected my family to accept her so easily, not because they were cold, but because I'd never done this before. I'd never introduced a woman to my sister or my father. And if Catalina brought a man around, I'd probably be the protective and judgmental one. I projected my own behavior onto her. "Stop saying she's hot."

"I've said it once."

"No, you said it last night too."

"What?" she asked incredulously. "I can't think someone of the same sex is hot?"

"Not when it's my girlfriend—"

"Ha!" She slammed both palms onto the table. "Told you."

I issued a quiet growl as I rolled my eyes.

HADES STEPPED into my office and set a stack of folders on the corner of my desk. He said a few things about clients and other projects as he slid his hands into his pockets. Then he addressed the real issue that was on his mind. "Haven't heard from him?"

"Not yet." I waited for Liam to pop out of a box like a demonic toy clown. "But I told Annabella that if it came down to his life or mine, it's gonna be his."

"And her response?"

"She accepted it."

"That's progress." He lowered himself into the chair, wearing a dark blue suit with a matching tie. His muscular arms rested along the sides of the chair, and he placed one ankle on the opposite knee, stretching out like he was lounging on the beach. "Getting laid?"

I gave him a scowl. "Did you really just ask that?"

"What's wrong with the question?"

"What if I asked about Sofia?"

"She's my wife. It's different. And I didn't ask for details. Just asked if you're getting laid." He adjusted the sleeves of his collared shirt under his jacket, so the collar stuck out just a little bit. "And judging from that pissed expression on your face, the answer is no."

It was a big fucking no. "I'm not gonna rush her."

"Yeah, I know how that is. You just have to wait for her to make the first move."

I didn't want to wait long to be with the woman I loved. I fantasized about her when I was awake, and when that wasn't enough, I dreamed about her. The chemistry we had was explosive compared to what she had with Liam, and in my eyes, she'd always been mine...even when she was married to him. He was just an obstacle standing in our way. Now that he wasn't there, we could finally break free of our restraints and be what we wanted.

But he was still in the way.

It would take time, and I just had to wait.

Hades could read the frustration in my eyes. "It'll be worth the wait, man. I promise."

AFTER MY WORKOUT AND DINNER, I sat on the couch with the TV in the background. My mind drifted to a lot of other things, from the bank to the streets, to the woman down the hall from me. Sometimes the scotch was strong enough to dull my thoughts, to get my brain to sleep while I was still awake. With the glass in my hand, I stared at the TV, not really paying attention to what I was looking at.

Then the door opened—and Annabella stepped inside.

There wasn't a drop of makeup on her face, and judging from her messy hair, she'd been nursing her hangover all day. She may have just woken up a few minutes ago. She was in a tiny pair of silk shorts and a t-shirt without a bra.

I stared at her in silence, finding her beautiful even at her worst.

She sauntered into the living room, running her fingers through her hair to pull it from her face. "Mind if I join you?"

"Never."

Instead of moving to the other couch, she took the seat directly beside me. Her arm grazed mine. Her thigh touched mine. The ends of her strands subtly brushed across my skin before they slipped away.

I froze in place, not having touched her skin in so long.

She tucked her feet behind her ass and leaned into me, her arm hooking through mine so she could rest her head on my shoulder.

The touch was innocent, but it made the low-burning fire inside me leap to life with sky-high flames. The booze lost all effect on my system, and my heart started to beat faster. Her scent entered my nose, a mixture of roses and pure woman.

My hands ached to grab her, to turn her face to me so I could kiss her with an embrace so strong that it bruised her mouth.

She sighed in comfort as she relaxed into me.

I stared down at her, feeling more alive in that moment than I had in forever.

"I feel terrible..." Her quiet voice escaped into the air, loud enough to be audible over the flames in the fireplace.

My arm pulled free of her grasp, and I wrapped it around her, pulling her close so she could rest her cheek against my chest. My hand slid into her hair, reuniting with my favorite feature she possessed. My fingers lightly touched her, pulling the strands away from her face but also massaging her scalp at the same time.

She sighed quietly, as if that was exactly what she needed.

Me.

She leaned farther into me and wrapped her arm around my waist.

Now, I watched her instead of the screen—and I paid attention to every subtle move, every breath she took, and I felt such a wave of peace, as if I could do this forever...until the sun set for the last time.

We sat together that way for thirty minutes. She closed her eyes and enjoyed the way I touched her, comfortable against my hard body even though I probably felt like a tree trunk. As long as she enjoyed it, I continued to touch her, to caress her like a precious doll.

She raised her head and looked at me, her eyes possessing a sleepy gaze. "I drank way too much last night..."

"I heard."

"I haven't drunk like that since..." Her eyes glazed over as she tried to think. "I can't even remember."

"Probably because you never have. My sister is a bad influence."

"She likes to have fun. Doesn't make her a bad influence."

"I disagree." My fingers never left her hair, continuing to glide through her softness. "Have you had dinner?"

She shook her head. "The last thing I want is food. I puked out all my intestines earlier today."

"Want a drink?"

She turned to give me an incredulous look.

"It helps, I swear." I smiled at her confusion because she somehow made that expression cute.

"Maybe it helps for you."

"Just take a sip." I grabbed my scotch off the table and handed it to her.

She hesitated before she took a small sip. Then she stuck out her tongue like she was disgusted. "Yuck. God, I'll never drink again."

"I hope that's not true. Drinking is one of the best things in the world." I'd been in a bad mood for weeks, but once I had her affection, my negativity slipped away. I felt better...a lot better.

She stuck out her tongue again. "I couldn't disagree more." She righted herself on the couch and pulled away so she could look at me better. Her knees still touched my thigh, and her scent still surrounded me.

My hand slid from her hair and rested on the back of the couch, but I was desperate to touch her once again, to feel the warmth of her neck, the pulse that trembled at my touch.

She stared at me for a while, her eyes filling with that silent intensity we shared. She felt the chemistry between us, the magnetic pull that wanted us to slam together with a noticeable bang. "I hope I didn't make an idiot out of myself yesterday."

"Only my sister did."

She chuckled. "She's a funny girl."

"Funny to look at, maybe."

She smiled slightly, like she knew I was teasing. "How are you?"

I miss you like crazy. "Fine. You?"

"Right now, I feel like shit. But otherwise...fine."

My fingers couldn't fight the urge, and they slid across the back of her neck, coming into contact with that heat. They touched the fall of her hair, slid up as they grazed across her beautiful brown hair.

She visibly melted at my touch, taking a deep breath at the contact. "I think I'm still a little drunk...because I want to kiss you."

"No. That's me, not the booze." I wanted to pull her into me to kiss her, but I had listened to Hades's advice to let her make the first move. "And you can kiss me whenever you want. I'm yours." I wanted those lips more than anything, wanted to actually feel the woman I'd worked so hard to enjoy.

She scooted closer to me, her hand moving to my bare chest so she could feel my heartbeat. She pressed her palm lightly, as if she wanted to feel the transfer of heat from my body to hers. Her forehead moved closer to mine, but she didn't kiss me. She just held me there, letting our bodies touch.

I wanted more, but I would settle for this. It was a piece of her. I would collect the rest of the pieces in time.

She came closer, her bottom nearly in my lap. Her hand slid across my cheek and into my hair, the way she used to touch me. Her eyes looked downward, and she stared at my chest as she held me. Moments passed, and neither one of us moved.

Our heartbeats slowed, and our breathing became so quiet neither one of us could hear it. The TV was ignored. The flames died in the hearth without another log to feed its hunger. The connection reminded me of what Hades had described with his wife, that there was an invisible connection stronger than anything else in this world. That was how I felt now, like nothing could ever diminish this feeling between us.

She pulled away, her eyes focused on where her palm rested against my chest. "Could I sleep with you...?" She didn't raise her gaze, as if she were afraid to ask the question, to give me the wrong impression of what she wanted. Her fingertips lightly pressed into my chest, her fingers cold in comparison to my naturally scorching skin.

I wanted her in any way I could have her, whether that meant I could touch her or not. "Always." I grabbed the remote and turned off the TV. My half-full glass was abandoned on the table, and I knew the fire would finish dying out on its own. When we used to be together, she liked staring at the fire as she fell asleep, so I let it be.

We left the couch, and Annabella immediately headed to the bed, the side that used to be hers. She pulled the covers back then slipped inside, making herself at home even though it'd been over six months since the last time she'd been there.

I closed the curtains so the sunlight wouldn't wake her in the morning. I was up at seven, so the sunlight didn't make a difference to me. I poured her a glass of water and set it on the nightstand beside her.

She was turned on her side, facing my usual position in the bed. She immediately fell into old habits, pulling the sheets to just below her shoulder. Her hand scooped her hair away, pushing it onto the pillow behind her.

I dropped my sweatpants then got into bed beside her. My body hit the soft mattress, and I could immediately feel the difference with her presence. The bed smelled like a woman, not a man, and the sound of her breathing filled the usual silence. The sheets bunched around my waist so my chest could feel the air that came through the vents overhead. I would normally pull her onto me or roll on top of her, but I kept my distance, lying on my back, with my gaze on the ceiling. I wouldn't even allow myself to look at her, because the sight of her in my bed would make me think of things I shouldn't.

She was still for minutes as if she was already asleep. Then she shifted toward me, snuggling into my side like it was too cold to sleep alone. Her face pressed into my neck, her nose right up against me, and she even placed her thigh over mine. Once she was comfortable, she released a quiet sigh, like she'd never been so comfortable.

Like this felt right.

I stared at the ceiling longer until I placed my hand on top of hers. Together, they rested on my chest, rising and falling slowly with my quiet breathing. Then she squeezed my fingers slightly, as if she wanted to make sure that I was real, that this moment wasn't a fictitious thought in her head.

"I'm tired of forcing myself to stay away...to sleep alone, when this is where I want to be."

"Then don't."

"Now that I'm here, I don't think I could anyway."

EIGHT

ANNABELLA

WHEN I WAS HOME ALL DAY, I DIDN'T HAVE MUCH TO DO. I worked on my laptop and kept up with paperwork, but there were other things I simply couldn't do, like give tours to potential clients who wanted to have their wedding at the hotel. But I sent them pictures and spoke to them on the phone, just as I would if I were sitting in my office all day.

But it was still lonely not to have Sofia across the hall, not to interact with the other staff at the hotel that cared about making the place as beautiful as possible. It was a sense of pride for everyone there, from the chef to the janitor.

Just when I shut my laptop, Catalina texted me.

Hey, were you as hungover as I was?

Worse, I'd imagine.

LOL. You wanna go to lunch?

Like, outside the house?

Patricia is a great cook, but you need to get some vitamin D. It's such a warm day. It's only spring but it already feels like summer.

I knew Damien didn't want me to leave the house, not when Liam could be waiting for the right opportunity to grab me. *I really shouldn't go anywhere...*

Because that asshole says no? Her attitude was obvious in her words. *Don't be one of those women who obeys their man like a dog.*

I'm not. I just know his concern is valid.

Look, if some guy bothers you, I'll take care of him.

Obviously, she thought this was all a joke. *I'm being serious, Catalina.*

As am I.

I stopped texting, unsure what to do.

It's just lunch, Anna. We'll walk a few blocks, eat, and then walk back. But if you're really that uncomfortable, I'll come by there.

Now that I had a friend, I didn't want to lose her. Hanging out at the house all the time wasn't fun for anyone. And I wanted to be close with Damien's sister, because I assumed my relationship with him might last forever. *Alright. Just give me fifteen minutes.*

Yaaaassssss.

SHE PICKED me up at the front door, and together, we walked down the street. She was in a short royal blue dress that had slits along the sides near her stomach, showing some skin but not enough to reveal her belly button. Her jean jacket hid most of it. She walked in wedges like they were flats, and she had a little brown purse that hung across her body. "It's such a beautiful day." She tilted her head back and held out her hands, as if she was absorbing the sun straight into her bloodstream. "Girl, if I could photosynthesize, I would."

I chuckled. "I'm a sun person too."

"I hate winter. Hate it. Hate it. Hate it." She lowered her arms and spun in a circle as she kept walking. "See? Isn't it nice to get out of the house?"

I had to admit it was. "Yes."

"The only good thing about winter is you can screw in the back seat of a car without getting hot. Otherwise, winter serves absolutely no purpose at all."

"I've never gotten laid in the back seat."

"Never?" she asked incredulously. "You've gotta try it sometime."

I could have screwed Damien last night in a comfortable bed with the fire crackling, but that didn't happen. It would eventually be inevitable, and I suspected it would grow more difficult to resist as I continued to sleep with him. But it was the best night of sleep I'd ever gotten, and I had no regrets. "I'll put it on my bucket list."

We walked two blocks until we reached a small bistro.

"You wanna sit on the patio?"

"Sure."

We moved to a table in the center of the seating area. All the other tables were taken, mostly by people who were there on their lunch break. Catalina opened her menu and looked through the options. "I want everything, but I'll order a goddamn salad."

"We came all the way here so you could order a salad?" I asked like a smartass.

"I know." She pulled off her sunglasses and rolled her eyes. "But I've got to keep my weight." She stuck out her tongue this time. "Trust me, if I could gain twenty pounds, I would do it in a heartbeat. I have no tits and no ass."

"That's not true."

"You haven't seen me naked, girl."

"I can see your tits right now." I looked down at her dress. "You've got something going on there."

She waved me off. "Well, thanks. I would quit ballet if I didn't love it so much. My feet are always blistered, and I have to stay at, like, eight pounds, but I won't be able to do it much longer, so I'll enjoy it while I can."

I wished I were passionate about something like that. "I want to watch you dance sometime."

"I have performance almost every weekend. Have Damien take you."

I doubted he would take me anywhere. "I'll ask him." I looked over the menu and didn't give a damn about my waistline. I decided on something big and delicious before I put the menu down.

The waiter took our orders before walking away.

Catalina sipped her iced tea and glanced at another table. "Ooh...that guy is hot."

I didn't look, not out of loyalty; it just wasn't instinct.

"He looks good in a suit." She took another sip and stared. "I bet he looks even better without that suit, if you know what I mean."

I chuckled. She was a woman deep in her youth, enjoying every second and savoring every experience. Not tied to any man and enjoying her beauty, she lived a young woman's dream. "I'm guessing you aren't seeing that guy anymore?"

"I am," she said. "But it's not serious." She turned back to me. "He wants it to be serious, but I definitely don't."

"What's wrong with him?"

"Nothing." She shrugged. "I'm just staying single until I'm twenty-eight."

I cocked an eyebrow. "Why?"

"Because that's when I need to meet my husband, date for like a year, and then get married to pop out those kids. Getting married any sooner is too premature, at least for me." She drank from her tea again. "I want a more mature man. They tend to need to be older to get that aged effect that I like."

"You could date an older man right now."

She shrugged. "I haven't met one I like." She glanced at the man she had just checked out. "He looks like he might be like twenty-eight, which is a good age, but I'm not ready to settle down yet anyway, so it doesn't matter."

"You're living the dream," I said with a chuckle.

"It's not for everybody. You got married young, and you were happy."

"Yeah...and that blew up in my face."

"But you were still happy," she said. "It's not like those years went to waste."

I wasn't so sure anymore. Sometimes I wished I could have met Damien sooner, because he seemed to be a better fit than Liam ever was.

"So, Damien tells me you're his girlfriend."

That didn't sound like something he would say, so I was surprised. "Really?"

"Direct quote."

He'd told me I was his, and that made me feel...a million emotions. He was loyal to me even though I had nothing to offer him right now. I wanted him and I missed him, but I was also overwhelmed with guilt, moving on from a marriage far too soon. The first time I got divorced, I waited months before I went on my first date. But now I was on the cusp of falling into a serious relationship, making love to a man who was already in love with me. It was so intense, it felt wrong.

"I've never seen my brother with a lady in my whole life, let alone living with one, so you must be the real deal."

"I'm not living with him. Just staying there until—"

"Whatever. It's still a big deal."

I didn't know what to say, so I drank from my glass of wine.

"That makes me happy, because I was afraid he would wait too long and end up alone. Then it would be totally up to me to carry the family lineage."

"I'm not sure if he even wants to have children."

"Don't you?" she asked.

"Yes." More than anything.

"Then he will." She turned back to the guy she was eyeing. "I'm gonna give this hottie my number. I'll be right back." She pulled out a pen from her purse and scribbled on a napkin. In her feminine handwriting, she wrote the number in large characters so the digits would be unmistakable. "Wish me luck." She left the table.

"I don't think you need it..."

JUST WHEN WE finished our lunch, I noticed a large man appear behind Catalina. With enormous shoulders, chiseled arms, and a pair of blue eyes that were brighter than a summer sky, he stared at me like a hunter that had just cornered his meal.

Oh shit.

"What?" Catalina signed the tab before she pushed it away. "You look sick."

I couldn't talk because I was in survival mode. My heart was pounding with adrenaline, my palms were so sweaty that I couldn't grab a rope to climb to safety. Damien wasn't there to protect me, and now that Liam has snapped, I wasn't sure if I could do anything to stop this. I couldn't reason with him. I wasn't his wife anymore, so I had no power at all. I shouldn't have come here. It was a mistake...a big one.

"Anna?" Catalina narrowed her eyes.

Liam came closer to our table and stared down at me, his eyes menacing. He ignored Catalina altogether, and the wedding ring on his left hand was terrifying rather than romantic. He stared at me like I was his property, like a cow that wandered past the boundary line. He'd come to retrieve me, to put a lasso around my neck and drag me home. "Get up." He didn't raise his voice because we were in public, but if I didn't obey, there would be consequences.

"Liam—"

"Get. Up." He leaned down so only I could hear. "Or I'll make you get up."

I breathed hard in my panic, unsure what to do.

Catalina raised both eyebrows and sized him up, looking from his head to his toes. "Who the *fuck* do you think you are?"

He ignored her. "Three seconds, Anna."

"Three seconds until I kick your ass, bitch." Catalina got to her feet, hands on her hips as she stood tall in her wedges.

"Catalina," I said quietly. "Let it go."

"Fuck no." Catalina shoved him in the shoulder.

Liam moved slightly, probably because he wasn't expecting a woman to actually attack him.

"Catalina." I got to my feet quickly. "You don't understand. He's a fighter—"

She slapped him across the face, kneed him in the dick, and then kicked one of his knees with her massive shoe. It was like a Jackie Chan movie, hit after hit happening within seconds. "I'm a fighter too."

Liam moved with all her hits, falling down because she'd struck him so quickly, hitting all his most vulnerable places.

Now everyone in the restaurant was staring.

"You've got three seconds to get out of this restaurant." Catalina stood over him, victorious. "Or I'm gonna kick you in the face and knock out those two front teeth."

He looked up at her, a scowl on his face and his expression full of the promise of retribution. "Fucking bitch." He rose to his feet, staring at her with menace. "I don't hit women, but I'm about to—"

She punched him so hard in the face, he fell back and fell on top of a table. The couple sitting there jumped out of their seats and backed away as the wooden table broke under his weight. Everyone gasped at the scene.

"Come near my girl again, and I'll pluck your balls off your body like cherries off a tree. Bitch." She flipped her hair then stormed off, strutting out of there like a queen who had just conquered a land.

I didn't linger. I followed her and got the hell out of there.

WHEN WE WERE in the entryway of the house, I finally spoke. "Where did you learn to do that?" I was disturbed by what had just happened because I knew Liam had intended to whisk me away, to make me disappear so Damien would never be able to find me. I couldn't believe we got away. The only reason we did was because Catalina surprised us both. I never would have moved against him that way because I knew I couldn't win. He would have grabbed me by the arm and dragged me out of there. But with Catalina...she knew how to kick ass.

She answered so nonchalantly, like it wasn't a big deal. "This guy I was seeing taught me a few things."

"Was he a professional fighter?"

"No. He was just really into martial arts."

"Maybe I should learn some things..."

"It wouldn't hurt." She pulled her sunglasses off her face. "Big men like that fight like brutes. But martial arts are about striking quickly and using the least amount of energy. He may be bigger and stronger than you, but you're much smaller and quicker. It's not about always landing a knockout punch. It's about wearing him down until he's incapacitated."

"Good to know."

"I'm sure Damien could teach you."

"He knows martial arts?"

She shrugged. "My brother knows everything, so probably." She pulled her hair over one shoulder and then returned her sunglasses to her face. "I should get going. If you see my dad, tell him I said hi. And sorry I asked you to lunch. Didn't think that loser was stalking you like that."

"Yeah...neither did I." That meant he was watching the house, waiting for an opportunity once I walked out the front door. I guess it was smart that I wasn't going to work anymore. If Liam had intended to grab me in the middle of a public restaurant, he wouldn't give a shit about the hotel. "Damien is gonna be so mad at me..."

"Why? Don't tell him."

"I can't not tell him."

"Whether he knows or not doesn't make a difference, right? He assumed Liam is watching the house, and he was right. My personal opinion is this. The less men know they're right, the better." She blew me a kiss before she walked out. "Don't stress about it. No point in worrying about things you can't change."

I HEARD Damien walk down the hallway. His footsteps were so distinct, it was obvious it wasn't Patricia entering his bedroom to make the bed and gather his dirty laundry.

I left my bedroom and joined him. I would have waited in there for him to come home, but I hadn't officially moved in to his space, so I didn't want to cross the line. It might be an invasion of privacy.

His back was to me as he stripped off the jacket to his suit and tossed it over the back of the chair. He must have heard the door shut behind him, but he didn't turn around. He loosened his tie and pulled it free from around his corded neck before tossing it on top of his discarded jacket. "I told you not to leave the house." His fingers moved to his chest, and he unbuttoned his white collared shirt, allowing the fabric to fall free and slide down his arms. His muscular back was tense, all the lines separating groups of muscles as distinct as if outlined by the ink of a permanent marker.

I flinched at the tone of his voice. I was somehow more frightened now than I had been at lunch.

His belt came next, sliding out of the loops before he tossed it aside. As if he expected me to say something first, he didn't turn around, like he was too angry to look at me.

I didn't know what to say. I'd intended to tell him what happened, but not the second he came home, and not like this. We'd spent the night together in bliss, and I'd never felt so comfortable my whole life, like it was where I was meant to be. But now that fairy tale was over.

When I didn't speak, he turned around. He looked at me with his fiercest gaze, his slacks falling low on his hips now that his belt wasn't keeping his clothes in place. His tanned skin covered his thick abs, and there was a noticeable vein that disappeared into his slacks.

Now I was terrified for the second time that afternoon.

He took a step forward. "I told you not to leave the house—and you did it anyway." His muscular arms were rigid in place, some of his muscles twitching as the adrenaline dumped into his blood.

I had no idea what he knew and how he knew it. Catalina could have ratted me out, but that seemed unlikely. She was the one who told me not to mention it in the first place. Put on the spot, I didn't know what to say. Damien and I had become closer last night, but that seemed nonexistent now.

He moved a little closer. "I'm waiting for your response." He stopped when he was a few feet away, both of his hands tightening into fists.

When I took a breath, it burned my lungs, like the oxygen was full of acid. "How did you know that?"

That was the wrong thing to say. One eyebrow slowly rose while ferocity entered his gaze. "Because there's nothing I don't know about, Annabella. I hope you have a good explanation. If not, this is going to be an unpleasant conversation." He didn't need to raise his voice to frighten me, changing his tone was more than enough.

"Catalina wanted to go to lunch…"

He stilled at the response, probably shocked that I'd risked my life for something so stupid. "That better be a joke."

I dropped my gaze.

"If you wanted to get out of the house so bad, I could have taken you. But you run off with my sister? The most oblivious person on the planet? Her arrogance makes her careless. That's the last person I'd want you to leave the house with."

"Well, we're fine, so…"

That wasn't the right thing to say either because his eyes narrowed farther. "You're fine…that's your justification?"

I was starting to wonder if he had no idea what happened at the restaurant. Because if he did, his reaction would be more severe right now. "I'm sorry, and I won't do it again…"

When he sighed, it was deep like a growl, and he turned away from me dismissively. "Get out." He stepped into his living room and took a seat. His scotch was waiting for him like always, and he helped himself to a full glass. As if I wasn't there, he stared at the fire.

Now I didn't know what to do.

"Did you not hear me?" He raised his voice slightly.

I moved to the living room and stood behind one of the armchairs. "Damien."

He wouldn't look at me.

"I said I was sorry."

"And that makes it all okay?" He swirled his drink. "When Liam said sorry for fucking someone, did that make it okay?"

My eyes narrowed at the insult. "Don't be an asshole."

He set down the glass and looked at me. "I'm trying to keep you safe, and I'm an asshole?"

"You're an asshole for throwing that in my face, and you know it. Be angry at me for my wrongs, but don't be angry at me for things I can't control. Don't use my pain as ammo to pump me full of lead."

His eyes were rigid and focused as he watched me, the green color of his eyes brighter because of the flames reflecting on the surface. There was no hint of remorse, so an apology wasn't on the horizon. "I don't want to fight with you, Annabella. So, you should just go."

Telling him what happened with Liam would just make the situation worse, but I felt deceitful keeping it from him. The situation would escalate and break us further apart.

"And yet...you stay." He dragged his hands down his face then looked at the floor.

"I need to tell you something."

He closed his eyes and sighed. "This should be good..."

"Catalina and I went to lunch...and Liam showed up."

"Of course, he did." He lifted his gaze and looked at me, livid.

"You were right. He was going to take me."

He was quiet for a long time, as if he were afraid of the things that would come out of his mouth when he spoke. "How did you get away?"

"Catalina."

"She talked her way out of that?" he asked incredulously.

"No...she kicked his ass."

He looked back at me, his eyes more furious than ever before. Seconds passed before he rose to his feet, his body visibly shaking. "So, you put my sister in danger now?"

"No. She slapped him around a few times before pushing him into a table. When he was down, we left. Liam wouldn't hit a woman. If he was going to, he would have hit me already."

He dragged his hands down his face again. "So, let me get this straight. You go out to lunch with my sister, get harassed by Liam, and the only reason you got away was because my sister threw a few punches?"

"Uh...I guess. I wouldn't put it that way—"

"Why didn't you just listen to me?" He threw his arms down. "What if he'd taken you, Annabella? What if he'd punched my sister and knocked her out cold?"

"He wouldn't—"

"Stop saying that shit. You said he wouldn't cheat, and he did. You said he wouldn't try to kidnap you, and he did. You're unable to see reality, to see what's right in front of your face. That's why you need to listen to me because I've got 20/20 vision. I have no idea what the fuck you have." He turned away and began to pace in front of the fire, walking off his rage. "I don't get it, Annabella. You could have just had lunch here."

I couldn't throw Catalina under the bus because he would scream at her next. It was my fault in the end—because I was the one who'd agreed to leave. "I apologized and said it wouldn't happen again."

"And that makes everything okay?" he asked incredulously.

"No...but we should move on."

"It's not easy for me to move on, Annabella. Because if things had happened differently, I would have lost you. And I would have lost my mind to the terrors of my imagination." He stopped pacing and stared at me head on. "So don't expect me to fucking move on."

NINE

DAMIEN

I POUNDED MY FIST AGAINST THE DOOR THEN TURNED back into the hallway so my face wouldn't be pressed into the peephole. When there was no activity, I slammed my fist against the wood again—this time harder.

Footsteps were finally audible on the other side, frantic and quick. Her body pressed against the wood as she examined the peephole and stared at me on the other side of the door. Then she opened it. "Jesus, what's so damn important right now?" She was in a black dress with a gold necklace around her throat. Heels were on her feet, and her brown hair was pulled back from her face.

I moved to go inside her apartment.

She blocked my way. "What are you doing?"

"You aren't gonna invite your brother inside?"

"Why would I? You have no right just to drop by without letting me know."

"No right?" I asked. "You literally do that every week."

"Not this late at night," she countered. "And I don't come to see you."

A man's voice came from behind the door. "Everything alright?"

My eyes narrowed on her face.

"What?" she asked angrily. "Yes, I have a life."

"I need to talk to you, so get rid of him."

"I'm not kicking him out. He's hot."

I rolled my eyes. "If he really likes you, he'll come back."

She sighed in annoyance as she gripped the door. "If you weren't my brother..." She turned away and headed farther into her apartment. "Could we do a rain check? My brother needs to talk to me."

He didn't make a fuss. "Sure. Call me." He moved toward the door then stopped when we came face-to-face.

I sized him up, my instincts unstoppable. I wanted to protect a woman who didn't need to be protected, to make sure this guy was worthy of her when his qualifications were none of my business. I didn't like my sister seeing men casually, bringing them to her apartment for privacy, but I had to remind myself she was a grown-ass woman. She could do whatever she wanted...and it was none of my business.

"Collin." He extended his hand to shake mine.

I took it. "Damien." He was a handsome man, well dressed, seemed like the business type. No red flags. "I apologize for ruining your evening."

"Family always comes first." He gave me a polite nod before he walked off.

I actually liked the guy...which made me dislike him.

I stepped inside her apartment, seeing the scowl on her face. A wine bottle was on the table, along with a tray of various cheeses and fruit and a sliced baguette. A single white candle glowed. "Where did you meet him?"

She crossed her arms over her chest. "The other day at lunch. I gave him my number."

"Seems like a nice guy."

"What did you want to talk about, Damien?" She sat on the sofa and blew out the candle.

I shut the door behind me and took a seat on the sofa beside her. "I'm pretty pissed off at Annabella right now."

She crossed her legs and gave nothing away.

"Since the two of you went to lunch yesterday."

She slowly turned to me, stunning as always. "So, she told you."

"Patricia did."

"Traitor."

"I'm the one who employs her. I'm the man of the house. She's loyal to me—not to you. Therefore, she's not a traitor. Don't call her that."

She sighed. "You're right. She cooks so well that I could never be mad at her..."

But her cooking wasn't good enough to stay home, apparently.

"Fine. Yell at me. Go ahead." She turned to me, both of her arms resting on her raised knee.

"I'm not here to yell at you, Cat."

"Then what?" she asked.

"Just want to make sure you're alright."

The defiance in her eyes slowly softened. She was naturally stubborn and difficult, but she melted right before my eyes, becoming vulnerable in a way very few people ever witnessed.

"Annabella told me what happened with Liam. I want to make sure you're okay."

"If you have to ask, she didn't tell the story right. I broke his nuts and forced him on his back."

"He's a professional fighter, Catalina. He could have killed you."

"Even if I'd known that before, it wouldn't have changed anything. I'm not scared of him. I'm not letting that asshole take my friend away. He spoke to her like a dog. You think I'm gonna let that shit fly?"

The things I loved about her were also things I hated. I loved that she didn't take shit from anybody, but I was afraid it would get her killed one day. "I appreciate what you did, but I never want anything to happen to you. So be careful in those situations. You have no idea what your opponent is capable of."

"We were in a crowded restaurant, Damien. Not in an alleyway."

"Then you understand to run in an alleyway?"

She shrugged. "Depends on the situation."

"Catalina."

"I'm just being honest."

I was glad she knew how to defend herself, but if she messed with the wrong guy, it could end badly. "Where did you learn to do that?"

"This guy I was seeing."

"And why did he think that was necessary to teach you?"

"It was probably just an excuse to keep seeing me, honestly." She straightened her back and brought her hands together on her knee, her gold bracelets complementing her tanned skin.

"I'm sorry Annabella put you in that situation. You are two of the three women in this world that I love, and I would die if something happened to any of you."

Her eyes narrowed slightly. "She didn't put me in that situation."

I stared at her.

"It was my idea. I guess she didn't mention that."

"No." Now I was starting to get angry. All of this was instigated by the person I'd assumed was innocent in the whole ordeal.

"She didn't have to cover for me like that, but I respect her for it."

I felt the adrenaline spike in my blood.

"I was the one who pestered her to leave the house," she said candidly. "I didn't think it would be that big of a deal since we were just going two blocks away. I didn't take the situation seriously, and after I knocked him on his ass, I still didn't. She'd wanted to stay home, but I talked her out of it." She held my gaze and told the truth without hesitation.

I bowed my head because I couldn't look at her.

"I'm sorry, Damien."

I shook my head. "You know what your problem is? You think you know everything." I raised my head to look her in the eye. "You think you've got everything figured out. Your ego misdirects you. You refuse to listen. Maybe people find your confidence attractive, but I know it's just arrogance." I rose from the couch and headed to the door.

"Damien."

"Goodnight, Catalina." I headed into the hallway.

She came after me and grabbed me by the arm.

I twisted out of her grasp but faced her, nostrils flared.

"You know I don't apologize unless I mean it...so you know I'm sincere."

"I don't care that you're sincere. I care about the fact that you put yourself and my woman in danger—for absolutely no reason. You expect me to be impressed that you fought him off? The only reason you're alive is because it wasn't a fair fight. But next time...maybe he'll feel differently about it."

Pain was etched on her face, sincerity so bright it was unmistakable. She was never apologetic about anything, but now she wore her heart on her sleeve, showed a sign of humility. "It won't happen again, okay?"

"Now I'm afraid he's gonna come after you."

"He has no idea who I am."

"Doesn't matter. And maybe it's not obvious to you, but I love you and would die for you. So, if I have to protect two women, it's gonna be a lot harder than protecting one."

"Then why don't you just kill him?"

I released a sarcastic laugh, feeling the pain all the way down to my feet. "I would if I could, Catalina. Trust me, I would..."

WHEN I ENTERED HER BEDROOM, she was sitting on the couch in front of the fire. Instead of watching TV or reading, she was staring into the flames, as if all she could do was sit around and think about our conversation.

I hadn't spoken to her since our fight because I was so angry. I was afraid I would say things I didn't mean, push her away when I should be pulling her close. Adding distance between us was the only solution I had at the time.

But now that Catalina had explained what happened, I realized I was being harsh.

When she heard the door shut behind me, she turned her head my way. She was in a baggy white t-shirt and sleeping shorts, her hair pulled over one shoulder with no makeup on her face. She obviously didn't expect company.

She was beautiful, regardless.

I moved to the couch she was already on, leaving a foot between us.

Her knees were pulled up to her chest, her tanned legs sexy as hell when she wore white. She stared at the side of my face for a while but didn't make a sound. She held her silence so I could speak first.

"Catalina told me she instigated the whole thing."

She released a quiet breath.

"I'm sorry I was so harsh with you."

"It doesn't matter what she did," she whispered. "I should have said no, so don't blame her for everything."

I let the heat warm my face. It was getting warmer with every passing day, and soon the evening fires wouldn't make sense anymore. But they were nice to stare at, nice to listen to when making love. "I respect you for not throwing her under the bus."

"She's my friend…"

Her loyalty was arousing to me, because I understood the importance of loyalty more than anyone. "Just don't let it happen again. We have to be smart. I suspect Liam isn't going to go away. I suspect he's going to become more aggressive than he was before. We need to be smart."

"I know."

I leaned back into the sofa and looked at her, watching the flames light her face with a beautiful glow. I wanted to ask her permission to end this war, but I couldn't bear to listen to her say no. It hurt every time, and I didn't want to hurt. I just wanted to be with her…to feel the peace she used to give me.

So, I said nothing.

She moved closer to me and slid her hand into mine.

My fingers gripped hers in return, feeling the warm softness. My thumb brushed over her knuckles, and I felt her distant pulse deep under the skin.

She rested her chin on my shoulder. "I don't want you to be angry with me."

"I'm not…anymore."

"Good. Because I missed you…"

I stared at the flames as I heard her confession. Then I turned her way and felt my lips move on their own. They pressed into her forehead, coming into contact with the skin I hadn't felt in so long. I closed my eyes as I treasured the touch, barely registering what I was doing. It just felt right, felt natural.

She closed her eyes and sighed quietly, like she enjoyed that kiss as much as I did.

Instead of pulling away, I left my lips there, let us stay connected that way. It erased my pain, erased my stress. It gave me a sense of peace I'd never found anywhere else, not in a stranger's bed and not in the bottom of a bottle.

TEN

ANNABELLA

"WE MISS YOU AT THE HOTEL." SOFIA WATCHED ME HOLD her son at the table. "It's not the same without you."

"I miss being there too." I spoke as I looked into Andrew's face, seeing the same eyes Hades possessed. "Being cooped up here all day is lonely. Richard invited me to play chess with him tomorrow, and I'll probably take him up on that offer."

"Make sure you kick his ass."

Damien sat across from me, and he was engaged in deep conversation with Hades, their voices low. His knuckles rested against his lips as he listened to whatever Hades said, his eyes focused with intensity. In a t-shirt and jeans, Damien was addictive to stare at, a beautiful man in a hard package.

When Andrew started to cry, Sofia took him back into her arms then grabbed a bottle. "I swear, this kid never stops eating."

"In his defense, I never stop eating either," I teased.

She chuckled and put the nipple into his mouth.

"How's the second baby?"

"Good. He's getting anxious—as am I. Only six weeks left."

"Wow...that's exciting."

"Soon, I'll have three babies to take care of." She cast a glance at Hades, who was staring at Damien.

I chuckled. "When are you going on maternity leave?"

"Whenever I have the baby. Want to keep working as much as possible." She rocked Andrew gently as she continued to feed him. "I just hate staying at home all day. So boring."

I knew that all too well.

"What's new with you?"

I assumed Hades had already told her what happened with Liam. "Nothing much." I didn't want to discuss my complicated feelings for Damien when he was right across the table from me. He didn't seem to be listening to anything I said, but still.

"Damien being good to you?"

He was much more than I deserved. "Always."

She gave a slight smile before she continued to rock her son.

Hades and Damien excused themselves from the table and took their drinks onto the balcony, as if they wanted to discuss business away from us. They stood outside and leaned against the stone railing, drinks in hand.

I watched Damien for a moment, admiring his sculpted features and that handsome face. "Damien told me Hades had to quit drinking."

"Yes. He wasn't happy about it, but too bad. He has to live a long time for us." She watched her husband out the window while holding the bottle.

"Sometimes, I worry Damien drinks too much."

"He does," she said immediately. "He'll fall into my husband's footsteps if he hasn't already."

"He told me I can't be concerned about his health unless I'm sleeping with him."

"As in, you aren't?" she asked, surprise in her tone.

"No..."

"You have the restraint of a monk." When Andrew was finished with his bottle, she set it on the table and wiped his mouth with a napkin. The second he got his drink, he went right back to sleep.

"I haven't been divorced very long... Don't want to jump into anything."

"Well, your ex-husband jumped into another woman's bed when he was still married to you—twice. If the reason you aren't doing what you want is out of guilt, then that's unnecessary. You owe him nothing, Anna."

"I know..."

"Then what's stopping you?"

"I don't know... I guess that is the reason."

"Then forget about it," she said. "You've wanted Damien the entire time you were married. You can have him now—so, have him."

"Exactly...that's why I feel guilty."

She gave me a confused expression.

"I blame Liam for our divorce, but it's really my fault."

"You didn't cheat, Anna. He did."

"I know, but it's more complicated than that."

She watched the guys out the window for a while before she turned back to me. "If you wanted another man while you were married, getting divorced was probably the best thing for both you and Liam. You were never going to last if you were head over heels for someone else. It's unfortunate, but that's what happened. And let's not forget, you got divorced in the first place because Liam was unfaithful. It's still not your fault."

I stared out the window a long time, not even really looking at Damien. My thoughts just started to wander, to drift away. "Can I tell you something?"

"You can tell me anything, Anna."

"And for it not to be shared with your husband."

"Honey, I don't share any of our conversations with him. I know he'll tell Damien every little thing."

"Well...I haven't really thought about Liam much."

She leaned back in her chair once Andrew was sleep. Nestled in one arm, he slept with his favorite blanket tucked around him. Instead of questioning me about my exact meaning, she let me continue to speak.

"I really wanted that marriage to work, but once he hurt me...I mentally checked out. I lived alone for a while, and I was upset. But now that I'm around Damien all the time, I don't think about Liam at all...and I guess I feel bad about that. I got over my marriage really quickly. Moved on to someone else like it never happened. It just... I don't know."

"I don't think you should feel guilty about that. If anything, I think you should feel excited."

I had no idea what that meant, so my eyes shifted back to hers.

"It means you know Damien is the right person."

My heart raced at the idea of getting what I'd always wanted, what I wanted the moment I met him. Our time together had been short, but the amount of love I'd developed in that amount of time was enormous...and it never went away.

"And since he's the right person...be with him."

AFTER WE SAID goodnight to Hades and Sofia, we returned to his bedroom, where the table was as clean as new because Patricia cleaned everything the moment we were gone. It was spotless, a vase of fresh flowers in the middle of the table instead of the bottle of wine.

The fire had been almost dead by the time they'd left, but now it was burning at full blast once again.

"It was nice having them over." I stood in front of the fire before I turned to look back at him.

He pulled his shirt over his head, eager to get his clothes off the second he wasn't entertaining. A lean body of muscle that rippled with his movements was visible. His tanned skin was kissable, beautiful. He tossed the t-shirt on one of the chairs then removed his jeans in the closet. When he came back out, he was in a pair of black sweatpants. "I knew you'd appreciate the company." He moved to the couch and sat down, his arms stretching across the back in both directions.

"You invited them here for me?"

He gave a slight shrug. "I thought you could spend time with Sofia. I know you get lonely home alone."

"That was sweet."

"I mean, I see Hades all fucking day. The last thing I want to do is talk to that guy."

I knew he was kidding, so I smiled. "Your father asked if I wanted to play chess with him tomorrow."

"Yeah? He's pretty good."

"I'm pretty good too." I moved toward the couch and stopped when I stood over him.

"But he's old. All he ever does it play chess. He's got a lot more experience than you do."

"Experience isn't everything." I sat on the couch beside him. "Do you play?"

"Not often. But yes."

"Did he teach you?"

He nodded. "Catalina is really good. She usually beats me."

"Wow. I'm surprised you would admit that."

"I'm not intimidated when a woman beats me at something."

A soft smile spread across my lips.

He continued to stare at the fire, his jawline sprinkled with a shadow. His thin lips were kissable in the firelight. His eyes reflected the dancing flames, making his bronzed skin glow like he was a god. "Why don't you join us?"

"Because I work for a living."

"Well, why don't we have dinner with your family tomorrow?"

"You want to subject yourself to that? I'm still annoyed with Catalina."

"She's your sister. Let it go." I scooted close into his side, wanting to snuggle his hard body.

Once he felt me touch him, his body tensed, as if it affected him as much as it affected me. His hand moved into my hair, touching me like I was his.

I stared into his face with my mouth close to his. His cologne was addictive, the smell of a real man. My hand slowly slid to his stomach, stroking that hard surface like a tabletop before I slid upward. My fingers grazed over his hard muscles, over his concrete chest, and moved up his neck until my fingers touched his soft cheek.

His gaze hardened as he felt me touch him, felt me touch him in a way I hadn't for almost a year. His fingers froze in my hair as he waited for something to happen, as he prayed he would get what he wanted. He couldn't hide the expression in his eyes, that he hoped tonight would be the night something more would happen, that we would do more than combine our hands together.

My fingers slid to the corner of his mouth as I stared at his lips, as I treasured this quiet moment with the man I loved. My heart beat for him as much as it ever had. I still dreamed of him, even when he was right next to me. Something told me he loved me in a way Liam never had, even at our best. Damien had hurt me before, but he wouldn't do it again.

I leaned in and pressed my mouth to his, feeling the fire leap higher in my throat. The skin of our mouths immediately stuck together at the embrace, like two magnets finding each other. I closed my eyes and treasured the contact, the way I felt so much with so little.

His lips didn't move, as if he wanted to see what I would do before he kissed me the way he wanted.

My fingers cupped his cheek, and I kissed him again, pressing his bottom lip with purposeful intensity.

He still didn't respond, but his breathing increased.

"Kiss me, Damien..."

He inhaled a deep breath before his fingers fisted a big chunk of hair and he pulled me tighter into him, kissing me harder. His mouth held mine delicately, but also with barely restrained passion. Between every kiss was a definitive pause, as if he wanted to treasure every step of this dance. He turned his head the other way to kiss me differently, to feel the other side of my mouth with the same desire. His fingers dug deeper, and his kisses became harder, more consuming.

It felt right...like always.

His lips parted mine before his tongue slipped inside. He moved until he felt mine, our tongues touching each other like two clouds bumping in the sky. He breathed deep into me, sharing his oxygen with me, and then he kissed me again...and again.

I couldn't remember the last time we'd kissed like this. The balcony at the charity event came to mind, but it was over so quickly that I never got to really enjoy it. But tonight, it was beautiful the way it used to be, deep, powerful, and spiritual. My fingers glided to the back of his neck, and I pulled at the short strands of his dark hair. A moan escaped my mouth, so quiet that I doubted he could hear it.

But he moaned back like he had.

He started to lower me to the couch, moving on top of me so he could pin me to the cushions below. His body turned to one side so he could keep the rest of his weight off me while one hand was still buried in my hair. The other slid under my shirt and felt the skin of my belly, gripping my hip and squeezing me.

My arm hooked under his shoulder, and I scooped him closer to me, my nails clawing at his back even though he wasn't inside me. The kiss was better than sex, better than any experience I had ever had with another man. It was because I was in love with a man who was in love with me.

I knew he would never hurt me. He wouldn't lie to me. He would never be unfaithful.

Because he was the one.

I slowed our kisses down until they came to a standstill. I wanted to kiss him forever, but I also wanted to stop, wanted to pause to appreciate the moment.

His eyes looked into mine, eagerness in his gaze.

"I love you..." It was the first time I'd said the words without being afraid of what he would say back. There was no guilt as the words escaped my lips into the air, into the world. My hand moved to the back of his neck, and I held him there, seeing those green eyes stare back into mine.

His fingers slid down from my hair until he cupped my cheek. Without blinking, without hesitating, he looked deep into my gaze and said it back. "I love you too, Annabella."

I LAY in bed beside him, my hand resting on his hard chest as it gently rose with his breathing. He was dead asleep, clueless to the morning light creeping through the cracks in the curtains and slowly reaching closer to the bed. The sunlight hit our feet, but the heat wasn't enough to stir him from sleep.

I was wide awake because I couldn't sleep. Not because I wasn't tired. Not because I was uneasy. I was just happy, being there with him, sleeping in that big bed the way I used. All we'd done was make out on the couch last night because I wasn't ready to jump into a deeply physical relationship, but it was still a level of intimacy I hadn't had with Liam once our relationship turned sour.

It was never magical like that.

Damien's alarm went off, beeping loudly.

He groaned and reached for the phone, swiping on the screen so the obnoxious noise would end. His fingers dove into his hair, and he sighed as the morning greeted him unkindly. His head turned back to me, and his sleepy eyes found mine. When he realized I was really there beside him, that the memory of last night wasn't just in his head, his arm pulled me tighter, and his other hand cupped my face as he kissed me on the forehead.

Wow, that was nice.

He took a deep breath as he touched me, as he woke up to the feeling of my body in his arms. "You're wide awake."

"I've been awake for a few hours."

"And you just lay there? You didn't go down and ask Patricia to make you breakfast?"

My hand rubbed his chest. "Why would I want breakfast when I can have you?"

He smiled slightly. "Good answer." He rolled on top of me, his large mass making me sink into the bed. Playfully, he grabbed both of my wrists and pinned them to the sheets before he leaned down and kissed me on the mouth.

I melted like a piece of chocolate over a flame.

His hand slid into my hair as he embraced me, his dick hard through his boxers as he held me close. He gently pressed it against me on purpose, as if he wanted me to know that I was the reason he was this way.

Oh, I knew.

When he broke our kiss, he gave me a gentle rub of his nose

before he got off me. He stood next to the nightstand, placing his arms over his head as he stretched. His muscles were chiseled and strong, and his boxers hung low on his hips because his big dick was dragging them down. "I'm gonna get in the shower."

"Do you have to go to work today?" I wanted to stay home with him all day, right here in this big bed.

He turned back around, his abs endless rivers of muscles. "Yes. But I'm yours after work."

I pouted my lips.

He smiled slightly. "If I didn't have an important meeting, I would blow it off. I'd probably quit my job on the spot if Hades would let me." He came back to the bed and kissed me once again before he walked into the shower. "But I'll make it up to you tonight."

"Yeah? Anything specific in mind?" I said after him.

He continued to walk. "You'll see."

ELEVEN

DAMIEN

Hades sat behind his desk.

I was in the armchair, flipping through paperwork with my legs crossed. Numbers were boring, even if they reflected my paycheck, but I smiled anyway, thinking about the sexy brunette waiting for me at home.

"What are you smiling about?"

I lifted my gaze but continued to turn the pages over.

"Gonna leave me hanging, huh?"

"You know I don't kiss and tell."

He turned back to his laptop. "Finally got laid. Good for you."

"No. Annabella kissed me last night."

He turned back to me, his eyebrow raised. "You're that excited about a kiss? Did she kiss your dick?"

I shot him a glare.

"You know I'm kidding, Damien. I'm happy for you."

"You better be."

"It's a start."

"Yeah." It wasn't sex or anything kinky, but that wasn't important to me anymore. I just wanted her. I grew impatient
waiting for Liam to leave her thoughts. After she'd stayed with
me a few weeks, that seemed to fix the problem.

We organized the stack of papers and put them into two
different files before we were finished. Hades looked at me,
giving me that familiar gaze I'd seen for a decade. "It's nice to
see you happy."

He wasn't a mushy kind of guy, so I appreciated those
comments whenever they came. "Yeah, it's nice. Never
thought I would be a one-woman kind of guy. But there's only
one woman I want. So, I guess I am that guy..."

He smiled slightly. "Yeah. I couldn't believe it either when it
happened to me. But the sex is so much hotter when it is with
that one woman, that one woman you can't get enough of. It's
better than all my nights in the alleyways, public restrooms,
and everywhere else I fucked around."

It'd been so long since I'd actually had Annabella, but my
memory hadn't faded at all. "I'm gonna head back to my office.
I'll meet you in the conference room for the meeting." I rose
from my chair and headed to the door.

Hades watch me go. "Good. I don't have to see your face for
another hour."

I flipped him off before I walked down the hallway.

I headed to my office, and I thought about how much my life
had changed. When Hades and I weren't friends, I didn't have
this camaraderie with anyone. No one to bullshit with. No one
who knew me well enough to make a joke that landed. And

now I had the one woman who'd ever meant anything to me in my bed at this very moment.

That high disappeared when I turned the corner and entered my office. A large man sat in the chair facing my desk, huge shoulders packed with layers of muscle and forearms that were thicker than mature tree branches. He didn't need to show his face to give away his identity. I knew exactly who he was.

Liam didn't turn around. "Your assistant's nice."

I stilled for just a second to digest the situation, but then I moved past him and walked over to my desk. With a slow beating heart, I lowered myself into the chair and faced one of my nemeses. My face was stoic, and I showed no fear because this man didn't deserve any reaction from me. He could have a gun in his pocket, a bullet with my name on it, and I still wouldn't care. "Yeah, she's delightful." I sat there with my hands together on my lap and leaned back into the chair, like this was a real meeting with a real client. My gaze was focused on his hard expression, and I waited for him to announce his intentions. He was probably there to kill me, but he wanted to give a speech first. "How can I help you?"

His eyes narrowed a little farther at my ease. "You should be scared, Damien. And if you aren't, you will be."

I was an asshole, so I responded like one. "I'll pass."

Liam let my words sink into the air around us for a few seconds, his eyes working like cogs in a machine. "Your plan is to keep Anna locked up in your home forever? You think your building can keep me out? You think your door and windows are thick enough to stop a man like me?" He stared at me like he knew he was making a valid point. They were difficult parameters to surround any relationship. And it definitely wasn't the best way to start a romance. "Damien, you are the reason my marriage failed. And here you are again, interfering. Walk away and let Anna and me work on this."

"Are you delusional?" I couldn't keep my voice down because I was exhausted by his insanity. "There's nothing to work on. She left you. You fucked somebody else, so she divorced you. She's ready to move on with her life, and you need to move on too."

"None of that would've happened if it weren't for you. We both know it."

"Doesn't matter. Let. It. Go."

A slight smile escaped into his lips, even though nothing about this was funny. "This only ends one way. I'm gonna kill you. I want to do it. So that works out for me, but that's not the best outcome for you. If you step aside, I'll grant you mercy. I'll let you walk."

"Even if I agree to that, what's the point? Annabella doesn't want to be with you. She's divorced you twice because she doesn't want to be with you. Your plan to take her away and lock her up until she falls in love with you is a stupid one."

"Isn't that exactly what you're doing?"

I let the insult simmer in my blood but didn't give in to it. "She can't be a prisoner if she wants to be there. And trust me, she wants to be there."

Both of his hands tightened into fists at my response. The skin stretched so far that his knuckles turned white. He twisted his head slightly to the side, needing to pull his gaze off of my face so his rage wouldn't explode. When he had the calmness to look at me again, he turned back to me. "Then fight me. Winner gets to live."

There was nothing I wanted more. I wanted to beat this man

to death with my bare fists. While I was happy that Liam had fucked up so I could have Annabella, I was also pissed that he'd hurt her at all. I wanted to get rid of him for good, but I also wanted to punish him. "There's nothing I want more. But Annabella doesn't want me to kill you, and I actually care about the way she feels—unlike you."

"You can come at me hard in the ring, face-to-face. Or I'm gonna come at you hard in every way possible. I've given you the opportunity to fight me like a man. But if you are too much of a pussy, that's fine." He rose out of the chair and gave me one more glare before he turned to the doorway. His heavy footsteps landed against the hardwood floor until he made it to the door. He turned back around and looked at me before he walked out. "Your sister has a stronger backbone than you."

The mention of my sister quickened my pulse, made me see the world with a distinct shade of red. "She gets that from me."

WHEN THE MEETING WAS OVER, the men filed out and disappeared down the hallway. Hades closed his laptop and placed his papers in the folder before he turned to me. "That was easier than I thought it would be."

I didn't rise from my chair. Truth be told, I hadn't paid much attention to the meeting. Even when I broke down the exchange rate for the bonds, I wasn't really aware of what I was saying. My mind was stuck on the conversation I'd had in my office just minutes before.

When Hades picked up on my sour mood, he set his things down and stared at me. "What am I missing?"

My eyes slowly turned to him. "Liam stopped by my office right before this meeting."

Hades was still as he heard what I said. His body always became more rigid when he was invested in my words. His muscles instinctively contracted in preparation for war. Once he finished digesting what I'd said, his hands slid into his pockets. "And how did that go?"

"He told me I can fight him in the ring, or he'll make my life miserable. Basically."

He sighed in irritation. "Just kill the motherfucker. Who gives a shit how Anna feels about it? The fact that this is still going on is absolutely stupid. You take your gun, point it at the back of his head, and pull the trigger. That simple."

"You know I can't."

Both of his hands flattened on the table as he leaned forward. "Tell her to get over it."

"She was married to the guy. I hate this asshole too, but her feelings are understandable."

"Not when he's trying to kill you." He stepped back and threw his arms in the air. "Who's she sleeping with? You or him? He's her past, and you're her present. It's time she showed some goddamn loyalty to the right man. The fucker is trying to kill you. Literally."

"She'll get there. She just needs time..."

"Well, hopefully she doesn't take too much time. Because you might be dead any day." He grabbed his stuff off the desk, prepared to walk out, his nostrils flared and his shoulders stiff. He used to be patient, but now he was livid about the situation. "You know I like Anna. But I like you a hell of a lot more. And if something happens to you because she can't get her shit together, I'll lose it."

It was a heartfelt thing to say, and of course, it meant a lot to me, but I decided to respond like a jerk. "I love you too, asshole."

With his laptop and folder under his arm, he stared at me. The sarcasm from my lips seemed to calm him down. "Are you gonna tell her what happened?"

I didn't want to spend my evenings talking about her ex-husband. I wanted her to kiss me again, kiss me everywhere, do more things. Talking about Liam would only slow down the process. It was time for us to be together. I could worry about Liam, but she didn't need to. "No. I'm the only man I want her to think about."

TWELVE
ANNABELLA

My clothes and other belongings were in my bedroom next door, but I spent my days in Damien's bedroom. That was where Patricia brought me lunch. That was where I watched TV in the afternoon. He allowed me to be in his personal space where I could violate his privacy all I wanted, but he trusted me, and I wanted to be where his presence infected the air. Not in the room next door that was so sterile, it felt like a hotel room.

The sun was out much longer now that summer had arrived, so he didn't come home when it was dark. The sun was still up, a few hours before sunset. The bedroom door opened, and he stepped inside. He looked like a sexy powerhouse in that gray suit, but what I noticed the most was the pizza box in his hand. I got off the couch and walked toward him. "Is that what I think it is?"

He'd worn a hard expression when he'd first walked into the door, but now there was a playful smile on his lips, a subtle joy that reached all the way to his eyes. "I told you I had a surprise." He carried it to the table and set it on top.

"Patricia won't be happy..."

"She gets a night off. That sounds nice to me."

I knew Patricia enjoyed serving Damien and anyone else in the house. She lived for it, thrived on it. That was why she was such a good housekeeper, because she cared about her employer so much. How could she not? He was such a beautiful man, on the inside as well as the outside. I opened the lid and took a peek inside. "The last time I had takeout pizza like this was with you..."

He stripped off his jacket and set it on the back of the chair. "And I only eat pizza when I'm with you." His hands worked his tie, and he got it loose within a few seconds. Then he unbuttoned his collared shirt, the white fabric slowly opening and revealing beautiful, tanned skin.

I stared for a few seconds, admiring that olive-toned shine that was part of his Italian heritage. His jaw was free of shadow because he'd shaved before he went to work that morning. I liked seeing every single groove along his mouth, but I also liked it when it was hidden under his stubble. Sometimes, I stared at him with infatuation, a powerful lustful feeling I could barely control. But other times, I looked at him like he was the most special man in the world...because he was.

His shirt fell from his shoulders, and he let it slide down his arms until he caught it and placed it on top of his jacket. He did all of his undressing with his eyes locked on mine. His smile was gone, just a distant memory at this point, and he gave me such a powerfully intense look that it was paralyzing. He looked at me as if I was a muse and he was the artist. His eyes were so focused on mine there was nothing else in the room that mattered. It was suddenly much quieter, our breathing much louder. My heartbeat was audible in my ears, and I swore I could hear his too...somehow.

Whenever these heated moments happened, I couldn't really think about anything concrete. I didn't think about Liam, if it was too soon after my divorce to be so intimately attracted to another man. Those thoughts were frozen, and all I could do was feel...feel everything. In that moment, I knew I wanted to kiss this man. I wanted to greet him with my lips when he walked in the door. My fingers wanted to feel those large arms, feel the heartbeat in the vein of his neck as I cupped his face in an embrace.

Damien could probably read every thought in my eyes like they were words on a page, but he didn't reach for me like he used to. He was patient enough to give me the power to decide when and how it happened. He didn't want to rush me because he only wanted what I wanted to give.

That made me love him so much more.

I ignored the pizza and slowly moved into his chest. I noticed the way he immediately took a deep breath once I drew near. He reacted to me exactly the same way I reacted to him. There was a skip in our heartbeats, a pause in our lungs, and every-thing around us went still. I came closer, and my palms landed on his stomach. My fingers fell into the rivers edged into his skin, the valleys of muscle that intersected one another. He was so warm to the touch, his skin the same temperature as summer air. My face came close to his, and I stared at his lips, immobile because I felt my heart beating so hard. There was so much adrenaline in my veins, as if I was about to run a marathon rather than kiss the man I loved. Liam never made me feel this way, even at our best. There was something about Damien that was different, something I never felt with anyone else.

Something special.

I fell in love with him overnight, and once I felt that way, it never stopped. I ran to Liam because Damien broke my heart, but even through that pain, I continued to love Damien more and more with every passing day. Now I adored this man in a way I couldn't describe. He was thoughtful, protective, kind, and everything else I wanted in a partner. He was also loyal, honest, and so brutally real, it was sometimes difficult to withstand. But I wouldn't have it any other way.

My hands slowly glided to his chest, and my right hand stopped over the steady beat of his heart. There was distinct thump over and over again, the feeling of his strength and vitality, a powerful vibration against my fingertips. But I could also feel his unique heartbeat, the heartbeat that drummed just for me. I didn't need to hear Damien say he loved me to know how he felt. I could feel it when I touched him like this. And when he looked at me like this.

He wouldn't touch me even though he clearly wanted to. He let me do whatever I wanted, let me use him whatever way I wished. He took another deep breath as I came closer to him then dropped his gaze to watch me feel his beating heart. He only wore his slacks and belt, his chest bare and strong. He watched my hands moving for a long time before he looked at my face again.

I stepped closer to him until our noses were practically touching. His heartbeat quickened at my touch, beating deeper the closer my mouth came to his. I rested my forehead against his and just stood there with him, because proximity was as good as a kiss. I could feel our souls connect without a physical union. They intertwined, as if they knew they would still have each other once our bodies were gone.

"You can kiss me, Damien." I stared down at his chest, looking at my own hands as they remain flat against his hardness.

He pulled back so he could look into my gaze. Then one hand moved to my neck, and he grabbed me like owned me. He didn't squeeze me the way he used to. It was just a touch, a way to get ahold of me. "What else can I do, Annabella?" His fingers slipped into the back of my hair slightly, and his hand was so warm, it was like a hot frying pan against my skin.

I kept my eyes down, thinking about his question.

When he didn't get an answer, he grasped the back of my hair and gave me a gentle tug, bringing my chin up so I could look him in the eye. "Answer me, Annabella." His fingers started pulling me closer, as if he were going to kiss me the second he knew what I wanted. It was obvious that he wanted everything right then and there, but he didn't expect to get it.

I knew I wanted him, but I didn't think about exactly what I was capable of handling. So, I played it safe. "You can kiss me. You can kiss me all you want."

Instead of being disappointed that he wouldn't get more, he seemed happy just to have some of me no matter that he couldn't have it all. His hand slid farther into my hair, and he guided me backward to the bed. His possessive eyes were locked on mine as he guided me toward the bed where we'd slept together the night before. When my knees hit the wooden frame, he dug his fingers farther into my hair and wrapped his arm around my waist. He moaned before he even kissed me, as if he imagined how this would go before it even began.

His hand gripped my lower back and bunched the fabric of my t-shirt before he squeezed. His other hand got lost in my sea of hair before he leaned in and gave me a gentle kiss on the lips. He gripped me like he wanted to take me roughly, shove me up against the wall and hike my leg over his waist, but he kissed me with such softness, it didn't seem like a man like him could produce a touch so gentle. He started off slow because he wasn't in a hurry to get anywhere else. He was happy to live in the moment with me, even if the moment never escalated into something more.

I closed my eyes and treasured the feel of his demanding lips. He pulled the air right out of my lungs, excited my nerves in a way I'd never felt before. I felt so weak but so strong at the same time. I could drop my guard and not worry about anything when he loved me like this. I trusted him without really having a reason, but not having a reason was how I knew it was true. My fingers slowly pressed into his skin as I felt my emotions get swept up in those phenomenal kisses. I let him do whatever he wanted to my mouth, and without thinking, I reciprocated. When he gave me his tongue, I gave mine back. When he moaned, I echoed the same noise. We were two different people, but we felt everything as one. I kissed him harder and deeper as a beautiful passion drew me in. My hands glided into the back of his hair as I drew him in for a deeper kiss. I even whimpered against his lips because it felt so right.

He kicked off his shoes and undid his belt as he continued to kiss me, not wasting a single moment as he undressed the rest of the way. When he was just in his black boxers, he removed my shirt and pulled it over my head. The second the fabric was over my face, his lips found mine and he picked up exactly where we left off. His hands got my shorts loose, and he pushed them over my hips until they slid down my legs.

His hand moved up my back to the center of my bra, where his fingers moved to unclasp the material.

But that was when the warning went off in my head, that this was too soon, that this was more than I was ready to handle. My hand moved to his forearm and I steadied him, but I didn't have to say anything else because he understood immediately. He dropped his hand, guiding me backward onto the bed.

My body hit the softness of his duvet cover, and a moment later, he was on top of me. Heavy. Strong. Sexy. His body covered mine and kept me warm like a thick blanket. He kissed me on the mouth, caressing each of my lips equally, making me moan and writhe from our heated kisses.

Our lips came together and broke apart in a beautiful dance, a soft embrace turning into chaotic passion. Kiss after kiss, each one was different and special, a conversation that required no words. It brought our souls close together, feeling each other in a deep, special way. They were only kisses, two people engaged in an amateur affair, but it was just like making love, at least for me.

His hand slid into my hair, and he cradled my face at the perfect angle for how he wanted to take my lips. He sucked my bottom lip into his mouth before he looked at me, wanting to show me how much he adored me.

As if I didn't already know.

His other hand slid up my leg and over my thigh until he traveled underneath the band of my underwear. He felt the bare skin, touching the place where he knew I had a single freckle that he used to kiss all the time. He still remembered everything about my body, as if there'd been no one else since the last time he'd had me.

The only time he broke our kiss was to glide his lips to my neck and kiss me all the way down to my collarbone. He even kissed my bra strap before he slid down to the cleavage of my chest. He gave each of my breasts kisses, his tongue tasting my skin. Then he moved to my stomach, kissing me and marking his territory.

I closed my eyes and breathed as I felt him kiss me everywhere, from the sensitive area between my thighs to the skin on my belly. He even kissed the inside of my knees because he found that place as beautiful as everywhere else. He slowly glided back up my body until he returned his lips to mine. "You're my woman, Annabella." He stopped kissing me so he could look

down into my gaze, seeing his expression reflected back at him.
"Mine."

I'D HAD dinner with his family before, but my relationship
with Damien hadn't been as concrete then as it was now. I
didn't even have my own bedroom anymore because I slept
with him instead. I was his girlfriend now, so being around his
family was a whole different dynamic. I knew I shouldn't be
nervous since Catalina and I got along anyway, and his father
seemed to enjoy my company, but I was nervous all the same.

Dinner was quiet and uneventful. Catalina talked about
rehearsals that week, and Richard hung on every word she
said. Both men seem to be fascinated by her, teasing her but so
proud at the same time. It made me wonder what Damien's
mother had been like, since her absence was constantly felt.

Damien was quiet, staying mute while the conversation
continued. He enjoyed his wine and his dinner and stayed
away from the bread basket in the center, not that there was
anything in it since Catalina and I had demolished it.

After dinner, Damien and his father went to the other side of
the room to play a game of chess. Richard stared at the board
so intently as he thought about every move before he made it.
Damien didn't even try, which was impressive because he
actually played pretty well. They left Catalina and me alone at
the dinner table, enjoying the tiramisu because Damien didn't
want any and Richard wasn't allowed to have sugar anymore.

"How's it going with that guy?" I knew she'd gotten the man's
number at the restaurant and called him, but I didn't know
what had happened after that.

"Good. He's good in bed, but he's a dull conversationalist. But
I guess it doesn't matter. I don't like to talk much either."

I raised an eyebrow. "You talk more than anyone I know."

"Well, I talk a lot to my friends. But guys I'm seeing? Not so much. I go out with guys for the D. Gossiping, shopping, dancing is reserved for only friends." She took a small bite of tiramisu but left most of it untouched, probably because she couldn't weigh more than a certain amount. Otherwise, her job would be in jeopardy. "I mean, are you really with Damien because of those long conversations over dinner? No. My brother is as dull as they come."

I appreciated her friendship and I wanted us to remain close, but I didn't want to bash Damien, especially when I didn't agree with her insults, even if they were jokes. "He's not dull."

She rolled her eyes. "Sure..."

"He's not. He's the smartest, most loyal, most interesting man I've ever met. He's my best friend."

"That's sweet. But I still think he's dull. And I also don't think there's anything wrong with a woman only wanting a man for physical reasons. That's exactly how men are, wanting a woman for the weekend as a lover and nothing more. It's how I feel about most men. They're fun for a while...but then I get bored."

I never got bored of Damien. And, even after a lifetime, I suspected I never would.

"So, have you heard from your douchebag ex-husband?"

I didn't argue with her insult that time. Liam deserved it. "Not for a while. I hope that last interaction will make him cool off. He pretty much got his ass handed to him by a chick."

"If he ever wants to go again, tell him he can call me." She took another bite of her dessert. "So how are things going with Damien? I don't want any details...if you catch my meaning."

"Really good." It was hard not to smile and think about the way I slept beside him every night, the way he kissed me goodbye in the morning before he left for work, the way we'd demolished that pizza together in front of the TV. I felt so right that I wondered how being with Liam had ever felt right.

Catalina studied me for a while, her brown hair pinned back into a pretty updo. "That smile on your face says it's more than good." She reached her hand out to my arm and gave it a gentle pat. "And I'm happy for you. I'm happy for my brother too because he's been alone for so long, and the older he gets, the grouchier he gets, like an old man. He needed to find a good woman before it was too late."

Damien was such a catch, and he could have any woman he wanted, regardless of his age. He was seeing a supermodel before I left Liam, and every guy wanted Charlotte to be the woman in their arms. I considered myself a major step down from her, but Damien wanted me instead.

"So, when are you going to be able to go outside? Because we should go get a drink sometime. I know you're tied down now, but you can always help me pick up a sexy guy."

I glanced at Damien on the other side of the room. He was focused on the game, figuring out the next move once his father finished his move. Whenever his father was taking his turn, Damien would watch him, as if he were trying to memorize his face so he could think of it when his father was no longer around. When they sat together, it was easy to see the similarities in their appearances. Both men had rugged jaws, hostile eyes, and strong physiques. Damien's father was in his seventies, and he was still handsome in old age. It made me realize Damien would always be handsome as long as he lived.

"Hello?" When I didn't respond, Catalina grew impatient.

I turned back to her, realizing I'd gotten so lost in my stare. "I really don't know. If I step outside the house, I know Liam will try to grab me."

"Then have Damien kill him. Problem solved."

I didn't want violence to be my only answer. Liam and I had nothing anymore, but I could never forget all our memories together. Allowing him to be murdered didn't sit right with me, even if he was forcing me to take that violent path. "I can't do that."

Catalina watched me but didn't press her argument. "Then you need to figure out something else to do. Because you should be out living life, not stuck in here like a princess locked in a tower. You should be going to work every day, going out for a drink with me every night, and just doing your own thing. You shouldn't let a man take that away from you. I know I wouldn't."

WE SNUGGLED TOGETHER on the couch while the movie played on the TV above the fireplace. I curled into his side with a blanket over my body. His body kept me warm like a heating pad, and the fire filled the entire room with heat, not that we needed it since it was summertime. We both just enjoyed looking at the flames. It was something we'd been doing since we met.

When the movie was over, I sat up and looked at him.

He seemed to know a serious conversation was coming because he grabbed the remote and turned off the TV. "Yes, Annabella?"

"I want to talk to you about something..."

Now that it was quiet with the TV off, he stared at me with his striking green eyes, the flames casting a beautiful glow on his tanned skin. Whenever he was home, he was always in just sweatpants, and it was sexy to see him walk around like that all night. He regarded me with an intense expression, waiting for me to make my point. "Alright."

"I know we haven't talked about it much, but what are we gonna do about Liam?" I liked spending my evenings in this castle like I had no cares in the world. It was easy to pretend we didn't have a problem. But this problem was only going to get worse the longer it was allowed to grow. "I don't want to talk about him, but I want to find a solution. I want to go back to work. I want us to go out to dinner together. I want us to have more of a relationship."

He processed all that with a blank expression, as if the mention of my ex didn't anger him. "How do you expect me to fix this problem? I can't kill him, so I'll never be able to stop him."

"There has to be another solution besides death."

"There's not." He lowered his voice, which made him sound more serious.

"He hasn't bothered us in a while…"

"Yes, he has. I just didn't tell you about it."

Slowly, I started to feel the dread growing in my stomach. I felt slightly betrayed because Damien had hidden this from me, but I knew he did it in my best interest. "What happened?"

"The usual. He threatened me, nothing out of the ordinary." His sarcasm showed how annoyed he was, how exhausted he was that this was a recurring issue he couldn't fix with his usual response. "He said I was the reason your relationship failed and I should step away so you guys can try again."

"Oh my god…"

"He doesn't get it. He keeps saying the same thing over and over again. His version of reality is so different from yours. I don't think this is ever gonna go away. And the longer we do nothing, the more likely it is that he'll be able to take you."

I didn't want to believe Liam would really do that, but I didn't know what to believe anymore. If he was going to get over this, it would've happened by now. The fact that he continued to bother Damien told me this was a problem with no solution. "I'm so sorry... I'm sorry you have to go through this. I'm sorry you have to put up with my baggage."

The anger in his eyes died away. "Don't apologize for that. It's not your fault, and I don't blame you. For better or worse, I'm here with you. We'll get through this together, no matter what. I'm just frustrated that you won't allow me to do what's necessary to defeat this problem."

"How can you sit there and ask my permission to kill someone I loved? Any other sane person would respond the same way."

"Not if the person they loved the most were at risk."

I studied his gaze for a few seconds, slowly realizing the implication of his words. "I hope you don't think I don't love you because I don't want you to kill him. I hope you don't think he means more to me than you do. If I tell you to kill him, you will. That makes me a murderer. Don't you understand that?"

"I do understand that. But I also understand that every day I don't do something, I become more vulnerable to an attack I can't see coming. You're giving him the upper hand by handicapping me. You're directly putting me in danger." He watched me with a dispassionate gaze, speaking with little emotion in his voice. There was a touch of resentment in his tone, obvious frustration, even when he tried to hide it.

"Damien, I would die if anything happened to you. That's the last thing that I want. I love you...so much." I moved closer into him and cupped his face. "If I had to choose, I would choose you over him in a heartbeat. But don't make me kill somebody, anybody, especially a man I spent half a decade with. I just can't tell you to kill him...I can't. Please understand." My hands slid from his face as I looked for a sign of sympathy or understanding.

It was there...but so faint I could barely see it. It was like a dim light in a cloud of fog. There was illumination, but it would never be bright enough to pierce through.

THIRTEEN
DAMIEN

I DIDN'T LIKE THE SITUATION WE WERE IN, BUT I'D HAVE to be naïve not to understand it. Annabella was as gentle as a spring flower, as harmless as a butterfly. She could never wish death upon anyone, even if they deserved it.

And I loved that about her.

I had to understand it wasn't about him or me. It was about her. And if he came at me with a bullet, knife, or fist, I'd just have to do my best and kill him first. If given no other choice, she would understand. Somewhere down the road, his demise was inevitable. We both knew it.

We'd deal with the consequences later.

Annabella was asleep beside me, wearing one of my t-shirts with just her panties underneath. Her hair was all over the place, my pillow, the sheets, and everywhere else, leaving her fragrance soaked deeply into my belongings. Sometimes she would sigh in her sleep, her lips slightly parted and so sexy. She would roll away to the other side of the bed, but at some point, she'd reach for me, making sure I wasn't too far away. She washed her face before bed every night, and I loved her plain look. Charlotte had to be caked with makeup to look anything like she appeared in magazines, but Annabella was stunning on her own. She never seemed to understand that, no matter how many times I told her.

I grabbed my phone off the nightstand and looked at the time.

I had to leave.

I slid from the bed as quietly as possible, doing my best to limit the creak of the wooden frame and the mattress. Once I was on my feet, I stepped into the closet and pulled on a pair of jeans and a t-shirt before I went to walk over to grab my wallet from the dresser.

Annabella was up in bed, sitting against the headboard as she looked around with sleepy eyes. Her gaze was focused on the bathroom, but when she heard me emerge from the closet, she turned her gaze on me. Once she realized I was dressed to go out, the concern emerged. "What are you doing?"

I'd hoped to slip out and come back in without her noticing. But I blew that. "I have to take care of something."

"At this time of night?" She leaned over and looked at the clock sitting on my nightstand. "It's three in the morning."

"My job never sleeps."

"Well...when will you be back?"

I moved back to the bed and sat on the edge. This was the reason I hadn't wanted to be with Annabella in the first place. My life had dangerous tangents. There were times when I wouldn't come home for days, nights when I would sneak out the door with a gun tucked in the back of my jeans. There would be nights when I killed people. I didn't want her to get mixed up in that. "Before you wake up."

Her eyes suddenly fell down, visibly disappointed. But she

didn't make an argument or guilt-trip me for leaving her so abruptly. "Please be careful."

"I'm always careful." My hand moved into her hair, and I stared at her for a while, treasuring the moment even though we would have so many other good memories in the future. This beautiful woman wanted me to stay in bed with her instead of attending to business. It was all I'd ever wanted.

I just hadn't known that until recently.

"Get some sleep." I leaned down and gave her a small kiss on the lips, a gentle touch that was purposely superficial. Anything more than that would get me back in bed again.

I grabbed my wallet and keys and headed to the door.

"Damien?"

I turned back around, my hand resting on the doorknob.

"I love you."

Paralyzed by her sincerity, I watched this woman love me with naked eyes. Those words always pierced me right through the heart. Every time she'd said it in the past, I'd always felt like shit because she should love someone better than me. But I would work harder to be a man worthy of her love, worthy of the heaven between her legs. It made me feel so much. And it made me want to leave her even less. "I love you too."

I TOOK care of a few things at the lab, collected a payment from my distributors, and I prepared my own payment for the asshole I despised.

I'd had a strong month, lots of sales, lots of drugs. The cash was stuffed into two black duffel bags set on the rug in front of my desk. Sometimes I considered skewing my numbers so he could collect as little as possible. But if he called my bluff, there would be repercussions. He had eyes and ears everywhere, so my secrets weren't safe. And now that I had someone to protect, I couldn't risk her for anything, couldn't make a single mistake for fear of her safety. My vendetta against him was officially over because I couldn't do anything about it. The risk wasn't worth the reward...not anymore.

He announced his presence obnoxiously, like always. "You came prepared this time." His heavy footfalls were audible even on the thick rug. "Good job. You get an A for the day."

I sat in my chair behind my desk and watched him saunter inside like he owned the damn place. There was so much violence in my blood, wanting this man dead for so many reasons, but his arrogance was the biggest reason of all. I despised myself for giving in to his demands, for rolling over like a fucking dog. But I knew I didn't have any other choice.

He crossed his arms and glanced at the two duffel bags on the floor. "Looks like you've had a good month. Or should I say, we've had a good month." He kicked each bag, as if that was an accurate way to count the cash inside.

I wasn't in the mood to deal with his bullshit, so I stayed quiet at my desk.

With his arms still crossed over his body, he stared at me as if he'd asked me a question that never got a response. His bright-blue eyes were the only kind feature he possessed, a pretty color that probably made women go weak. Everything else was rigid, hard, and thick like steel. He was in a dark blue t-shirt and black jeans, his thick muscles filling out everything he wore. "You're no fun tonight."

My fingers scratched against the scruff of my jawline as I

dragged my hand across my lips. "Take your money and go."

He pressed his thin lips tightly together. "Bad day?"

"No. It didn't go to shit until you walked in."

He chuckled and looked from side to side, as if people were standing there with him, mocking me along with him. "You really hate this, don't you?"

"Would you enjoy being robbed?"

"Trust me, if I were robbing you, you'd know. You wouldn't have a cent in your pocket right now." He moved to the doorway, snapped his fingers, and two men came inside and picked up the heavy bags of cash. "And this is my money. I earned this shit, asshole."

I fantasized about shoving a knife through his throat all the way to the back of his skull. His body would go limp first. His eyes would turn dull quickly afterward.

"Maybe your life would be a bit easier if you weren't screwing another man's wife." He turned to join his men in the hallway.

I didn't react to his statement initially, but after a few seconds, I understood the implication of his words. My heart started to beat fast as if a battle was about to rage. Even my palms were a little sweaty. I jumped out of the chair and followed him out the door. "What the fuck are you trying to say?"

He took his time turning around, and when he showed his face again, he was grinning like he enjoyed how this had played out. "It means what it means. You aren't my only client. Everybody in this town is my fucking client."

Annabella had mentioned the Skull King once before, that he did business with Liam. I never put too much thought into it until now. Heath was already a major enemy of mine, but if he was teamed up with Liam, I had a serious problem on my hands.

"All you had to do was pay me." His smile faded away as his gaze became hostile once again. He'd never forgive me for using his own brother against him, for embarrassing him in front of his soldiers. This wasn't about money. It was about so much more. And I was going to pay for it. "But you didn't. You thought you were better than everybody else. But you're the worst one."

WE USUALLY TOOK our lunch together in the office. We had the usual, protein shakes and salads, and our assistants ran out and picked them up for us. So, we sat together, Hades behind his desk while I sat in the leather armchair. We were both uncomfortable in our suits because of the summer heat. We usually had the AC running, but if it was too low, everyone else in the office froze, so we had to suffer instead.

Hades finished his smoothie and most of the salad was gone. He leaned back into the chair, both of his hands on the edge of the armrests. "What are you going to do, then?"

It was one of the rare times when I shrugged in response to a question like that. "No fucking idea."

"Now that you're with Anna, are you going to drop your war with the Skull King?"

"I'm not sure I can, even if I wanted to. He implied that he'd spoken to Liam about Annabella's situation, and obviously, that's concerning."

Hades shook his head. "I told you to drop it."

Now I wished I had listened when Hades had originally asked.

But how was I supposed to know it would bite me in the ass like this? Over and over again?

Hades spoke again. "The good news is, he makes too much money off you. He's not going to kill you."

"And what about Annabella?"

"I don't see how taking her would benefit him," he said. "He wants to keep making money, not to piss you off and stop the gravy train."

"But do you think he'd team up with Liam?"

Hades considered it as he tapped his fingers on the edge of the armrest. "I don't see him actively working against you, but he wouldn't hesitate to help one of your enemies."

"And if I die, he doesn't get paid."

"Not necessarily. He could take over your business."

"He could do that now too."

Hades shrugged. "But that's a lot of work for him. Why would he do the work himself when he can just have you do it?"

So far, this conversation hadn't made me feel better. We'd just determined anything was possible. "Then maybe I should kill them both."

"Well, if you try and don't succeed, then he really will burn you to the ground. He'll take your father, Anna, even your sister..."

"Then what the hell am I supposed to do?"

"I already said it. You should have paid him in the first place."

"Asshole, that's not advice." He was just saying I told you so, but I'd already gotten that message. Loud and fucking clear.

He shrugged slightly. "I'm just saying..."

I relaxed into the chair and put my hands together on my lap. Heath had always been my enemy, but now I wasn't sure what part he would play in this game. I could kill him first and then do Liam later, but that was very ambitious for one man. It was very ambitious for someone who had a woman at home. Hades's domestic life had never looked so appealing until now.

Hades watched me with sympathy. "I'm here if you need anything, Damien."

"I would never drag you into this."

"But if you don't, you might die."

"I'd still rather die than you risk yourself and your family. You turned in the keys on this lifestyle and walked away. This is my problem, not yours."

He massaged the knuckles on his left hand as he looked out the window, thinking about every word I'd just spoken. When enough silence had passed, he returned his focus to me. "You're right. But I'm still your friend, so I'll always be your ally."

WHEN I WALKED in the door, Annabella was in a dark blue summer dress, tight around her waist and flaring out along her hips. It showed off her beautiful tanned skin, her natural curves, and it was an all-around nice color on her. Her hair was in curls over her shoulders, and the mascara on her lashes made her eyes look so big. She seemed to be more stunning every time I saw her, so all my thoughts about Liam and Heath vanished the moment I looked at her.

Dinner was already on the table, white candles lit along with a small vase of red roses. Patricia never added that stuff, so I assumed Annabella was the one behind it. I loosened my tie as I came farther inside because it was way too fucking hot to wear all this shit.

Annabella walked up to me and slid her thumbs underneath my jacket so she could push it over my shoulders and let it fall down my arms. She took the jacket and folded it up before she placed it on the table.

Whenever she touched me, I grew weak. I stood still on the spot, enjoying every touch as if it electrified me. I'd never been a tame lover, but she made me so gentle, made me make love rather than fuck.

When she came back to me, her hands cupped my cheeks, and she rose on her tiptoes so she could kiss me. She didn't greet me with a hello or ask about my day. All she wanted to do was feel my lips on hers, show me exactly how much she missed me all day. Soon, her gentle kisses became more demanding, and with every breath she breathed into my mouth, she became more anxious, her touch more desperate.

My hands moved around her waist and pulled her close, exploring her sexy curves and that beautiful dark hair. I cupped the back of her head and tilted her chin back so I could deepen the kiss, so I could give her my tongue and feel hers dance with mine. My other hand moved to her ass and gave one of her cheeks a masculine squeeze. All the stress in my shoulders disappeared instantly. I could worry about that bullshit later. Right now, I just wanted to enjoy her, appreciate the woman I'd worked so hard to earn.

She pulled away first, her hands dropping to my chest. Her fingers undid every single button of my collared shirt and popped each one open so she could get to my naked skin underneath. When she was halfway to the bottom, her eyes flicked up and looked into mine. Shy. Sexy. Confident. She was a good lover because she was so enthusiastic, so desperate to have as much of me as she could. She wasn't necessarily kinky or willing to do things most women wouldn't. She just loved to be with me...and that made me feel good.

When the shirt was loose, she pushed it over my shoulders just as she had with my jacket, but this time, she let it fall to the floor. Her hands were on my bare skin, her fingertips feeling the heat of my flesh. She stepped closer and placed a kiss over my heart, her tongue dragging over my nipple before she moved to the other side of my chest and did the same to the other. Her face disappeared under her thick hair, and her fingertips dug into me harder as if she couldn't get enough of me.

Then she slowly dropped to her knees, kissing my stomach all the way down.

I couldn't fight the excitement that spiked in my blood. Anytime her mouth was anywhere near my dick, my mind went in the gutter. I was already hard at her first kiss, but now my dick was so swollen I could barely fit in my slacks.

She undid my belt, pulled down my zipper, and then tugged everything to the floor.

My dick hung out, so hard it was almost embarrassing.

On her knees, she stared at my length above her, thoroughly impressed by my size. She rose slightly on her knees and then kissed the fat vein along my shaft.

I closed my eyes and suppressed the moan that wanted to explode from the back of my throat. I hadn't realized how much I wanted this until it was right in front of me. I hadn't been with anyone else in a long time, and since she was my ultimate fantasy, this was a dream come true. I was just as enthusiastic about her as she was about me. If I could have any woman in the world right now, I would always choose her.

Always.

Why Liam ran to other women when things got tough, I'd never understand. What did he hope to find in a bar that was better than what he had at home? As far as I could tell, Annabella was the sexiest, kindest, and most amazing woman on this earth.

Period.

Annabella took her time and placed kisses along my shaft and balls. She moved slowly, like she didn't want to rush to the end, like having a big-ass dick in her mouth was enjoyable rather than exhausting. Sometimes she would close her eyes when she kissed the head of my cock, and sometimes she had the confidence to look right into my gaze as she gave me her sexy kisses.

My hand slid under the fall of her hair as I took a deep breath, enjoying the feeling of her pebbled tongue as it slid over my crown. I watched her lick away my arousal every time it started to bubble from the tip. Instead of acting like a gentleman and asking if she was ready for this, I took what she offered.

Because I wanted it so bad.

What I wanted most of all was sex. Not to get laid, but to finally make love to the woman I'd fallen so deeply in love with. I've never made love to a woman in my life, and I wanted her to be the first.

The only, preferably.

She finally put my dick in her mouth and pushed forward until my entire length was buried in her throat.

My fingers tightened on her neck, and I released a loud moan. "Jesus..."

She moved forward and backward, slow and gentle, giving

my dick a chance to enjoy it before making him explode. Instead of giving it to me hard and making me come right away, she pulled away and edged my orgasm because she wanted to make it last. She didn't mind letting her knees hit the hard floor. She didn't mind craning her neck over and over again to make me feel good. She didn't mind the tears that leaked from her eyes and streaked down her cheeks. She wanted to make it last because she enjoyed it as much as I did.

I appreciated the gesture, but damn, I wasn't gonna last long enough.

I'd had blue balls every night she'd slept with me. We made out like two young kids falling in love for the first time, but I hadn't seen her completely naked since the last time we were together. I wanted to pull her panties off her body and slide between her thighs until I felt heaven wrapped around my dick.

My hand remained against the back of her head, and I started to thrust deep into her throat. My breathing was uneven, and I couldn't stop myself from groaning every thirty seconds. I forgot how good it felt to be in her mouth, to glide along that small tongue to reach the back of her throat until her eyes began to water.

I felt like a goddamn king.

I felt the heat start in my stomach, right beneath my abs. It was an orgasm that rivaled a hurricane, destroyed everything in its path, including all logical thought. I moved closer to her and grabbed her hair like reins of a horse and thrust into her throat faster because it felt so good. I turned into an animal with a single desire. I wanted to fill her entire mouth with my come, erase every trace of the man who came before me. I breathed hard and felt sweat drip down my chest even though she was the one doing all the work.

And then I came. "Annabella..." My hand held her lips to my cock, and I squirted everywhere. I closed my eyes as I finished, feeling every muscle in my back tighten until they cramped. The pleasure in my brain was so extreme. It made me wonder if I'd ever really felt pleasure before now. It was a sensation that made a man fell to his knees, that completely incapacitated him.

Jesus Christ.

When I was finished, I pulled my softening dick out of her mouth. There was so much come on her tongue that she had to swallow at least twice.

The sight made me hard again.

She wiped her mouth with the back of her hand then got to her feet. Her cheeks were red, either from exertion or embarrassment. But she wouldn't look at me, as if her enjoyment were something to be ashamed of.

Definitely not.

I grabbed both straps of her dress and pushed them over her shoulders so the fabric fell to the floor.

A surprised look came over her face, as if she hadn't expected anything else to happen. She sucked my dick because she wanted to. No other reason.

We were far from finished.

She didn't have a bra on underneath her dress, so I could see her tits right away. And they were just as beautiful as I remembered. Small. Perky. Round. She had small nipples in the center, perfect size for my mouth and to lick with my tongue. Her soft stomach still had curves, a natural hourglass shape that made her the most desirable woman in the world. All she wore was a thong, black in color, as if she'd come prepared for this moment.

I stared for so long because I was hypnotized by the woman in front of me. I could honestly say I'd never been more attracted to anyone else in my life; I'd never been so turned on. I'd just exploded in her mouth, but looking at her now made me even harder. It was the beginning of an addiction, and I knew I was going to get lost in this disease.

I maneuvered her back toward the bed as I gripped the straps of her thong and pushed it over her hips. She didn't stop me, just as I expected she wouldn't, and once I reached her thighs, it fell the rest of the way down.

When the backs of her knees hit the frame of the bed, she stilled and watched me stare at her.

How could I not stare when she was so damn beautiful?

I laid her back on the sheets before I gripped her hips and dragged her to the edge of the bed, as if I were about to take her the way I used to when I would come over in the middle of the night.

But if she were ready for sex, she would've told me.

It didn't matter anyway because I had something else in mind. I leaned over her and finally kissed the tits I missed. I went straight for her right nipple and sucked it into my mouth. I gave it a slight bite and made her wince, but I knew she liked it.

She always liked it.

She arched her back, forcing more of her tit into my mouth. At my first touch, she was already writhing, as if my caresses were already orgasmic. Her fingers dug into my hair, and her thighs squeezed my torso. Her breathing was so deep and loud, as if she lost herself the moment I hit her buttons.

I moved to the other nipple and did the same. Warm. Sweet. Perfect. I loved being the recipient of pleasure, but giving it back to her was somehow more enjoyable. I wanted to please my woman every night, all the time, because it was my purpose in life. I wanted to make her smile. Make her happy. Make sure she never thought about anyone else except me.

I dragged my tongue right through her cleavage to taste the sweat that formed there minutes ago. The salt was strong on my tongue, and it reminded me of all our past nights together. She tasted exactly the same. Felt exactly the same.

I moved down her stomach into the space between her thighs. My lips found hers, and I gave her most sensitive area a gentle kiss. The touch was so soft, but her hips bucked instinctively, her breath shaky. When she released her moans, they echoed off the ceiling and reverberated throughout the entire room. Our warm dinner got cold, but I'd rather eat her than whatever was on those dishes.

I started to kiss her harder, drag my tongue over the areas she wanted to feel me the most. She was so sensitive because every move made her react so passionately. It took less than a minute to make her breathe hard, to make her body twist and turn because she couldn't sit still. She clawed at the sheets, and her moans got so loud, it sounded like she was being tortured rather than pleased.

I knew when she came because everything increased tenfold. She slammed her hands down onto the bed then yanked the sheets until they came loose. She pushed her pussy farther into my face because she wanted every single ounce of pleasure my tongue could give her. "Damien…"

I kept circling her clit with my tongue until she started to calm once more, her high fading away. I'd missed the taste of this cunt. I used to feast on it on a regular basis, and now that it was mine again, I wouldn't stop eating until I was full.

I pulled my mouth away then moved on top of her so I could get a good look at her face. Her cheeks were red, and her eyes were watery as if she'd cried when she came. She massaged her fingers through her hair and slowly brought her breathing back to normal. She made a deep sigh of satisfaction then looked at me head on. "I forgot how good that felt."

I tried not to think about her physical relationship with Liam, but I assumed that meant he never did that to her. He never went down on his wife, and that made him a bigger asshole in my eyes. I didn't do that with any woman unless we had some kind of relationship, but now that I was a committed man, I'd definitely do it all the time.

I certainly enjoyed it.

She reached out her arms to me because she wanted to pull me close. She was satisfied, but still desperate to have more of me. It was love that drew her to me now that her lust had been quenched.

I moved on top of her and felt her tits press against my chest. My hands moved into her hair because that's where I loved to touch her the most. My lips were soaked with her arousal, and my come was probably still in her mouth, but that was so sexy to me. I rested my forehead against hers and just held her close. I never wanted to lose this feeling, never wanted to let her go.

"You're the sexiest man alive, you know that?" She looked into my gaze with so much emotion in her eyes, like she couldn't believe she was really there with me. Her fingers played with my hair before they slowly glided down to the side of my face. She liked to touch me, liked to explore my body.

"Actually, yes. I did know that."

She smiled because she knew I was teasing, and it seemed to make the affection in her gaze stronger.

"And you're the sexiest woman in the world. I hope you know that."

"Sometimes I do...when you look at me like that." She moved her palms to my shoulders and squeezed the muscles. Her eyes drifted over my features, as if she was looking at a sculpture rather than a real person. Then her eyes came back to mine, filled with so much love, it was hard to believe she'd ever loved anyone else but me.

"Then I'm doing my job right." I separated her thighs so I could get closer to her. Anytime my dick was near her pussy, I thought about fucking her. How could I not? I was a man. But I also wanted to feel her heartbeat against my chest, feel us wrapped together as closely as possible.

I'd never been so satisfied without sex. I'd never been so satisfied with one woman. But there was nowhere else in the world I'd rather be. Lying with her, looking at her, was the best thing I could possibly do.

I CAME HOME LATE that night. It was a long day at the bank, and an even longer one on the streets. Some of my guys told me one of my distributors was trying to undercut me, so I had to take care of that in my usual way. Threats. Violence. The norm.

When I stepped inside my bedroom, it was four in the morning. I was careful as I walked across the carpet, my boots making an audible thud against the rug from my weight. I ducked into the closet and shed my suit jacket so Patricia could take it to the cleaners tomorrow. My tie was tossed in the laundry basket, and I got rid of the rest of my clothes piece by piece. When I was stripped down to my boxers, I walked over to my nightstand and placed my phone on the surface.

Annabella was asleep on her side of the bed, so tired she didn't stir at the sound of my movements. Her hair was a mess on the pillow, and she had the sheets pulled all the way up to her neck because she was cold without me beside her.

When I looked at my nightstand, I noticed the folded white paper sitting on top. It was folded four times, a single sheet of printer paper made into a square. I knew I hadn't left it there, so I grabbed it and quietly opened it until it was readable.

My eyes scanned over the results of a procedure until I understood what it was. Annabella got tested and wanted me to know the outcome.

She was clean.

And she was ready.

My heart started to beat a little faster as I understood the implication. My eyes moved back to Annabella, who was dreaming about a faraway place. This note told me everything I need to know.

I was hard instantly.

I folded the paper back up and inserted it into my nightstand drawer. I'd just received great news, but for now, there was nothing I could do about it.

Just had to be patient a little longer.

FOURTEEN
ANNABELLA

DAMIEN NEVER MENTIONED THE RESULTS I'D LEFT ON HIS nightstand days ago. Maybe nothing needed to be said. Or maybe he decided to be a gentleman and not question me about it. Instead of assuming I was ready to hit the sheets right away, he treated me the same. Gentle. Loving. Patient.

But a part of me wondered why we continued to wait.

When he came home every night, we had dinner at the dining table, sometimes with his father, but most of the time, it was just the two of us. The curtains were always open so I could enjoy the sunshine outside while I was home during the day. There was patio furniture on the balcony so I got to sit outside in the middle of the day and let the sunshine tan my skin. Then when he came home, we watched movies and whatever was on TV.

But most of the time, we fooled around.

We did everything but the actual act of making love. We kissed each other all night, our fingers digging into each other's hair, my ankles locked around his waist as I fantasized about feeling him inside me. Before we went to sleep, he always kissed me good night and told me he loved me.

If felt like we'd been together forever.

It felt right, like we should've been doing this years ago. Like I never should have married Liam, like I should've been with Damien this whole time. It was a feeling I couldn't describe, a closeness I'd never had with my ex-husband, not even on our wedding day. I didn't believe in fate or soul mates, but I started to wonder if Damien was meant for me.

I sat on the couch and watched TV alone while I waited for him to come home. Sometimes he had to work late, and even though I hated it, I never complained. I trusted him, so whatever he was doing out there wouldn't hurt me. He left me because he didn't want to put me in danger. If I ever expressed concern about his criminal enterprise, he might leave me again.

I would never ask him to sacrifice his livelihood for me.

We never discussed it, and I assumed we never would.

The bedroom door opened, and Damien walked inside. He was dressed casually in jeans and a t-shirt, because he'd left the bank long ago and headed to his other commitments. He sauntered inside with a pizza box tucked under his arm.

"Ooh...is that for me?"

"Definitely not for me." He walked to the sitting area and placed the box on the table in front of the couches. "I don't want to deal with Patricia's look of death for any reason, so I always tell her it's for you." He slipped off his shoes then sat next to me on the couch.

"I thought she liked having the night off."

"She does. But seeing a greasy-ass pizza walk into this house is borderline insulting, especially when all her cooking is home-made and fresh."

"Well, if she tried it, I'm sure she'd change her mind." Who didn't like layers of cheese on a crispy crust with fresh marinara sauce? It would change her life.

"She's just old-school. You know, family should always eat at home together. They should be talking loudly in the kitchen, spilling wine everywhere, and devouring fresh bread, with recipes that have been in their family for generations." He looked at the TV to see what I was watching before he turned his gaze back to me. His arm moved over the back of the couch so he could wrap his fingers around the back of my neck. Now he was staring at me as if that was what he wanted to do all night.

"Traditions change."

"Our family can make new traditions." His fingers moved to my jawline and into the space at the bottom of my cheek. He touched my soft skin as if he were memorizing it. His eyes dropped down to my lips, and he stared for a while before he lifted his gaze and looked in my eyes again.

My hand moved to his chest, resting on top of the fabric of his black shirt. I could feel the hardness of his pectoral muscles, feel the heat of his body constantly radiating every second of the day. "Our family?" I couldn't make children with Liam, and that had always made us feel incomplete. When Liam betrayed me, I felt so alone. I'd lost everything and everyone.

Damien's hand cupped my cheek as his thumb traced my bottom lip. "Yes."

I felt like I belonged with him, like the perfect size glove for his hand. His home felt like my home. His friends felt like my friends. He already shared everything with me, and I wasn't even his wife. I felt his loyalty, respect, honesty. It was a family

I wanted to be a part of, a family I was proud to represent. "Damien...I know this is a bit presumptuous, but we've never really talked about it. I'm not sure if I can have children..." I'd always pictured my future with kids, two or three. So, if I couldn't have them naturally, I would adopt or do anything possible to make my family grow.

Damien stared at me with no visible reaction. He didn't cower at the mention of the future, of babies and marriage. He didn't run like most men would. He continued to adore me with his eyes, as if his feelings for me hadn't faltered, as if he believed I was still the most desirable woman on the planet. "Whether you can or can't doesn't matter. I want to be with you, regardless."

It was hard to look at him without needing to cry. When Liam and I had tried to have a baby and failed, I felt responsible for the loss. He never blamed me verbally, but I could feel his accusation every single day. And when he went out and screwed somebody else, I knew he felt entitled to it...because I'd lost his son. It made me feel like less of a woman, like a waste of life. I'd let him down, and I never forgave myself for it. But now that Damien treated me this way, like it made absolutely no difference, it made me realize this was really love. True love. "You've never told me if you want to have children or not."

He considered my words a long time, like he had to be careful with his answer. "I've never thought about it, to be honest. I've been alone a long time...until you. But I want you, no matter what, so if children are important to you, I'll do it."

"But you don't want them?"

"I wouldn't say that. My father continues to pester me about continuing the family line, and being around Andrew makes me less afraid to be a father myself. Never in a million years did I think Hades would be the family type, and it turns out he's pretty damn good at it. Do I want to have kids tomorrow? Not really. But someday? Why not." He continued to outline the bow shape of my bottom lip, to caress me like a treasured belonging. He didn't say exactly what I wanted to hear, but it was good enough.

"You talk like you picture us getting married..." That was the future I imagined myself, but it seemed too soon to assume. We hadn't even slept together yet, and I already visualized my first name with his last name. I'd barely been divorced for a few months, and I was already imagining the style of my wedding dress. Damien was nothing like me, and I doubted he fantasized about these sorts of things.

"I don't know much about love, but I know it's rare, unusual, and impossible to find...especially for someone like me. When I realized how I felt about you, I knew that feeling would last a lifetime. There will never be a day when I suddenly don't want you, when I get bored of you. I imagine us being together forever. And yes, that probably includes marriage. It's not like I'm ever gonna let you go anyway." His hand moved to my cheek then to my strands of hair. He gently pushed it back, tucking it behind my ear so he could see my face with no obstruction. He wasn't a romantic man, but when he said things like that, he was as gifted as a poet. He spoke from the heart, a heart that had never loved anyone else, and that was what made it so beautiful.

"This feels right to me. Like I should've been with you all along."

"I feel the same way." He leaned in and gave me a kiss on the lips, a gentle touch that was packed with emotion. He sucked my bottom lip into his mouth for a gentle caress before he let me go. "That's why I'm willing to do anything to keep you. That's why I won't kill him, even though I should. Because you're the only thing that matters to me. And whatever you want...I'll give it to you."

I had no idea what to say to that. What had I done to earn his heart? He could have any woman he wanted, so what was so special about me? I wasn't a supermodel. I wasn't a billionaire from a noble family. I was just a woman...nothing special. But my mediocrity told me this love was true, because he loved me for no real reason at all. I looked into his deep green eyes and spoke the words in my soul. "I love you..." I wished I had something stronger to say, but I couldn't think of any other pairing of words that could do my feelings justice.

"I know. You loved me from the beginning. You loved me despite my impulsiveness, my unpredictability. You trusted me when you had no reason to, when your trust had been shattered before. I should've stayed. I never should've left you... and I will always regret that." He reached into his pocket and pulled out a folded white paper. "But I'm here now. Forever."

I already knew the contents of the paper without opening it. We were both ready for this, and there was nothing holding us back anymore. I should feel guilty for being over my marriage so quickly, but I wasn't thinking about my ex at all. I was completely invested and devoted to the man staring at me. And even though it made me a terrible person, I confessed to myself that I was happy Liam had betrayed me.

Because if he hadn't...I wouldn't have this.

Damien's eyes stayed on mine and never glanced down at the paper between us. Heartbeats passed as he waited for me to say something, to either open it and read it, or disregard it altogether. When nothing happened, he spoke. "Annabella." He said my name with ownership, with a tone so deep and sexy. "May I make love to you?"

My fingers suddenly felt sweaty and numb, and my heart was

beating so fast, I felt like a virgin. My nipples hardened in my bra, and my toes curled from excitement and anxiety. There was no reason to say no, and even if there were, it wouldn't be enough to stop this from happening. I'd given him my papers because I wanted all of him, not just pieces of him. I was so anxious, I felt my head spin, felt the floor shake underneath my feet. "Yes..."

NAKED, we got onto the bed with the sheets kicked to the very bottom. My head was on a soft pillow, and he immediately pulled the strands of my hair away from my face so he could see me perfectly.

I was all bare skin, my nipples hard and pointed straight at his chest. There were bumps over my arms and legs because I was nervous, even though I had no reason to be. This was Damien...the man I've been in love with since the first time we kissed. Being with him was right, so there was no reason to be uneasy. I was just so excited, so aroused by this moment that my body could barely contain it.

There were no kisses. No whispers. We both breathed deep and hard as we looked into each other's gazes. It was the sound of two people at maximum exertion, except we weren't moving at all. We were both on the precipice of the most important moment in our lives, and it made us both lethargic.

Damien knew exactly how he would take me, part my thighs with his so he could have me in the position he'd already fantasized about. His warm dick immediately came into contact with my clit, and that simple touch was enough to make me shiver. He lay over me more fully, his shoulders and chest blocking my view of the ceiling. He dominated me, cast me in shadow, and stared down at me like he couldn't wait to possess me. He was calm and ready, and his heavy breathing was just a byproduct of his excitement.

My hands immediately flattened against those pecs, preparing for the enjoyment I was about to feel. I was bracing myself for impact, prepared to get whiplashed harder than ever before. My heart pounded so forcefully I swore he could hear the beat. My breathing couldn't be controlled, no matter how much I tried. My desire was almost shameful. I'd never wanted another man this much, and it was a bit humiliating that I could be this aroused by someone, this excited, this out of control.

Instead of kissing me, he continued to stare at me. This was a moment for our souls to touch, not our bodies to come together with a deep kiss. It was meaningful, as if it was our first time together ever.

He tilted his hips and pressed down on his hard shaft so his swollen head could slide into my soaked opening. It was tight in the beginning, but once he got his fat crown past my lips, he was able to sink in slowly.

Deep. Deeper. And so deep he would never come out again.

I closed my eyes and clawed at his skin because he felt exactly as I remembered. He filled me horizontally as well as vertically, exciting my nerves and bringing me pleasure, which was also mixed with a little pain. It felt so good, so different from any other man I'd been with. It was like our bodies were made to combine just like this.

Damien watched my performance, watched every subtle expression I made in reaction. He could read my pleasure like words appeared on my face, could sense when he was in too deep by seeing my watery eyes. When he was at the perfect spot, he stilled. "Annabella."

My arms moved around his neck, and I brought head face

close to mine. "Oh god..." I breathed into his face as I got used to his thick size inside me, and I felt my body stretch to accommodate him. I was squeezing him so tight, and it took a long time for me to let go, for my pussy to relax around his throbbing dick.

With his forehead against mine, he started to thrust slowly, to slide in and out of me with strokes that were smooth. He didn't shake me or make my tits move up and down the way they used to when he pounded into me. He took me gentler than he ever had before, like it was the first time I'd ever been with a man at all.

My hand went to his back, and my nails clawed deep into his skin. My ankles wrapped around his waist and locked together so he couldn't escape, so he had to stay inside me until we were both finished.

He pushed into me after every thrust, rubbing my clit just the way I liked. My breathing grew louder, and I pressed on his back every time he was inside me, like I wanted just a little bit more even though it hurt when he came too close to my cervix.

"Damien...I love you." I moaned when I felt another thrust deep inside me, when I felt how much he desired me with his impressive hardness. I'd wanted to tell this man I loved him so many times, but I never could. When we were naked in my bed, I'd felt it then, felt it any time we were together. Now I actually got to say the words, say them as much as I wanted without repercussion.

This man was mine.

My hand went to his ass and pushed on him harder and harder because I was so close to my release. He brought me to the edge so quickly, excited my clit with his hard body. I moaned and gasped because it felt so good, far better than I remembered it. I'd been living there for over a month, and now that time seemed wasted because we hadn't been doing this all along.

His strong arms held his body above mine, his fists pressing into the mattress on either side of me. He held his frame still so his hips could make those deep and smooth thrusts. He wasn't working at a fast pace, but that smoothness was even more exerting than quick pounding. His skin became sticky with sweat, and the red tint to his face showed his desire.

"I can't wait for you to come inside me…" I wasn't trying to talk dirty or make him come soon. I was just excited to feel his seed inside me, to fell his come drip between my legs the second I got up to use the bathroom. It was a sexy feeling, to feel him inside me long after he was gone.

He moaned without pausing his thrusts. It was a deep, animalistic sound in the back of his throat. His tone was possessive and masculine, like there was nothing more he wanted besides giving me what I asked for. "Baby…"

I knew I was going to come the second he was inside me. I'd been fighting off the climax because I wanted to enjoy him a little while before I gave it up. My quick rise to orgasm was embarrassing when it shouldn't be. I shouldn't be afraid to show him how much I wanted him, how much I desired him, because he already knew how obsessed I was. It would just make that fat ego bigger, bigger than his already fat cock.

Damien seemed to know every thought in my mind. "Come for me."

I bit my bottom lip and dragged my nails down his back as I felt the explosion begin at every extremity. The fire burned all the way down to the area between my legs, and when our paths met at the same time, I exploded so hard, I lost my sight for just a second. "God…yes." I held him harder and buried my face in his neck so I could finish while hiding my tears. I wasn't sure how long I moaned and cried for, but it seemed like a life-time. I didn't realize how good an orgasm could be until Damien increased the threshold.

He pulled my face from his neck and forced my head back onto the pillow so he could look at me. "Do you still want that come?"

"Please..." My nails dug deep to show my enthusiasm. My climax hadn't quenched my thirst for this man.

His eyes darkened again, and he gave his final thrusts before he shoved his massive length inside me, making me wince because he was buried so deep, and released with the sexiest moan I'd ever heard. He suddenly dropped his guard and enjoyed the high I'd just experienced. He was vulnerable. Masculine. Passionate. He moaned over and over again until every drop was between my legs.

I cupped his face and felt my fingers wipe away the sweat that formed in his dark hair. I kissed him everywhere, the corners of his lips, his jawline, his neck. I cherished him everywhere, because I still wanted him even though he'd already given me everything.

After the climax, he should be soft inside me, but he was still just as hard. "I'm far from done, Annabella."

FIFTEEN

DAMIEN

My phone kept ringing on the nightstand. It was on vibrate, so I heard it tap against the wood with every single ring. It wasn't loud enough to wake me up ordinarily, but since the noise refused to stop, it was incredibly distracting.

I partially woke up and heard Annabella sigh beside me.

My arm flung out to the nightstand, and I grabbed the device so I could shut up the person who wouldn't leave me alone. Without checking to see who was calling me, I answered and put the phone to my ear. "What?" My tone was clipped and sleepy at the same time. My eyes were still closed because I refused to fully wake up.

"Are you coming in today or not?" It was Hades, his tone bursting with annoyance. "We're supposed to meet the Salvatore brothers today, and you're thirty minutes late. And I shouldn't have to be your fucking alarm clock."

Couldn't care less about whoever the hell he was talking about. "Take care of it."

"Me?" he asked incredulously. "These are your clients, asshole."

I grew tired of the conversation, so I hung up. I put the phone back on the nightstand and went right back to sleep.

But he called back anyway.

The phone rang over and over, so I was forced to answer. I took the call and growled into the phone. "Yes?"

"What the fuck are you doing?"

"I'm taking the day off, alright? Vacation day...sick day. Whatever you call it."

"Pussies get sick days. Now get your ass in here."

"I know you can handle it. Don't call again." I dropped the phone on the nightstand and got comfortable once more.

Now Annabella was awake, and she scooted closer to me on the bed. She wrapped her arm around my stomach and rested her head on my shoulder. "Morning..." She pressed a kiss to my warm skin, moving from my shoulder to my neck.

"I'm sorry that asshole woke you up."

"Don't be." She moved farther on top of me, kissing me all over the place. Her hair dragged across my skin, and her smell was intoxicating in my nose. She kissed my abs and went farther south until she found my hard dick under the sheets. "I'm happy to be awake." She started to kiss my shaft, dragging her tongue over the tip and down along the vein until she placed a few kisses on my balls.

All I could do was enjoy it. Now I was happy that Hades had obnoxiously ruined my morning. I had the hottest pair of lips against my body that very moment because of it. My hand moved into her hair, and I relaxed as I watched her suck me off and appreciate my morning wood.

After I moaned a few times, I felt my body grow excited and

anxious to release, so she pulled her lips away and got on top of me. Naked from head to toe, she was sexy in her tanned skin. She had nice, small tits, a flat stomach with a cute belly button, and the sexiest thighs I'd ever seen. One hand moved into her hair, and she pulled the strands from her face in the most arousing way before she planted both hands on my chest and tilted her hips so she could slide herself onto my dick.

Like a fucking pro.

I'd already had her the night before, but this felt like the first time all over again. My dick wasn't used to the softness of her wet flesh. I wasn't used to feeling her so intimately, claiming her in a way I'd never claimed another woman. I had to close my eyes and take a deep breath to steady my excitement so I would last as long as she needed.

I watched her move up and down, arching her back and playing with her tits. Her hand squeezed her breasts, and her fingers pinched the nipples to make herself moan. She kept going, kept rolling her hips, taking every inch of my dick like it didn't sometimes hurt her.

I couldn't wait to do this for the rest of my life.

Now I understood exactly what Hades was talking about. I understood the fiery obsession, the unstoppable lust, the enormous love that beat in the heart of a man. There was no one else, and I never wanted there to be anyone else.

My hands went to her hips, and I guided her at a slower pace because I wouldn't last if she continued to ride me like a damn cowgirl. My threshold for climaxes hadn't been restored because I wasn't getting laid on a regular basis. It would take time, especially when there was nothing separating us like this. She needed to be patient, need to give me time to become the man I used to be.

And watching her bounce on my dick with that look in her

eyes wasn't helping.

I guided her body to grind against mine, to drag her clit over my hard body so she could bring herself to climax sooner rather than later. I needed her to shoot her load before I shot mine, because that was what I was known for. I had far too much pride to finish before my woman did.

"I want you to come..." With her palms flat against my chest, she leaned forward and let her hair hang over my face. "You can make me come before or after. Doesn't make a difference when we have all the time in the world."

WE SPENT the day in bed, making love in different positions, getting hot and sweaty against the sheets. There wasn't much conversation because our bodies did all the talking. I felt like a married man on his honeymoon, spending all his time fucking his wife instead of going out to dinner, sight-seeing, and whatever else people did on their vacations.

When we were both starving well past noon, we finally had Patricia send up a tray so we could eat lunch at the dining table. Sex was a powerful distraction to make us forget about food, but when our stomachs began to growl, we couldn't keep going.

We sat together at the dining table, eating the fresh salads and sandwiches Patricia had prepared. We shared a bottle of wine and enjoyed the freshly baked bread from a recipe that had been in Patricia's family for generations. The sun came through the window and made the room hot, but I knew Annabella loved the sunshine so I didn't close the curtains.

Her hair was such a mess, it looked like it had gotten stuck in the spinning blades of a fan, and her baggy shirt had sweat stains because she was still warm from all the fucking we did.

Her face was free of makeup, but she'd never looked more beautiful. She sipped her wine and smeared jam across her French bread before she took a loud bite, the crunch audible.

A part of me felt guilty for ditching Hades, but when I explained later why I'd bailed, he would understand. I never took a vacation or sick day, but after Annabella wanted to be with me, I didn't want to go back to the real world until I was fully satisfied. I wanted to be in bed with her all the time, to catch up on all the time we'd lost.

I finished the last few bites of my food and spent my time staring at her, the beautiful brunette who fell in love with me for reasons I'd never understand. The gypsy said only one woman would love me for me, my soul and not my money. There was no doubt in my mind Annabella was the woman in that prophecy. And I somehow got her...despite that foreboding warning the gypsy had given to me.

I considered myself lucky to end up with her. I'd never imagined I'd fall in love at all, let alone with a woman who had already been married—twice. But it felt right. It felt true. And now all I had to do was be happy.

Well, I had to take care of a few things before that could really happen. It was easy to forget sometimes.

When I looked into her beautiful face, I forgot all about her ex-husband who wanted to kill me. I forgot Heath could be his ally. I forgot I had a target on my back and Liam would pull the trigger at the first opportunity.

But I didn't want to think about that right now. I just wanted to look at her instead.

She smiled when she realized I was staring. She took another bite of her food, a subtle blush to her cheeks. "Yes?"

I couldn't hide my own smile. "What?"

"Is there something I can help you with?"

"I can't stare at you?" I grabbed my glass and took a drink. It was early in the day for wine, but I didn't care. It wasn't like I was drinking scotch. "You're my woman. I can stare at you whenever I want."

She finished her bite and couldn't contain her playful smile. "That's a two-way street."

"I doubt you would ever want to stare at me as much as I want to stare at you, but I hope so." I was a handsome man, fit and strong, not to mention rich, but I was nowhere near her stratosphere. She was perfect. I was flawed.

"So, you aren't going to work today?"

I shook my head.

"What about tomorrow?"

"Why? Trying to get rid of me?"

"No." She chuckled like my question was ridiculous. "I just want to know how long this is going to last."

Forever, I hoped. "I'll be home a few days. I never take time off, so I thought now would be a good time."

Her plate was empty because she enjoyed Patricia's cooking so much, and she continued to pour the wine like alcohol had no effect on her. She smiled between drinks, visibly pleased that I was there with her. "That makes me happy. I want to see you more…" She seemed to want to say more but kept it back. She was probably tired of being confined to the bedroom for weeks on end. She wanted to get out of the house, go out to dinner with me, travel with me. But she didn't say that out loud because she didn't want to ruin this moment. Like me, she wanted to continue to pretend that Liam wasn't a problem, that we didn't still need to find a solution so we could be together safely.

I wasn't ready to deal with it either, so I put it to the back of my mind and decided to enjoy her instead.

I OPEN a new bottle of scotch and poured myself a glass. My back was to the couches and the fire, while Annabella watched the movie on TV. We'd spent the whole day in bed, but now we both needed a rest. I capped the bottle then took a drink before I turned around.

I came face-to-face with Annabella, who emerged behind me without making a sound. I was hypnotized by her beauty, so I stood there for second and stared down at her.

She took the glass from my hand. "No more of this." After taking a sip, she stepped around me and poured the contents back into the bottle. Then she placed the booze and glass back into the liquor cabinet. "I'm fucking you now, so I get to nag." She gave me a look of attitude before she walked back toward the couch.

I watched her go, a bit turned on by her bossiness. "Hades has a medical issue. I might be as healthy as a horse."

She got to the couch and took a seat. "Until we know for sure, you're cutting back." She faced the TV and stared up at the screen for a while before she noticed my silence. Then she turned her gaze back to me, unapologetic.

I didn't appreciate being told what to do, but damn, it was pretty hot when she did it. I sat down on the couch beside her.

"Fine. I said you could nag at me when you're fucking me. So, I guess that's fair."

"Damn right, it's fair. I want you to live a long time, Damien."

I'd never known how much I would enjoy being loved by one woman, but it was pretty sexy to see a babe care about me so much, that she would stand up to me to make sure I was healthy and safe.

My arm moved over the back of the couch so my fingers could slide into her hair. "If we go to the doctor and everything is fine, am I off the hook?"

"No. Even if you're healthy now, you won't be healthy soon if you continue to drink like that. So, no more."

"Ever?"

"Yep."

"Baby, that seems a little harsh..."

She must've known her demand was unrealistic because she softened right away. "All right...but you need to cut back significantly."

"You've got a deal." I brought my face close to hers and rubbed my nose softly against her cheek. My other hand moved into her hair so I could grasp it, control her completely. I forced her lips my way and looked her in the eye before I kissed her. I'd had her all night and all afternoon, but as if those sessions had never happened, I wanted her more. My hand moved to her left hip, and I grabbed the strap of her thong so I could pull it down her long legs.

She dropped her attitude instantly, becoming aroused like the fight was long over.

I pinned her to the corner of the couch and pulled down my

own sweats so I could fuck her while I pressed her into the cushions.

With her top still on, she opened her legs and pulled me to her. She was tucked into the corner of the furniture so she could barely move. All she could do was take it, whatever I wanted to give her.

I got between her legs and gave a hard thrust, pushing myself inside like I owned her, could do whatever the hell I wanted.

Which was true. As far as I was concerned, I did own her.

I started to fuck her hard against the couch. Lovemaking was over, and now I just wanted to have her. I wanted to take her good and hard because that was what a man was supposed to do with his woman. It wasn't just slow and smooth strokes, quiet whispers filled with promises. It was aggressive and possessive, right to the point, and with just enough hardness to make her scream.

But we didn't get far because the main window shattered.

The window that overlooked the balcony was enormous, a large arch fifteen feet in height. Made of solid glass that was bulletproof, it was indestructible. But it fractured into a million pieces, as if a bomb had just gone off and crushed it to dust. My home had been breached with weapons of warfare, the safety my castle once provided long gone. The sound of shards hitting the floor was so loud and distinct I would never forget it because it was such a cacophony, such a distinguished assault.

I immediately went into fight mode. Danger was around us, and I needed to get my gun and get Annabella the hell out of there. I was off her in a nanosecond, my pants up as I dashed to the nightstand where I kept my pistol.

"Move, and I'll shoot you." The sound of broken glass had

disappeared, and now it was quiet. A man was behind me, and his voice was easy to recognize. I should've made my move sooner, and now I was out of time. A barrel was pointed right at my back, and with one squeeze of the trigger, I'd be dead on the floor. My nightstand was still seven feet away, and I wouldn't be able to get to it without him piercing my skull and spraying my brains on the wall. "How did you break through the glass?"

"That's the least of your worries right now." He moved his fingers and cocked the gun.

Annabella was still in the living room, and when she realized what was happening, she gasped. "Liam, what the hell are you doing?"

The terror in her voice made me turn around.

Liam glanced at his former wife, then turned back to me, raising the gun a little higher. "I told you not to move, asshole."

I should shit my pants right now, but I wasn't afraid. In the most dangerous situations, I was oddly calm. Whereas the same thing scared most people. "You're going to shoot me anyway." Shirtless and in just my sweatpants, I had nothing to protect me from the bullet that was about to puncture my heart. My mortality wasn't important right now. The only thing I cared about was the frantic woman watching her greatest nightmare take place.

"Good point," he said. "Final words?"

I should resent Annabella right now. I was about to die because she wouldn't allow me to do what was necessary. But instead of feeling anger or pain, I felt something else entirely. "Yeah." I turned my gaze to Annabella, who was already crying. "I love you." I turned my gaze back to him. "Now, do it."

The gun started to shake in his grasp because of the rage heavy in his veins. Now, he wanted me dead more than before, and I only had a few seconds before I turned to worm food.

"Liam." Annabella slowly moved closer to him, standing in the area between us, being balanced and diplomatic. "Look at me."

His face was red with rage, and a bead of sweat started to form on his forehead. But her voice was enough for him to turn his gaze back to her.

"You were right." Tears still welled up in her eyes, and the tears that had already fallen reflected like shiny rivers down her cheeks. She was only wearing one of my shirts, long enough to cover her body to her knees. "It's my fault that our marriage didn't work. I was in love with somebody else, and that wasn't fair to you. The person you should punish is me, not him."

Liam lowered the gun slightly. "You mean that?"

"Yes." Her breathing started to slow once Liam began to calm down. "And I'm so sorry for hurting you. You and I can work on this. Let's go somewhere quiet and talk. Just don't kill Damien."

The last thing I wanted was for Annabella to do something she didn't want to do, especially on my account. She only offered him that to spare my life, but I'd rather die than let her be forced to do something against her will.

Liam lowered the gun altogether. "That's what I wanted from the beginning."

I considered rushing him and knocking him to the ground, but I couldn't risk accidental casualties. There was only one life in the room that mattered, and I couldn't risk it for anything. So I'd have to keep being patient and wait for a better opportunity.

"Then, let's go." Once Annabella successfully calmed Liam, the tears stopped altogether and her shoulders weren't so tight. She stood in just her underwear and my t-shirt, but she didn't seem uncomfortable in a provocative outfit, even though it implied we'd just been screwing.

"Sure." Liam raised the barrel and pointed the gun at me again. "I'll just kill him first."

"Liam, no! I said I would come with you."

"I already gave you the opportunity to spare his life, and you refused." He placed his forefinger over the trigger. "My generosity has expired."

My heart started to race once I reached death's doorstep. There was nothing I could do to stop the bullet when it left the barrel. I was cornered near the back wall, so there was nowhere to run. I'd have to take death like a man and accept it.

He pulled the trigger.

My eyes immediately closed as I prepared for the pain. I'd been shot before, but the adrenaline usually masked the immediate agony. I didn't feel it now because my body was in survival mode. I kept my pulse slow so I wouldn't lose all my blood too soon.

"Anna!"

I opened my eyes and grabbed at my chest. There was no drop of blood, no sign of red. My fingers felt my perfectly healthy body, and I didn't feel the intrusion of a bullet. My eyes moved over to the floor, and that was when I saw my white shirt covered in red blood.

Now, I panicked.

Now, the pain hit me hard.

Now, something worse than death had happened.

She was still, her eyes open as she stared at the floor beside her. She breathed hard as she processed the bullet that had just hit her in the gut, and she was clearly in shock based on the emptiness in her gaze.

I didn't have the luxury of getting upset. I couldn't fall to my knees and sob at the sight before me. I couldn't pull out my gun and shoot Liam for what he'd just done. There was still time to save her, and I needed it to haul ass to make that happen. Vengeance would come later.

I moved to the floor beside her and pressed my hand over the bleeding wound. My fingers and palm were soaked in her blood, and I realized how much of it she had already lost. That could only mean several organs were pierced...that was very bad news. "Annabella, you're going to be fine. I just need you to stay with me, okay?" I lied to keep her calm, to make her remain positive so she was more likely to live. I scooped my hands underneath her body and lifted her as I rose to my feet.

Liam was a mess. He sobbed uncontrollably and was so upset he couldn't do anything at all. Filled with self-loathing, he just stood there and watched me take her away. "Anna...I'm so sorry."

I headed to the door, prepared to run down three flights of stairs to get her into the car. But I stilled when I heard Liam's words.

"That bullet was meant for you..." He stood near my bed and didn't know what to do with himself. He was overwhelmed by the grave mistake he'd just made.

I faced him, so livid I could barely breathe. "Then you should've aimed better."

I GOT her to the hospital in record time and handed her over to the trauma team. Letting her go was so damn difficult because I was giving her to strangers, but they were the only people who could help her right now.

There was nothing I could do.

All I'd been focused on was getting there as soon as possible, and once that mission was complete, I had no other purpose.

Other than to wait.

The adrenaline never disappeared. It was still fresh in my veins. Sometimes I sat on the couch, sometimes I paced just to move, and I even read the newspaper without understanding a single word...all in an effort to pass the time. I was in a state of panic, waiting for news that I wouldn't receive for a long time.

Unless she didn't make it.

They took her to surgery right away without giving me much detail about their plan to help her. They had no idea the extent of the injury until they got their scans and opened her up, and they didn't have time to waste telling me all those things. Their only option was to move as quickly as possible to fix the damage right then and there.

So I waited...and waited.

A LOT of bad things had happened to me.

I'd lost my mom too soon. I'd lost my best friend over my stupidity. I'd killed people who were innocent, and I'd gotten my hands dirty more than I wished.

But this was definitely worse than all of those occasions.

Worst day of my fucking life.

I sat in the waiting room, and my heart continued to pound violently in my chest. At some point, I called Hades and told him what happened, but I couldn't recall exactly what I said.

Just a blur.

Now, he was beside me, Sofia on the other side of me. They'd brought me a change of clothes since my sweatpants had been wet with Annabella's blood. At first, they asked questions, and I answered in a dreamlike state. But then I turned quiet because my body couldn't respond anymore.

Hades was silent for hours, but when the waiting room started to empty, he said something. "No news is good news."

I stared at the linoleum beneath my feet. "Not sure if I agree with that."

"It means she's still alive. Otherwise, they would come out here and deliver the bad news. That means her heart is still beating, she's still fighting, that she'll pull through this." He rested his arms on his knees with his hands together in front of him. He was in jeans and a t-shirt, probably throwing on whatever he could find after I called. It was late at night, eleven when I finally reached out to him.

Pretty sure he was asleep by nine.

So domesticated.

Sofia locked our fingers together, and she held me with a soft touch. "She's going to be okay. I can feel it."

"But if she's not…" I had no idea what I would do if Annabella didn't pull through. First things first, I would execute Liam. I wouldn't honor her last wish to spare his life. But after my need for vengeance was satisfied, what would I do then? I'd finally found a woman I loved, and then she was gone. There wouldn't be somebody else. Time wouldn't heal that kind of pain.

Hades turned his gaze on me, watching the side of my face. He didn't give me false promises or try to make me feel better with unrealistic hope. "Whatever happens, it wasn't your fault."

I pulled my hand away from Sofia's. "None of this would've happened if I'd just killed him…" I didn't have a lot of regrets in life, but now that was at the top on my list. Even if Annabella came out of this relatively unscathed, she shouldn't have been forced to endure it in the first place. I should've done my job and protected her. I shouldn't have allowed her feelings to complicate the situation. Liam had always been an enemy, and I should've killed him like all my other enemies.

Hades kept his voice low because people were still around. "You'll get your chance, Damien. And you know I'll be there if you need help."

I released a sarcastic chuckle even though it was completely inappropriate. "I won't need help. Trust me."

Sofia refused to accept my coldness, so she rested her hand on my forearm, lightly touching me because she wanted me to know that she was there. "Everything is going to be okay. We just need to get through this first…and then take care of everything else."

I couldn't imagine my life without Annabella. I'd been alone for so long, but now that I'd shared my soul with another person, I didn't know what to do without her. I'd never been so scared. "But what if she—"

"That won't happen." She squeezed my arm. "She'll get through this. I know she will."

❄

DUE TO THE complications of the bullet, the surgery took twelve hours. It included a team of three surgeons, assisted by a staff of nurses and medical personnel. The bullet had pierced her stomach, liver, and kidney, so they had to fix all the damage and remove the bullet, while keeping her alive.

But she would live.

That was all that mattered. We could sort everything else out later.

When the doctor told me the news, I stood still and just stared at his face. It was difficult to process the information he'd just delivered, but I wasn't going to lose her, and that was what I focused on. It seemed too good to be true. "When can I see her?"

"In just a bit. We need to transfer her to a room." He shook my hand before he walked away.

Hades and Sofia were standing off to the side, in earshot so they could hear whatever was about to happen. Hades came to me and wrapped his arm around my shoulders. "Thank god."

Sofia hugged me and squeezed me tight. "Oh...I'm so relieved." She rubbed the back of my neck before she pulled away, tears in her eyes. "She didn't deserve this, and I'm so glad it's not going to claim her life."

I was still in a dream, still hollow and empty. Of course, I was thrilled she would be okay, but I was traumatized this had happened to her in the first place. There was a lot of rage, a lot of guilt.

Hades patted me on the back. "What is it, Damien?"

"I don't know," I answered. "I'm still in shock, I guess." I placed my hands against my face and cupped my nose as I closed my eyes. I couldn't get the image of her on the floor out of my mind, the feeling of her blood on my hands. I almost lost the person I cared the most about.

What would I have done if I had lost her?

Even if Annabella asked me not to kill Liam, I would anyway.

I fucking would.

I dropped my hands and sucked in a deep breath through my teeth. I didn't realize my eyes were wet until a tear streaked down my cheek.

Hades didn't react to my emotion. He'd cried in front of me before, when his wife was taken away from him. He wouldn't judge me for feeling this way now, for being so relieved and so emotional at the same time. "She's going to be okay. The worst part is over." He pulled me in for a hug, his hand on the back of my neck.

I hugged him back, this time holding him tight and giving in to my tears. I let myself explode, let all the pent-up tension and sorrow escape. He became my crutch, my friend, my brother. "I know..."

SHE WAS unconscious for thirty-six hours.

I sat at her bedside and watched her breathe with a ventilator, looking so small in a bed that was already small. I got used to the sound of the machines, the hourly hum of her blood pressure cuff, the beep of her pulse, and everything else that made up the background of a hospital room.

Hades joined me and set a white Styrofoam box on the table in the sitting area. He also put down a coffee. "Thought you might be hungry."

I kept my eyes on Annabella as I shook my head.

Hades sat in the chair next to her bedside. "You haven't slept in days. How about you go home and at least shower?"

"I'm not leaving her." It was only a matter of time before Liam showed his face. I wouldn't be surprised if he was still listed as her emergency contact. How often do people change those? I wasn't letting him anywhere near her, and if he did show up here, at least he would have immediate medical attention once I was done with him.

"I'll stay."

Hades had been there with me the whole time. Sofia came and went, because she was pregnant and had a little boy at home. But Hades was there...always there. "I can't do it. Liam will show his face at some point."

"And I'll kill him."

"That's my job." I pulled my eyes away from her pale face and looked at him instead. She'd lost so much blood and had required a blood transfusion, but somehow, she still looked pale as a ghost. "I'll be fine. Don't worry about me."

"Hard not to. That's my job."

"Well, you're fired."

He chuckled. "Think about it. She's going to wake up and see you looking like hell. You haven't showered in days, you haven't shaved, and you look like shit. At least go home and shower and change your clothes. I can watch her for a couple hours."

It was like asking a parent to leave their child. It was the hardest thing to do. I knew Annabella didn't have any family, so I was her family. There was no one else to sit by her side other than me.

Hades saw my hesitation. "It's fine."

"I'm afraid I won't be here when she wakes up."

He pulled back his sleeve and looked at the time on his watch. "Doctor said you still have twelve hours. You'll be back long before then."

I wasn't comfortable in these old clothes, and I hadn't brushed my teeth in days. I didn't need to sleep, but the lack of hygiene was making me uncomfortable. And I definitely didn't want her to see me at my worst. "Alright. I won't be gone for long." I rose to my feet and patted him on the shoulder. "Thanks, man."

"No problem."

I leaned down and kissed her on the forehead before I headed to the door.

"Damien?"

I turned back to Hades.

He nodded to the meal he'd just brought. "Are you going to eat that?"

I gave a slight smile. "It's all yours."

WHEN I RETURNED, I was much more comfortable in a new set of clothes and a shaved chin. Annabella was exactly as I left her, sleeping soundly. Hades stuck around for a bit and we talked, but eventually, he went home to his family.

And I stayed with mine.

She slept longer than the doctors anticipated, and it was nearly a day later before she woke up. I slept on and off in the uncomfortable armchair, and when I heard her shift in the bed, I opened my eyes and immediately scooted forward.

She started to move, her hand reaching for the ventilator that breathed on her behalf. The nurses warned me she would be agitated when she woke up because the tubing was extremely painful. I grabbed her hand so she won't pull on it and hit the button to call for the nurse.

She opened her eyes and looked at me, and when she recognized my features, she stopped fighting. She was unable to speak, but her eyes conveyed so much. She was so happy to see me, so emotional, and she grabbed my hand and gave it a tight squeeze. Now, she stopped fighting the discomfort in her throat and focused on me.

She made my heart grow a million times in size.

The nurses removed her from the breathing tube and situated her in bed before they checked her vitals and left.

The second she was mine again, I grabbed both of her hands with mine. I looked into her hollow face because she'd been eating through a feeding tube and had already lost weight she'd never needed to lose in the first place. Her hair was oily because all she received were sponge baths, and she didn't look her best. But to me, she was perfect.

She was always perfect.

Now that she was there with me, I was at a loss for words. I had no idea what to say because I was caught off guard by the look in her eyes. Without any warning, tears sprung to my eyes, and I finally allowed myself to celebrate the victory. She survived. She was still here. And soon enough, she would come home with me.

Even when the doctor told me she would be okay, I couldn't

bring myself to accept it. It was too good to be true. It had to be a sure thing before I dropped my guard.

Now it was.

When she saw my tears, hers started to form too. She squeezed my hands back with limited strength and breathed through the emotion in her veins.

She took that bullet for me. I never would've wanted that...but it meant the world to me that she had.

No one else would've done that. Not even Hades. What had I done to deserve a love like this? I'd hurt her so many times. I wasn't the man she deserved.

But now, I would be.

AFTER EVALUATING HER, the doctors said she needed to stay in the hospital for a few days before she could be discharged. She stayed in bed the entire time, had meals when they were brought, and spent most of her time conversing with me.

For the amount of pain she was in, she was oddly delightful, even when the pain meds wore off. She was just happy to be with me, just to be alive.

"I got you this." I opened the lid and revealed a slice of chocolate cake. "Thought you might be tired of hospital food."

Her eyes open wide. "Ooh...getting shot isn't so bad when you get a fat piece of cake."

I smiled slightly even though I didn't feel that same joy in my heart. I set the dessert off to the side before scooting closer to her bed so we could hold hands. It was the most affection we could have because I couldn't hug her or get her out of bed. It was important for her incision to heal, for the rest of her body to begin working normally again.

Her eyes turned apologetic as she realized the pain her words caused. "Thank you."

"You're welcome. I'll bring you anything you want."

"Anything?" she asked playfully.

"Yes." I squeezed her hand. "Anything at all."

She stared at me for a while with a slight smile on her lips. Her eyes were full of endless love, and she looked at me in a way no one else ever had. Because it was love, not infatuation, not lust. And I could honestly say no one except her had ever loved me.

I wanted to take her home and take care of her myself, but I had to keep waiting for the permission of the doctors. I tried to make the best of it by bringing her different foods and games to keep her mind busy.

"Damien?"

"Yes, Annabella?"

"Why don't you go home and get some rest? You look exhausted, like you haven't slept since the very first night when all this happened."

My gaze fell down to our joined hands, and I stared at her small fingernails. "I won't leave you."

"I'll be fine, Damien."

I shook my head. "I'm not leaving you alone. Ever. Not until we get home..."

She stared into my eyes as if she could see the effects of my exhaustion from the accumulated days. My shower and change of clothes weren't enough to mask my fatigue, my bloodshot eyes, and my aged skin. "Hades can sit with me."

I tried not to lose my temper because she meant well, but there was no way in hell I would let some other man watch my woman so I could fucking sleep. "You're my woman. Not his."

She would normally continue to argue with me, but she let it go this time. She probably understood how much I'd been through since Liam pulled the trigger. Her thumb brushed across my knuckles as she held me. "Did the doctors say when I could leave?"

"Two days."

"Well, maybe you can sleep in here with me." She patted the sheets.

I gave a slight smile. "Yeah. Maybe."

She hadn't mentioned Liam or the circumstances of the gunshot that had almost claimed her life since she woke up. Maybe it traumatized her, or maybe she knew it traumatized me. But now, she brought up the subject neither one of us wanted to discuss. "Did you kill him?"

It was a loaded question, and I had to take my time before I responded. "How would you feel if my answer was yes?"

Her playfulness drained away as her eyes turned serious. "I don't know... Did you?"

That wasn't the answer I wanted to hear. "I got you here as quickly as I could. Haven't seen him since."

The relief was unmistakable. "It was an accident..."

I tried to keep my anger in check since she was lying in a hospital bed. "That bullet was meant for me, Annabella. If you hadn't jumped in the way, he would've hit my femoral artery, and I would be dead right now. That wasn't a fucking accident."

She couldn't handle the rage in my eyes, so she looked away. "You're right…"

Finally.

"I hope after all this, he finally lets it go and moves on. And if he doesn't…you have no choice."

I finally got her blessing to do what I should've done in the beginning. She shouldn't have almost died for it to happen, but at least it did. I could remove the biggest obstacle to our happiness guilt-free.

"I'm surprised he hasn't come to the hospital."

"He knows I'm here. And he knows I'll kill him if he shows his face."

She dropped her gaze, her tone turning softer. "I'm so sorry. If I hadn't asked you not to kill him, none of this would've happened. I could've died…or you could've died. It was a mistake, and I apologize." She had so much guilt, she couldn't look me in the eye. Full of shame and sadness, she was a mess.

I wanted to stay mad at her, but I just couldn't. She'd dragged her feet with Liam and denied me what I wanted, but at the end of the day, she'd jumped in front of a bullet to spare my life. She chose me over him, unequivocally. "It's okay, Annabella. It was a complicated situation, and anyone else would've struggled, given the same parameters. You guys had a long relationship, and it's hard to wish death on anybody…even if they deserve it."

She slowly lifted her gaze to meet mine.

"I wish I had taken that bullet instead of you. But…it means a lot to me that you did."

"I love you, Damien. I can't live without you. I would do it again in a heartbeat...and I wouldn't do it for anybody else." Her eyes became coated with moisture, but they didn't form tears. She squeezed my hand, wearing her heart on her sleeve. "I loved Liam with my whole heart. Before anything bad ever happened, I was very happy. But even then, I didn't love him the way I love you. This is different. This is special. You're the person I was supposed to be with all along. Maybe all those terrible things happened because they were supposed to...so I would find you."

HER MEDICATIONS MADE HER SLEEPY, so there were several times throughout the day when she would nod off and rest for a few hours. I would utilize that time to take care of emails and business and, occasionally, take a nap.

I stepped into the hallway outside her door and spoke on the phone to Hades. "They're supposed to discharge her tomorrow."

Hades was at the bank covering my ass while I was out. He took care of my clients as well as his own. "Good. You must look like hell right now."

"A little," I said sarcastically.

"I mean because you haven't slept."

I was so fucking tired, I almost couldn't see straight. Getting a few hours throughout the night simply wasn't enough. But I couldn't go home and leave her there, especially since she was awake. I wanted to enjoy every minute with her, given that I'd almost lost her just days ago. "I'll sleep tomorrow."

"I'm guessing you won't be back at the office for a while."

My eyes drifted down the hallway when I noticed a large man heading my way. My guard was sky-high, so I noticed everything around me. And since I'd been expecting this, I anticipated the situation quickly. My heart started to race as adrenaline became readily available for my body to utilize in a fight. Hades was an afterthought at this point. "Liam is here."

He paused. "I'm on my way."

"Don't bother. I'll handle it." I hung up and shoved the phone into my pocket. I was in the center of the doorway, blocking the path to Annabella entirely. There was no way in hell he was going to get past me to see her. Motherfucker had no right.

His eyes locked on mine as he moved forward, undeterred by the murder in my gaze. He was in jeans and a shirt and didn't seem like he was packing a weapon in the back of his pants. He kept going until he stopped a few feet away from me.

I wanted to kill him for everything he'd done to Annabella. I honestly believed the world would be a better place without him in it, without the man who'd shot an innocent woman while she protected the man she loved. I couldn't bring myself to speak because I was so livid, flashbacks of that night hitting me.

This man almost killed my woman.

Liam glanced at the entryway to her room before he turned back to me. "How is she?"

How could he ask me that after what he did to her? "Your bullet pierced her stomach, liver, and kidney. How do you think she's doing?"

At least he had the humility to look devastated. He wasn't the aggressive serial killer anymore. Now he was just a heartbroken man. "Tell me she's going to be okay."

"I don't have to tell you a damn thing."

He didn't have the same blood lust anymore. His murderous desire had been tamed by the tragedy. Otherwise, he would probably choke me on the spot. "Then step aside."

"No." He would never be in the same room with her again. "You aren't her husband. You aren't her friend. You're the man who broke in to my fucking house and tried to kill me—and instead, nearly killed her. Get the fuck out of here." The stakes were high now that I was no longer restrained. I didn't have to fight with one arm tied behind my back. I could kill him the second the perfect opportunity arose. I wanted to fight him, just not near her, not in a hospital with innocent bystanders.

Liam stared at me for minutes, the tension rising like smoke from a fire. He was bigger than me, but he knew that wasn't everything. I was quicker, smarter, better than him in every way but size.

"Leave. Before I kill you."

His eyes narrowed on my face.

"She gave me her approval. Give me any reason to do it, and I will. Come near us again, and I'll slit your throat." I spoke quietly so the passing nurses and doctors couldn't hear the threats leave my lips. "The situation has changed. You aren't fighting a man who will spare your life. Now you're up against a monster that will tear you to pieces without mercy."

He had the audacity to look hurt, as if that was a blow he never expected to receive, like Annabella would still protect him even though he'd fucking shot her. Pain was etched into his expression, and he even looked weak once he heard the truth. "It was an accident. I'd rather kill myself then let anything happen to her. She knows that."

"But you tried to kill me. And in case it wasn't obvious, she jumped in front of the bullet to save my life, not yours. She loves me, will do anything for me, and I'm the man in her life now. Not you."

I DIDN'T MENTION what happened with Liam to Annabella. When we got home, I would tell her, but I didn't want her to get upset while still in a hospital bed.

Now she was asleep, taking her midmorning nap after her dose of painkillers. It was too bright in the room for me to sleep, so I continued to stare at her, to keep an eye on her even though she would be alright.

A nurse walked inside, a blonde I'd never seen before. "She must be excited to go home."

"Yeah." I was even more excited. "She's been here long enough."

She checked all the vitals and made notes in her computer before she walked around to my side of the bed. Nurses never came to this side because all of their equipment was placed on the other side, so it was odd.

I grew suspicious.

She walked behind my chair and grabbed the curtains. "It's awfully bright in here."

"Yeah." Now that I understood her intentions, I relaxed. "But she likes the..."

I suddenly felt a needle slide into my neck and the liquid pump into my flesh. My instinct was to turn around and fight, but I was quickly overcome by whatever was just injected into my body. It was either a sedative or poison, and the world started to spin until my body slumped in the chair. I saw the nurse cross my vision and approach Annabella, but there was nothing I could do to stop it. It was a powerful dose, more potent than normal because I usually was immune to those kinds of drugs. I wanted to scream, but I was already falling into slumber. My thoughts were incoherent, but I managed to deduce one thing before I went under.

Liam did this.

SIXTEEN

ANNABELLA

WHEN I WOKE UP, I NOTICED MY SURROUNDINGS. THE large windows weren't to my left like they'd been last time I was awake. Sunshine didn't stretch across the room. Now the curtains were closed, and I was in deep shadow. There was no medical equipment near my bed, no blood pressure cuff on my arm. I wasn't in the hospital at all.

I was in a bedroom I'd never seen before.

Had Damien taken me home? If he had, why wasn't I in his bedroom? Why was I moved when I was unconscious in the first place?

Why was there this fear in the pit of my stomach?

I looked around and saw the drapes covering the windows. The bed I slept on had a gold comforter. There was a vase of flowers on the nightstand and a few paintings on the walls.

Where was I?

Had Damien taken me to a new location so Liam couldn't find me?

I got out of bed and opened the curtains. Sunlight splashed into the bedroom, and the view of the Tuscan hillside was gorgeous. Vineyards were visible in the distance, the grape leaves crisp and bright as they were blanketed in sunlight. It was a beautiful summer day, and for a second, I forgot everything that had happened to me.

Then the view started to look familiar...as if I'd been there before.

I turned around and left the bedroom. I was in a shirt and sweatpants, clothing I didn't recognize. Someone must've put it on me because I'd been in a gown for days. Once I entered the hallway, I stilled.

I knew this place.

I kept walking until I reached the end of the hallway. The narrow staircase was there, leading to the first floor. It'd been so many years since I'd been there that it took a while for me to notice the details. It was a small cottage in the Tuscan hillside, hidden well from the road because of the hills around it.

My heart started to slam in my chest. My mind understood I was in immediate danger. Instead of waking up in my home, I quickly realized I had been kidnapped.

By my ex-husband.

I was so weak from my injuries that I couldn't fight back. Even at full health, I was no match for a monster like him. There was a lamp on the nearby table, so I grabbed the cord and tugged it from the wall before I picked it up. Now I was prepared to kill this man for what he'd done to me. He took me out of the hospital bed and hid me away where no one would find me.

Killing him was my only chance.

Why hadn't I listened to Damien? Why hadn't I let him kill Liam in the first place?

This was a cruel way to repay my mercy.

I crept down the stairs quietly because I could definitely hear the sound of the TV. The place was small, a summer home we used to get away from the crowds of tourists. I held on to the banister as I made my way down, the adrenaline masking the pain I felt in my stomach. I shouldn't be creeping around in stealth mode to kill a man several times my size.

But I wasn't going to lose Damien like this.

Unless he was already dead...

When I made it to the ground floor, I looked around for any sign of Liam. I kept heading for the living room, following the sound of the TV. When I rounded the corner, I noticed him standing in the kitchen. He was making dinner...like we'd gone back in time.

I crept up behind him so quietly and grabbed the lamp with steady hands as I prepared to slam it down on his head. He would be knocked out, potentially dead, and I could find the car keys to get out of there. I'd even go on foot if I had to.

My feet were so silent against the tile, and I didn't breathe a single breath because I didn't want to give away my position.

He stirred the contents of the skillet, his bare back muscular and strong. He was in just sweatpants, oblivious to my intent right behind him. "Good. You're awake." He turned off the burner before he faced me.

I quickly stepped back, the lamp still in my hands.

He didn't seem the least bit surprised. "I have your medication here." He walked to the other counter and grabbed the meds from a bag. There were several bottles, all labeled. He must've gotten them when he took me from the hospital, but since he'd kidnapped me, I wasn't sure how he'd orchestrated that. "You should put that down." He nodded to the lamp. "It's heavy, and I don't want you to hurt yourself."

Since my only advantage was the element of surprise, I lowered it to the kitchen island. There was no way I could come at him now and possibly win. And if I really engaged in a physical battle, not only would I lose, but it would probably rip my incision.

He watched me from across the room. "You hungry?"

Floored by the question, all I could do was stare. "Am I hungry...?" Did he seriously just ask me that? "Am I fucking hungry? Is that a joke?"

He grabbed one bottle of pills and read the label. "You're supposed to take most of these on a full stomach, so yeah, it's not a joke."

My frustration built until I broke like an overflowing dam. My hands went into my hair and dug the strands from my scalp because I was overwhelmed by this reality. This was a man I could never get away from. Death was really the only solution. "What the fuck, Liam? What the fuck did you do?"

He stayed calm, trying to convince me this was normal when it was anything but. The doctor said you were free to go. I decided to bring you home and take care of you."

"Exactly. *You* decided. What the fuck is wrong with you?" I threw my arms down and knocked over all the dishes sitting on the table in front of me. They crashed to the floor in pieces.

He watched my movements without reacting, as if he expected me to behave this way.

"Where's Damien?" If Liam had killed him, I really would hang myself and take my own life. I couldn't live with the guilt of what my stupidity had caused. I already hated myself for ever loving Liam at any point in time, for being faithful to somebody who never deserved my loyalty.

He leaned against the counter and crossed his arms over his chest. "Alive."

My hand moved across my chest, and I bowed my head as relief released the pain in my heart. "Oh, thank god."

Liam wore his best poker face as he stared at me.

"Let me go."

He moved to the cabinet and pulled out a new set of plates.

"Liam."

He scooped the food onto the plates and ignored me.

"You can't keep me here. What do you think that's going to achieve? I don't love you anymore, and now my indifference is quickly turning to hatred. The only way you're going to have me is if you force me. And if you do that...you'll definitely never get what you want." I couldn't imagine Liam doing something like that, but then I realized I couldn't imagine him kidnapping me either...and that happened. I had been blinded by his handsome and charming ways. He'd been a monster the whole time—I just never noticed.

He turned around and set the food down. "You said you would give me another chance. So that's what we'll work on."

"I only said that so you wouldn't shoot Damien. And you did anyway...then missed."

He finally showed his shame by looking away and closing his

eyes. He gripped the edge of the table and turned quiet, accepting the loathing that accompanied the consequences of his actions. "You know that was an accident. You know I would never hurt you."

"You tried to kill the man I love. That was no accident...and I'll never forgive you." My eyes started to water because I was so hurt by his betrayal. I'd asked Damien to let live Liam live, and he did. But when I asked Liam the same thing, the man I was married to, he refused. It hurt. Bad. "You can lock me up here for fifty years, and I'll still despise you. There's nothing you can do to make me fall in love with you ever again. I will try to escape. And if I can't, I'll try to kill you."

He lifted his gaze and looked at me again.

"Damien will find me. And when he does, he's going to kill you. Don't expect me to stop him."

With his hands on the edge of the table, his eyes shifted back and forth as he absorbed what I said, as he processed all the threats I'd just thrown at him. "If you don't want me to kill him first, I suggest you be cooperative."

He was trying to control me with another threat, but I wouldn't fall for it. "I told Damien to kill you, so go after him if you want. I know he'll win."

I KNEW Damien would rescue me.

I just didn't know when.

I barricaded myself in my bedroom and didn't leave. Liam tried to lure me downstairs with food, and when I refused, he said he would let me starve until I changed my attitude. But I never did, not even taking my medication because of it, so he caved.

He left my food outside the door so I could grab it once he was gone.

I had no phone and no means of escape. Liam was always at the house, and he set the alarm at night so I couldn't slip out the back door. The cars were in the garage, which had its own alarm system, and there was no phone in sight. Sometimes I stared at his jeans to see if his phone was in his pocket, but he didn't carry anything at all.

The only way I was getting out of here was if Damien set me free.

I sat on my bed and stared out the window because I had no idea what else to do with my time. I was just letting it pass, allowing my wound to heal. All I was supposed to do was rest, so I was at least doing that.

But I should be resting at home...with Damien. He was probably so worried about me. When he realized I was gone from the hospital room, he probably figured out who took me within a few seconds. Now he would comb the streets, asking anyone who knew Liam where he could be hiding.

I wasn't sure who knew about our Tuscan home, so I didn't know what kind of information Damien would find. But if he looked up our asset information with the province, he would find the deed to this house under Liam's name.

I was certain Damien would figure it out...eventually.

I took comfort knowing he would never give up on me. It was only a matter of time before he broke down that front door and took me away.

There was a knock at my door.

Liam always announced the tray by tapping his knuckles against the wood. When I resisted conversation, Liam didn't force it. Maybe he assumed I would have a change in attitude on my own.

Never going to happen.

I opened the door and looked at the tray on the floor. It was always a nutritional home-cooked meal, the perfect ingredients to help me heal and get the inflammation down. I bent down and picked it up.

He appeared in the doorway, catching me off guard.

I flinched at his appearance, my hands still gripping the handles of the tray. My heart skipped a beat before I turned away and carried the tray to the bed. I could hear his footsteps behind me. "I still don't want to talk to you, Liam. I'll never want to talk to you."

He helped himself to the armchair by my window. His massive body lowered until he took up the entire seat. One ankle rested on the opposite knee, and his hands got comfortable in his lap.

I sat on the bed with my tray in front of me. I was hungry and had nothing else to do, so I grabbed the sandwich and took a bite, ignoring him by the window. We hadn't spoken much in the last week. Every time he tried, I ignored him. Nothing that came out of his mouth would change my mind about anything.

He watched me with those blue eyes, watching me take little bites of my sandwich before moving to the bag of chips. He was in a relaxed position, so even-keeled and calm, he didn't seem like the man who'd tried to kill Damien and shot me instead.

I didn't bother asking him to leave. I knew he would never listen.

"Anna." He stared at me until I met his look. "I'm so sorry for what I did to you. You have no idea how horrible I feel. Sometimes I want to take my own life just to make the suffering stop."

"No matter how bad you feel, it'll never feel as bad as being shot in the stomach." I brushed off his apology, cold as ice, and kept eating. I used to melt every time Liam became vulnerable, but now, those days were long gone. I'd learned my lesson —finally.

He dropped his gaze.

"And if you were truly sorry, you wouldn't be keeping me here as a goddamn prisoner." I grabbed the bread and took another bite. The only thing I enjoyed about being with Liam was his cooking. He was no Patricia, but he was pretty damn good. "I understand you're hurting, but I'm with Damien now, and that's where I should be."

He lifted his gaze again, this time unapologetic. "That man sabotaged our marriage—"

"No, bitch. I did." I dropped the food onto the plate. "I was in love with another man while I was married, and that was wrong. Even if I was honest about it, it was wrong. I put us both in a bad situation, made us both do things we regret. You fucked around and broke our vows time and time again, but my heart broke those vows too. We were never going to make it, Liam. And we're definitely not gonna make it now, trapped in this fucking house."

His expression remained calm as he listened to every word.

"We both need to move on."

He straightened in the chair, his knees stretching apart. "That's what you don't understand. I can't move on. You're the only woman I love, will ever love, and I've always imagined us growing old together. Yes, I fucked up with those other women, but they never meant anything to me. I want you to have my money, have my ring, to be buried next to me when we're gone."

I shook my head. "Stop it."

His deep voice was defiant. "No."

I started to get so angry. I looked into his eyes and felt my frame begin to shake, my temples throbbing with blood. "You can't keep me here forever, Liam. I'll either kill you, or Damien will find me. And then he'll kill you."

With confidence in his gaze, he said, "You would never hurt me."

I shook my head slowly. "After what you tried to do to Damien, fuck yes, I will hurt you. You could've killed him. My loyalty belongs to one man, not the psychopath that kidnapped me from a hospital bed and boarded me up in the middle of the vineyards. This isn't normal, Liam. Let me go."

There was no interest in his eyes as he listened to me speak. "No."

"Is that all you know how to say? No?"

Like a smartass, he said it again. "No."

If I weren't so hungry, I would throw my tray at him. "What do you hope to achieve, Liam?"

When he was given an open-ended question, he leaned forward slightly. "We always find a way to work things out. We just need to talk. Spend time together."

This man was ludicrous, not romantic. "I don't want to work it out with you, Liam. I'm in love with another man. I don't know how to make that any clearer. I took a bullet for the man, for fuck's sake. I'd rather die than live without him. That's the bedrock of *Romeo and Juliet*."

There was always a slight look of anger on his face when I spoke of Damien that way. Liam tried to ball it inside, but steam rose from the ears. "You've known me for years. You've known him for days. Your feelings will fade."

"I was in love with him the entire time we were married. And it never faded. It will *never* fade." I pushed aside the tray because I couldn't eat another bite as I was sick to my stomach. "And even if I weren't, I'll never forgive you for cheating a second time. Your constant infidelity is unbearable. I don't care if you have an excuse for it, there's no excuse for disloyalty. And then you broke in to a man's house with the intent of killing him because I'm in love with him, to get rid of him so I can't have him. Do you think I'm just gonna forgive you for that? There was a bullet inside of me because of you." I felt my rage rise like a phoenix from the ashes. "Do you think anyone would forgive you for that?"

He must've been rendered speechless because he didn't say a single word. His eyes were focused on me, unable to blink.

"This is pointless."

Still, nothing.

"We're done, Liam. You can keep me locked in this room for years, and I'll never change my mind. You can't brainwash me."

"I'm not brainwashing you. Just reminding you where you belong."

That comment pushed me into a blind rage. "There's only one place I belong. And that's with him. Not you." I got off the bed and picked up the tray before I threw it down at his feet. All the dishes cracked and broke, and the food got all over the rug. Ants could swarm it, and I still wouldn't pick it up. "Fuck you, Liam. Keep me hostage. Rape me. Brainwash me. But none of that will work. I know where I belong, and it's definitely not with you."

SEVENTEEN

DAMIEN

There was only one person in the world who knew exactly what I was going through.

And he was in my bedroom with me, pacing in front of the recently repaired window while he spoke on the phone. "Ask everyone we know. I want Liam de Luca's head, and I'll pay any price for it." He hung up and stared out the window.

I couldn't believe this was happening. It was like a bad dream that never ended, a nightmare that continued to torture me even though I tried desperately to wake myself up. When I'd come to in the hospital room, her bed empty beside me, I hoped none of it was real.

But it fucking was.

Liam took her. I knew it was him. He staged everything, paid off everyone at the hospital to pull it off.

I was too fucking stupid to prevent it.

I sat in the wooden chair at the table, staring at the stained wood beneath me. A bottle of scotch was in front of me, but I didn't pour myself a drink because it felt too painful.

Annabella wanted me to quit, and now that she wasn't there, I couldn't allow myself to have a drop.

I couldn't begin to describe the emotions pounding in my chest. I was furious, bloodthirsty, murderous. But I was also stricken with grief, so upset that I even cried. I was supposed to protect her, and I'd failed twice in a row.

What kind of man was I?

Now I was tormented by the fear of what he was doing to her. Was he punishing her? Was he forcing her against her will? It was too much to handle, so I tried to think about something else. But since she was the only thing that mattered, I really had nothing else to think about.

Hades walked back to me and sat down. "I've got everyone looking. He hasn't been on a plane, unless he chartered a private one, but I doubt that. I think he's in the city."

I maintained my blank stare.

"He couldn't have gone far with her unconscious. And when she's awake, it'll be impossible to move her. She'll fight like a dog."

None of that made me feel better. "Doesn't matter. We have no idea where she is...and no idea what he's doing to her."

Hades stared at me from his chair across the table, his expression a mixture of many different emotions. He was angry about what happened to Annabella, but he was also hopeful for a return and also concerned about my sadness. He knew exactly how it felt to be in my shoes, to feel the overwhelming fear. Some other man took my woman, and those memories were still fresh in his mind. "We'll get her back."

"I know." I just had no idea when or how. I had to figure this out soon, because the longer I waited, the longer Annabella would be subjected to whatever Liam was doing to her. The thought of him... I couldn't even think about it.

"Liam isn't like other men. He wouldn't hurt her. And I don't think he would do anything else...that might upset her." That was the most he was willing to say on the topic that was in both of our minds.

She'd been gone for a week, and I had no idea where she went. Their house was abandoned. Nothing had been touched, no clothes had been taken. I was only unconscious for a couple hours, and that was enough time for him to disappear with no trace. That was what made me wonder if he was nearby. We checked the activity on his bank account and his credit cards, and he hadn't done anything that we could detect. That meant he was only using cash.

"Everyone's a snitch for the right price. Someone will give us a clue."

"Unless Liam didn't tell anyone at all..."

Hades looked out the window, as if he feared the exact same thing but just didn't want to say it. "I'm sorry, Damien."

"Not your fault. It's my fault."

"If I'd been at the hospital with you the whole time, that wouldn't have happened. They can't take us both down."

"Doesn't matter. She's my woman to take care of, not yours. I should've had you watch her while I went out and hunted him down. It would've been the last thing he expected. I would've taken him out so easily."

"We'll still take him out, Damien."

"I know we will." I couldn't wait to aim the barrel between Liam's eyes and pull the trigger. I couldn't wait to get rid of the man who had been a fucking wedge in my relationship since the day I met her. When he was gone, we would have what we deserved.

Finally.

DAYS PASSED, and information didn't turn up.

"Thanks. Call me if you hear anything." Hades circled my bedroom before he hung up. His loud sigh said everything his voice didn't need to. After his phone was shoved into his pocket, he planted his palms against his face and slowly dragged them down until his fingertips reached his chin. "Fuck."

I stood at the window and looked outside. My eyes combed the buildings and streets, as if I were a hawk surveying his prey from a distance. With every passing day, hope dwindled and anger grew. I probably wouldn't even kill Liam with a gun, choosing to use my bare hands instead.

Hades came to my side. "No one is rolling over on Liam."

"Because he didn't tell anybody."

It was the middle of the day, and Hades looked out across the scenic view of Florence. "There has to be somebody..."

"As far as I can tell, he doesn't have any friends."

Hades crossed his arms over his chest, and his finger supported the bottom of his jaw. He was lost in thought for a long time, his eyes scanning the horizon.

I hadn't given up, but this would be much harder than I'd ever realized.

"The Skull King." Hades turned and stared at me, a vibrant

look in his eyes like it was the answer we both needed. "He mentioned something to you. Brought up Liam and Anna."

Yeah, he did. It was so random, so passive-aggressive. The only way Heath would've known about that was if Liam mentioned it, and it wasn't a secret that Liam was one of the Skull King's clients. When my body became rigid and I felt a sudden excitement in my veins, I realized we were finally on to something. "Shit."

"Liam couldn't have pulled that off alone. The only person who could do something like that is Heath."

All the blood drained from my face and escaped to nowhere in particular. I felt like I was losing all my vitality, all my strength. The answer was right in front of me, but I was too upset to see it on my own. "He's supposed to collect his monthly taxes tonight."

"Perfect opportunity to ask him."

"Even if we're right, will he help me?"

"No. Not unless you make it worth his while."

HEATH PREFERRED to meet on my territory. He never invited me to his, so he showed up at the lab that night with his to cronies to collect his cash. If I didn't believe he was the key to finding Annabella, I wouldn't be able to handle the meeting at all. Hades or one of my men would have had to do it on my behalf. Paying an asshole money wasn't at the top of my priorities at the moment.

I leaned against the desk with my arms over my chest as I watched him walk in, carrying himself like he was a king presenting himself at court. And he wore the most obnoxious grin. I looked him up and down, noticed the bulge in the back of his pants where he kept his gun. He was in all black, his fair skin covered with dark tattoos.

"Why the long face?" He kneeled down and unzipped each bag to see the cash inside. Most of the time, he never checked the contents, but this time, he actually pulled out a bundle of cash just to examine the bills.

"You know exactly why."

He dropped his smile and fingered the currency, checking the different denominations. "Looks like you had a good month... you know, despite everything." He didn't even have the audacity to play ignorant. He wanted me to know he was part of this, that it was payback after I'd defied him, humiliated him. "Take it away, boys." He rose to his full height and snapped his fingers, like his men were dogs.

His henchmen came inside and picked up the heavy bags. They carried them back out into the main warehouse.

Heath stared at me like he knew something was coming, like the anger inside me was about to come out full force. He thrived on it, wanted to see me lose my shit.

"Tell me where he is." I didn't give any specifics because it was unnecessary. He knew exactly what I was talking about, and he was the kind of man that wanted to listen to me beg and plead. I had no pride at this moment, no vanity. I was willing to do anything to get my woman back.

A slow smile came over his expression. "I don't betray my clients."

"You're betraying me, and I'm your client."

He shook his head slightly. "No. You're just my fuckboy." He turned to walk out of my office.

Instead of getting angry at the comment, I was only disappointed. I was terrified I would never get Annabella out of this situation. And I was even more terrified that Heath was my only option. "I'll give you anything you want."

He stopped and turned around in the doorway.

"Take my business. Take my money. Take my house. Whatever the fuck you want." Annabella and I could live in a tiny house with no money and be perfectly happy. I already knew she loved me for me, not the zeros in my bank account, and not just because the gypsy told me that.

He gave me a final look before he turned away. "There's nothing I want more than revenge. And my revenge can't be bought."

EIGHTEEN
ANNABELLA

Two weeks had passed, and there was no sign of Damien.

Liam came to my bedroom and sat with me, as if his presence would be enough to warm me up. Sometimes we argued, sometimes I screamed, but most of the time, we sat in silence because I refused to speak to him.

I was afraid he would force me to be with him, but he hadn't tried. Maybe it was because I still had an injury...or maybe he was a better man than I gave him credit for. Either way, I was grateful, because being with him would be rape. Nothing less.

I sat in my bedroom, my stomach rumbling because I refused to eat the lunch he'd brought earlier. When he'd carried the tray inside, I slapped it down with my palm and told him to fuck off. The mess was still on the floor.

I was free to go about the house because I didn't have chains on my wrists or ankles, but I chose to sit in my bedroom alone. I'd rather be alone than breathe the same air as that asshole. I'd rather be lonely than subjected to his nonsense.

But I decided to leave and go downstairs to make something to eat in the kitchen, because I was so hungry I'd started to get a headache. When I reached the top of the staircase, I heard him talking to somebody.

"Grab Catalina. That's the only person that Damien will trade for. But just to warn you, she's a spitfire. She's small, but she knows a couple moves. Make sure you catch her alone because she won't go easy. She'll make a scene."

I heard every word, and I'd never been so terrified. Liam was conspiring to take my friend, Damien's sister, and do something horrific. I didn't bother to be quiet anymore, and I ran down the stairs, taking them two at a time, and ignored the pain in my abdomen. I might rip the stitches, but that wasn't important right now. I got to the living room and saw him standing near the couch.

He watched me, rigid and defensive, like there would be repercussions after what I just heard. He didn't even have the humility to look guilty, to possess a hint of shame. If anything, he just looked annoyed that I'd overheard his master plan.

"How dare you?" I marched up to him, unintimidated by his large size. I shoved both of my palms into his chest and forced him back, oblivious to the scream of my wound once I exerted myself. "Call it off. Now."

He staggered backward after my push but showed no resistance at all. He stayed back with a stoic expression, like he was prepared to handle anything I threw at him without an ounce of care. He looked like a martyr, doing something terrible for the greater good. He held his head high when he should be bent over in humiliation.

"Leave her out of this. She's my friend."

"Nothing will happen to her if Damien isn't a piece of shit."

The phone was still in his hand, and I knew I needed to grab

it if I was going to get out of here, if I was going to save
Catalina, if I was going to save Damien. "What are you trying
to do? You're bringing an innocent person into something she
has no part of." I crept closer to him, my heart beating so fast
because there were so many people on the line, including
myself.

"If Damien cares about his sister, he'll show up."

"And then what?" I tried to keep him distracted.

"I'll release his sister...then kill him." With no apology in his
gaze, he stared at me with a look made of steel. He wouldn't
change his mind, no matter how I felt about it. He wouldn't
spare Damien because he considered him to be the root of our
problems. "With him dead, we can finally have what we
deserve."

There were no words to describe everything I felt in that
moment. It was the first time I'd actually wanted to kill somebody, watch the light leave his eyes for good. I was a different
person, dark and maniacal, a disturbed soul. "I told him not to
kill you..." Why was I so stupid? Why did I say something so
naïve?

"You told him that because you love me."

Damien was really going to die because of my stupid decision.
I couldn't let that happen. "Liam." I came closer to him, kept
his gaze fixed on mine. "If I had a gun right now, I'd shoot you
in the stomach, just as you did to me."

Then I made my move.

I lunged forward and grabbed the phone out of his hand. I fell
forward and lost my footing, but I grabbed the armchair and
pushed myself back up. I had to run away to get ten seconds to
make the call that would save everyone's lives.

Liam was faster. He grabbed me by the ankle and dragged me to the floor. "Anna, stop."

I kicked him away and started to crawl.

"Stop." He got on top of me and pinned my arms down. "Calm down. You'll hurt yourself." He pulled the phone out of my tight fingers and slipped it into his pocket.

I knew I'd had no chance, but I was devastated that I'd lost. Damien would sacrifice himself to save his sister because I knew how much he loved her...and then I would lose him forever. Tears streaked down my cheeks, and I lost my mind. "Please. Please don't do this. I'll do anything."

There wasn't a flicker of emotion in his eyes, no indecision whatsoever. "I'm sorry, Anna."

Damien did nothing wrong. He met me at the bank and wanted more. He tried to leave me, but I wouldn't let him go. All this was happening because of me... It was all my fault. I sobbed harder than I ever had before, not looking at Liam even though he was right on top of me. "Please..."

"I have to do this, Anna." He finally looked conflicted, finally had a soul. He knew how much this hurt me and could at least feel that. "I have to do this for us."

NINETEEN

HEATH

Cast in shadow along with everyone else in the auditorium, I watched my target glide across the stage on the tips of her toes, a focused but poised expression on her face. Her dark hair was pulled back into a tight bun, making her soft features far sterner than they needed to be. It was her solo, and while the other dancers paused, she continued to move across the floor, jumping into the air, spinning, and landing on a single foot without making a sound on her landing—because she probably only weighed a hundred pounds.

Catalina was easy to spot.

Every guy was dressed in sport coats and suits, but I walked in there in jeans and a shirt.

Because I didn't give a fuck.

That was how you knew not to mess with someone, when they completely disregarded societal norms. They didn't care about anyone else, and if you fucked with them, they wouldn't care about fucking up your life either.

Catalina was such a beautiful and talented dancer. I almost felt bad for what was about to happen to her.

Almost.

THE CURTAINS CLOSED with a round of applause, and when Catalina took her curtsy, red roses were tossed on the stage, making it perfectly clear she had numerous admirers.

Everyone filed out of the auditorium and headed to the bar so they could discuss their opinions about the ballet, even though no one really gave a damn about opinions like that.

I left from the main entrance but waited in the back. Dancers and crew members entered and exited from a different area, a door that opened from the inside but not the outside. Anyone coming backstage had to knock and hope someone answered.

I leaned against the wall and waited.

One by one, dancers and crew left. Most girls left in a group of at least two, walking to their cars together to stay safe.

I was in shadow again so I was practically invisible, and I was also lucky that my target had an inflated ego. She knew a few self-defense moves and assumed she was invincible, that the rules didn't apply to her like everyone else.

She was about to find out how wrong she was.

Almost two hours after the curtains closed, she walked out.

Her hair was free from the bun, so long that it seemed impossible that it had all been stuffed inside that small bun just a few hours ago. She was in a yellow dress and heels, which was perplexing because I thought ballet dancers had painful feet, especially right after a performance. Why would any dancer put on five-inch heels after dancing for two hours? Her shoes tapped with a regular cadence as she walked down the sidewalk to her car parked somewhere at the curb.

My eyes moved down her silhouette, sizing her up. She was a very petite woman, so thin she couldn't be more than 110 pounds despite her above-average height. She had lean muscles in her arms and legs, a figure that was both athletic and strong. Maybe she was tougher than most girls, but she was still nothing compared to me.

Someone four times her size was still nothing compared to me.

I followed behind her with my hands in my pockets because this was a casual grab. I would cup my hand over her mouth and silence her screams before I choked her out and made her body go limp. Then I'd throw her over my shoulder and take her home like a deer carcass I'd shot in the woods.

Easy.

I came closer to her, my footsteps slightly audible if she was paying attention, but her heels were so loud, I doubt she noticed. A green purse hung off her shoulder, and she looked down and riffled through it to find her keys, the number one thing women should not do.

Ignore her surroundings.

Liam described this woman as having some kind of intelligence, but I didn't see any sign of it anywhere. All I saw was a dumb girl in a sundress and heels, completely oblivious to the enormous man behind her who could do some seriously terrible things.

Dumbass.

She stopped walking altogether because finding her keys in that big-ass purse was quite a task that required minutes rather than seconds. It was probably stuffed with lipstick, hair ties, old receipts from cafés, and a bunch of other bullshit that turned her purse into a trash can.

And now it would cost her life.

I moved behind her and started to make my move.

With lightning speed, she turned around and swung her purse like a weapon. She smacked it hard against my face, hitting me with her heavy pile of trash that struck my cheek so hard I actually felt it sting.

Bitch.

But that wasn't all. She pulled her purse back and revealed a decent-sized knife in her grasp.

That was what she was looking for—not her damn car keys.

She held it with confidence, the blade pointed down so she couldn't accidentally stab herself. It was a move someone had taught her, not something she'd picked up on her own, unless she watched a lot of YouTube videos. Carved into her serious features was the look of a madwoman. Her eyes were full of menace, and she actually showed her teeth like a threatened dog. She didn't warn me to run away or threaten to call the cops.

Instead, she tried to kill me.

She stabbed me in the arm, not waiting for me to get my footing after being hit in the face with a goddamn purse. She dug the blade right into my arm like a maniac. "Don't fuck with me, asshole." The blade sank deep into my flesh before it was ripped out again, and then she slammed her heel into my stomach, knocking the air out of my lungs.

Jesus Christ.

I fell back, my face on fire, choking for air, and my arm bleeding all over the fucking place.

But that wasn't enough for her. When my guard was down because I'd just gotten my ass handed to me, she came at me again.

Should've taken Liam seriously, apparently.

Now, I stopped paying attention to her bright dress and her long, done-up hair. I looked at her as a man and finally treated her like one. When she jumped on me, the blade was aimed right at my stomach.

This bitch was actually going to try to kill me.

I threw up my arm and braced her so her hand couldn't drive the knife inside me a second time. I threw her off of me, making her hit the pavement with a loud thud.

That didn't slow her down—at all.

It was enough time for me to get to my feet and look her in the eye with my hands up and ready for a fight.

She was just as ready, that knife so steady she could be a surgeon. "Come on, fuckboy."

What the fuck did she just call me?

"You better run, or I'll skin your ass alive." She spun the knife around her wrist, trying to show off her handling skills. "You're lucky I'm in heels because I can't run as fast as you. I suggest you take advantage of that."

I could say I'd assaulted a lot of people, but never had it gone like this. Even if people didn't know who I was, they were so scared of my size, they shit their pants, and they were never brave enough to talk shit like this. And she was a woman, to top it off.

She made a fake lunge, trying to scare me off with that big, bloody knife. "Who the fuck do you think I am?" She started to shout, probably in the hope someone would hear the commotion and come to her rescue.

I quickly jumped back, not wanting another wound that might actually make me bleed to death. One cut in my arm wouldn't slow me down. I had at least twenty minutes before it became a problem. But if she landed another blow, like in my stomach or my thigh, near major arteries, I'd be in trouble.

She danced in her heels like she was in flats, probably because she was a professional ballerina. She jumped to the right and swiped at me, aiming right for my stomach.

Shit, she was going for my artery. It was fucking intentional.

"I ain't no average bitch, boy." She struck again, trying to get that same spot.

I had the opportunity to twist her arm back and get that knife free, but I was so bewildered by what she'd just said. "What?"

"I'm gonna bounce on a dick, boy." She tried to stab me again.

I took a couple steps back. "Are you paraphrasing Beyoncé right now?"

"Hell yes, motherfucker. And I suggest you run before I kick your ass just like she would." Her green eyes were fearless, like a hunter in ancient times that couldn't afford to be afraid. She had to kill the animal to feed her family and survive, to win the battle to preserve her tribe. Nostrils flared and lips pressed tight together, she was savage, ice-fucking-cold. She spun the knife again around her wrist then made a move. This time, she went for my neck.

Crazy-ass bitch.

I stopped focusing on all the stupid shit flying out of her mouth so I could finally disarm her. I grabbed her wrist and spun her around, grabbing her by the neck and slamming her hand down onto my thigh so she would drop the blade.

But she didn't.

My arm wrapped around her mouth so she wouldn't scream.

But then she started to stab me in the leg without seeing where she was aiming, just frantically trying to get me in whatever way she could.

I moved my body away and kept hold of her, and while I was distracted, she bit down on my arm as hard she could.

I ground my teeth together and screamed from the back of my throat, suppressing the noise as much as possible so people wouldn't run over to see the commotion, but damn, that hurt more than the knife wound. "Alright, I'm sick of this shit." I grabbed her wrist and spun it around until it was about to break it. With my other hand on the back of her neck, I bent her over like a dog. "Let go."

"No."

I pushed harder on her wrist, bringing the bone to the breaking point.

She didn't whimper. "That's all you got, fuckboy?"

I lost my temper and threw her into the nearby car, and her body flattened against the solid door. She landed with a heavy thud. Thankfully it was an old, dusty car that didn't possess an alarm system, so an obnoxious noise didn't ring out. She groaned when her body slammed into it, but she still didn't drop the knife.

I pushed my chest against her back and kept her pinned in place so I could yank the knife from her hand. It still dripped with my blood. Now that the battle was over, there was blood everywhere. Drops from my cut were on the sidewalk, grass, and all over this piece-of-shit car. It was on my clothes, on her dress. It looked like a murder scene.

I slipped the knife into my pocket. "We can do this one of two ways. Easy way or hard way."

"Hard. Always hard." She bucked her hips against me as she tried to throw me off.

She was quite the adversary with a knife, but when it was just her body against mine, she stood no chance. It was like throwing herself against a brick wall. All she would do was hurt herself and leave me untouched. "Alright." I wrapped my arm around her throat and squeezed, cutting off her air supply so she would eventually black out. I could've given her a syringe full of sedative and that would've been a lot more pleasant for her, but I wasn't in the mood to be polite to this psycho.

She struggled to the very end, fighting with a strength that was so fierce it was a mystery where it came from. She fought harder than most men, didn't give up even when hope was pointless. And she lasted a lot longer than anyone ever would.

Then she finally went under.

I released my arm from her throat and supported her body. "Jesus fucking Christ." I sighed in relief because the bullshit was finally over. We were both covered in blood, and I was irritated that the whole thing had taken fifteen minutes when it should've taken fifteen seconds. I threw her over my shoulder and carried her to my truck farther down the road. Thankfully, no one was out because it was so late, so I did all of it unseen. I opened the passenger door and propped her inside before I shut the door and came around to the driver's side.

The passenger door opened, and she sprinted away. Her heels

were gone because she must've slipped them off when I walked behind the truck to get to my side, so now her bare feet slapped against the pavement with the speed of an Olympic runner.

"You've got to be fucking kidding me."

TWENTY

CATALINA

Drenched in sweat, I ran all the way to my apartment without stopping. My purse had fallen to the ground at some point in the battle, so I didn't have my keys to drive my car or my phone to call the cops. So, I had to use my landline, even though no one in this day and age had a fucking landline. Luckily, my apartment door had a keypad lock.

I paced my apartment, bloodstains on my favorite dress, and I spoke to the police about the nightmare I'd just experienced. "This fucking asshole snuck up behind me on my way to my car. I tried to fight him off, but he got my knife and choked me out."

The officer stayed calm over the line. "Can you describe the man?"

"Yes. He looked like a fucking asshole."

The officer didn't find that humorous at all. "You can't file a report without a description, miss."

I spat out the words, rapid-fire. "He was tall—like six-three, six-four—Caucasian, covered in black tattoos, blue eyes. Did I mention he's an asshole?"

He ignored my comment. "Anything else?"

"I thought he was just trying to rob me at first, but he was trying to take me. He might be a trafficker or a rapist, so we have to get this motherfucker. Life behind bars. Death by firing squad. Whatever. Guy has got to pay."

In a bored voice, he said, "We'll do everything we can, ma'am."

"Uh, I'm twenty-five. I prefer miss." Was going to hold on to my youth as long as I could.

"Do you have any other information that could help us?"

"Yeah. I memorized his license plate when he carried me to the car." I read out the letters and numbers and used my abnormally strong memorization skills. That was something that would make it so easy for the police to catch this guy. Looking up his plates in their database would lead them right to his address, and they would put cuffs on that jackass. I moved back and forth between my two couches, one hand on my hip with blood still splattered up and down both arms.

The officer typed in the information then turned quiet for a bit. "His plates aren't popping up..."

"You must've typed it in wrong."

"Or you're just wrong," he said coldly.

"Sir," I said condescendingly, "I have a photographic memory. I'm not wrong."

He sighed into the phone. "Well, it's not here. If we need anything else, I'll let you know—"

"Are you fucking kidding me?" I continue to pace, blood still on my arms because I hadn't even had a chance to wash up. I somehow fought off a guy three times my size, and I wasn't gonna let him get away with this. If the police didn't handle it, which was their job, I would take matters into my own hands. I'd kill him myself or ask my brother for a favor. No way in hell was I letting that piece of shit go free so he could do this to someone else. "The plates are right. You better check again and again because the information is solid."

He still had the same bitter attitude. "I said we'll do everything we can..."

I stopped in the center of the living room when I heard the knob turn in the front door. After a couple wiggles, the locked door was pushed free. "Who the hell are you?" Was someone breaking in to my apartment? Or was one of my lovers trying to surprise me? The chain on the top of the door was intact, so they couldn't get it open farther than a few inches.

"Ma'am, is everything okay?"

"It's miss, alright?" I said through clenched teeth. "And I think someone might be breaking in to my apartment."

Bolt cutters appeared, and the chain was snapped in one clean break. Then the door was pushed open to reveal the man who had just assaulted me fifteen minutes ago.

Now I was fucking scared. "He's here! He's in my apartment right now!" I crept backward and looked for a weapon to put this asshole in the ground. "He's going to do something. Send someone right away."

The officer never said anything because the line went dead.

I pulled the phone back and glanced at the keypad as the speaker beeped. "Did he just hang up on me?"

The asshole kicked the door shut behind him, and he looked even more threatening now than he had earlier. His hands were in tight fists, and he was still covered in blood. His arm was wrapped in gauze he must've had stored in his truck. "The police won't help you." He started to move toward me.

I dashed to the kitchen where the small window over the sink was located. It led to the fire escape. My best chance was to run, not fight, not in this small apartment. I jumped onto the tile counter, flung the window open, and I got most of my body through before he reached me.

"Jesus, stop running!"

He grabbed me by the arm, but I managed to twist away from him and get free. It was a small window, not meant for a big man like him to squeeze through, and I could barely make it out myself. It would definitely slow him down.

I sprinted down the pathway and pushed down the ladder so it lowered to the next level of the building. Without glancing behind me to see if he'd figured out a way to follow me, I just kept going, moving as fast as I could. Any neighbors who looked out the window and saw me running, caked in blood, would probably call the cops at any moment.

I hurried and climbed down the ladder until I reached the very last rung. I was ten feet off the ground, and I'd have to let go and land on the concrete before I could escape. It was a long fall, but I could handle it as long as I didn't lock my knees. With no money and no phone, I'd need to get a taxi and ask for a ride to Damien's. He could pay the fare when I got there. I glanced at the ground one more time and saw nothing but bird shit stains between the cracks. Then I looked at my hands before I closed my eyes and found the courage to let go.

The fall was only a second or two, and it wasn't a hard collision. It was actually soft.

Because the asshole caught me.

I stared at him blankly and couldn't process how this had

happened. How did he get to the bottom quicker than I did? Why wouldn't he leave me alone? It only took me a few moments to start pounding my fists into his face. "Bastard! Leave me alone!"

A needle slipped into the back of my neck, and then there was a hot injection of fluid.

Oh no.

He let me hit him as he carried me away. "Relax."

I kept fighting, but I felt my mind begin to slip away. I was growing weak, tired, so fatigued I couldn't think anymore. My body suddenly drooped, and I collapsed against his shoulder. "Leave me alone..." I closed my eyes and went straight to sleep.

I WOKE up to the sound of my captor's voice.

"I got her." His voice was deep, masculine, and quiet. He was much calmer than he had been earlier, borderline indifferent.

A man's voice responded through the speakerphone. "Good."

"Good?" His voice dripped with bitterness and sarcasm. "That's all you have to say? The bitch is psycho. She tried to kill me."

"I warned you, man."

"No," he snapped. "You said she knew a few moves. You didn't say she would cut me into tiny pieces."

The guy over the line chuckled. "Did she beat your ass?"

He took a long time before he responded. "She was just a pain... is all."

I was aware of my body lying on concrete. All my muscles

were sore, I could feel the ache in every single place. The muscles in my arms were so sore, I felt like I'd lifted a car off my body. I was an experienced dancer, but my thighs felt like I'd had the hardest workout of my life. My eyes slowly opened, and I saw the world tilted on its side. Everything was concrete, so it seemed like I was in the basement. Then I realized I was in a cage.

Made out of iron.

My eyes focused on the man sitting in the chair on the other side of the room. His phone was on the table beside him, screen facing the ceiling and bright. He rubbed his fingers against his temple as if he had a migraine, and the rest of the room was filled with various metal objects, like shackles that hung from the ceiling, metal shelving full of odd tools, and a couple drains in the floor that were stained a weird color.

His right arm was wrapped with white gauze, and I must've stabbed him pretty deep because the white material was stained a pink color as he bled through. He was in a black shirt and black jeans, the clothing fitting his muscular frame to show his undeniable strength. He was a large man, covered in muscles and ink, and it was no surprise he'd defeated me. "She came at me with a knife and started quoting some song by Beyoncé...fucking weird. Then I choked her out, and when I thought she was under, I put her in my truck...but she'd been faking and took off."

"Sounds about right."

"I chased her down to her apartment, but then she crawled through a fucking window the size of a cat door and sprinted down the fire escape... This bitch doesn't quit."

The guy chuckled. "She's got bigger balls than Damien."

He shook his head and stared at the ground. "No comparison."

The mention of my brother made me sit up. I squinted because the fluorescent lights overhead were so harsh on my eyes. I felt weak because of the drug that was still in my system, but I fought it off and prepared to rise to my feet.

When he heard me moving around, he lifted his gaze and looked at me. "Great...she's awake."

The other man spoke. "Let me know what Damien decides." The phone clicked when he hung up.

I grabbed the bars and used them to pull myself to my feet. I felt the metal of the cage, shook it with my hands, and was deflated to know it was completely solid. There was no give at all, as if it were a cage from medieval times rather than a modern apparatus. "Let me out of here. Now."

He relaxed back in the chair and spread his knees farther apart. With his arms crossed over his chest, he tilted his head slightly and stared at me with bright blue eyes. On his right hand was a large diamond ring carved into the shape of a skull, with two eyes and a slight indentation for a mouth. It had to be worth a billion euro.

"Who the hell has a cage like this?" I tried to shake the bars again with my hands. "Do you think you're a knight or something?"

"Knights serve their king, and I don't serve anybody."

Now that I was trapped, I was truly scared, but the worst thing I could do was show that fear. It gave my captor all the power, only made his ego bigger. If I acted like a victim, he would treat me like one. I had to convince him to let me go, to see me as his equal rather than his prisoner. "It sounds like you serve the loser on the phone."

He looked at me with intense eyes, staring at me in a way he hadn't before. He seemed perplexed by my existence, as if he didn't understand me at all. "Business associate."

"And what kind of business are you in? Raping people?" I could deal with being mugged, I could deal with someone taking me for every single cent I was worth, but I couldn't deal with someone stripping away all my rights and forcing me to do something against my will.

He was still as a statue in response to my accusation. "Do I look like someone who needs to rape women?" He tilted his head again, and this time, the hardness etched into his features showed he was actually offended by my assumption.

I didn't pay much attention to the attractiveness of my captor because he was my enemy, but yes, he was a handsome man, a guy I would probably hit on in a bar if I spotted him across the room. But that wasn't our situation. "Not all monsters are ugly."

He rose from the chair and came closer to me, his heavy boots thudding against the concrete as he approached, his heavy arms still crossed over his chest. When he was near the cage, he stopped far enough away so I couldn't grab him. "No. I'm not going to rape you."

I had no reason to trust this guy, but the answer made me feel better anyway. I could handle anything else, even death, but not that. "Good. Because I'd kill you if you tried."

"Pretty bold thing when you're inside a cage."

I gripped the bars and pressed my face through an opening so I could get as close to him as possible. "Then unlock the door." My threat was unmistakable. Maybe it was stupid to provoke a man like him, but I had nothing left to lose right now.

It was the first time we'd had a conversation because up until now we'd been fighting for our lives. It was a strange feeling, disconcerting, to talk to this monster like we were having a simple discussion. "You're no match for me."

"Open the door, then. Let's find out."

He smiled slightly, and it was a shame because he actually looked nice as he did it. On the street, he was a handsome man enjoying a warm afternoon. He even looked harmless. But in here...he looked like the devil. "I can't tell if you're brave or just crazy."

"Both, definitely." I hated feeling powerless behind these bars. There was no weapon in sight and no way for me to fight for my freedom when I was enclosed in solid iron. "What does my brother have to do with this?" I knew my brother dealt with shady people, did sketchy things, but I'd never worried I'd get involved in it. Yet here I was, a pawn in this violent game of chess.

"Everything."

"Be more specific." I continued to hold the bars as a crutch, needing to do something with my hands. I'd tried to run from this man so many times, but now I was stuck in one place. The cage kept me inside, but it also kept him out.

"My client wants something from Damien. So, we'll make a trade—you for him."

So, I was being held hostage. All I had to do was wait until Damien came for me. "When my brother gets here, he's going to kill you."

"Unlikely."

Was he stupid or arrogant? "Why do you say that?"

"Because I have someone else just as important to him. He makes a move...he'll never get her back."

I immediately realized I was a part of a much bigger plot. "I don't understand..." If Damien would trade himself for me, what did they want with him? And where was Annabella? "What are you going to do with him?"

He lowered his arms to his sides and slid his hands into his pockets. He looked away for a second, as if he needed time to figure out how to phrase his next words. He returned back to me eventually. "You already know."

I felt a shiver move down my spine, and there was this over-whelming feeling of hopelessness that exploded inside me. Damien was my brother, my friend, my family. I didn't want him to sacrifice his life for me. The only reason I was in the situation was because of the decisions he'd made in his life, but that didn't matter. He was my family...and I would do anything for him. "Why are you doing this? Just to make a few bucks?"

He shrugged. "It's complicated."

"It's not that fucking complicated," I snapped. "If Damien takes my place and I get out of here, what do you think will happen to you?"

He raised one eyebrow slightly as if he didn't understand the question.

"I'll come after you. And I won't stop until my knife is through your heart."

TWENTY-ONE

HEATH

I SET THE TRAY ON THE GROUND IN FRONT OF HER CAGE.

Instead of being grateful for the meal, she stared down at it with disgust before she looked at me again. "Do you expect me to eat that?"

"Eat it. Don't eat it. I don't care."

She looked down to examine the dinner I'd made myself upstairs, and she reached out to grab the glass of water sitting there, but the size and shape of the glass couldn't fit through the bars, so she tugged and spilled liquid all over the floor. "How do you expect me to drink this?" She copped an attitude every single time she spoke.

I turned around and opened a cabinet to grab a straw. When I returned, I threw it at her. "There."

She let it bounce off her dress and fall to the floor. "Are you at least going to give me a change of clothes?"

"Do I look like I have women's clothes?"

"I just said clothes, asshole. Men's or women's, I don't care. Expect me to eat when I'm covered in blood?" She lifted her arms and looked at herself. "Your blood? That's fucking gross. At least let me wash my hands first."

I was onto her game now. Never would I underestimate her again. She was trying to think of a way to get me to open that cage door, to get the hell out of there and kill me on her way. "No."

"Then I'd rather not eat."

"Fine." I picked up the tray and carried it to the table. I sat at the table and picked up the fork to take a bite. "It's a shame. I'm a pretty good cook."

She stood with her hands gripping the bars. She still in the short yellow dress, thin straps over her shoulders. Her long hair stretched out on either side of her, so long that the strands almost reached her belly button. She must've been a size zero because she had such a tiny waist. Her tanned skin made the yellow color perfect on her, when it would wash anyone else out. She flipped her head back to get the hair out of her face then continued to stare at me.

She was such a pain in the ass, but I couldn't deny that she was beautiful. Her concern about being raped wasn't ridiculous because most guys probably would do that. Luckily for her, that wasn't my thing.

She sighed loudly, wanting me to know exactly how annoyed she was. "Expect me to sleep in here?"

I nodded.

"On this little roll?" she asked incredibly. "I'm gonna throw out my back."

I kept eating.

"And where am I supposed to go to the bathroom?"

"There's a bucket."

"Oh my god, hell no. I'm a lady, asshole."

"Really?" I asked. "Because you don't sound like one."

She narrowed her eyes and let out a loud groan of irritation. "How long are you going to keep me here?"

"Until Damien shows up."

"And when will that be?"

"As soon as I call."

"What are you waiting for?"

I sliced my fork into the tender chicken and took a big bite. It was a shame she was missing out on this delicious meal. "I thought you didn't want Damien to come down here."

"Well, maybe he won't."

"You really think he'd leave you here to die?"

She lowered her hands down the bars until they were at her sides. "So that's what you intend to do with me? If he doesn't take my place?"

I didn't answer.

"I assume that asshole ex of hers has Anna. If Damien does make this trade, he'll never save Anna. Did you think of that?"

This wasn't my plan, so no, I hadn't thought it through.

"So maybe he won't come after all."

"And that's what you want?" Was she really that brave? Was she really that selfless? Because I had a few men who weren't so loyal. "To die in this basement? To die in this cage?"

She backed away from the bars and leaned into the opposite

wall, covered in red blood with patches of yellow between the stains. She looked like a hot dog slathered in mustard and ketchup. Her arms crossed over her chest, and she looked away. "I'll die for what I believe in. I'll die for love. That's the dream, right? For your life to mean something? For your death to mean more?"

I set down my fork and continued to stare at this bizarre woman. She was so poetic without even realizing it, speaking like a soldier about to fight for his country in a bloody war. Maybe she wasn't that brave...but maybe she loved that hard.

IT'D BEEN A LONG FUCKING night, so I went to sleep for a couple hours upstairs. I knew I needed to contact Damien, but this woman put me in such a sour mood, I didn't want to deal with one of the men I hated most right this second. After a shower and a meal, I went down to the basement with a bagel and cream cheese.

She was against the wall with her knees pulled to her chest. "Oh thank god..."

"Hungry?" I put the plate on the ground with the water so she could reach it.

"No. If you don't let me go to the bathroom right now, I'm gonna die."

I stopped at the bars and stared at her, giving her a cold look. "Pretty sure you can't die from that." Fucking drama queen.

She placed her palms over her flat stomach and groaned. "No, bitch. You can." She leaned forward and growled again. "Seriously, my bladder is gonna explode, and your plan will be pointless. Just let me use the damn toilet."

I nodded to the bucket.

"That's not a toilet. Come on, have you no compassion?"

"You'll try to escape. You put me through the wringer, and I'm way too tired to do that shit again." She was smarter than I'd given her credit for, faster than I'd expected her to be, and she moved so quickly that she was a formidable opponent. Unpredictable. I had no idea what she would do. A man would face me, would fight to the death. But she was like a rabbit, dashed under boxes and hid in holes so I couldn't find her. She was so small, she slipped from my grasp every time I grabbed her.

"Reasonable assumption, but I really do just need to use the bathroom. It's right there, isn't it?" She glanced to the other side of the room, where the door was slightly ajar. "You obviously let other prisoners use it. Don't be sexist now."

"What makes you think I haven't had female prisoners before?"

Her only response was a long stare.

"The answer is no. Eat your breakfast."

"That is not a breakfast. That's a piece of bread, and I'm not a duck."

Jesus, this woman had a comeback for everything. "In case you've forgotten, you're a prisoner. And prisoners don't get shit."

"Uh, no. According to the Geneva Convention, prisoners have the right to basic necessities, like food, water, the toilet, and no unusual torture and punishment. So, let me use the goddamn bathroom. I'm haven't washed my hands in sooo long."

Now I wanted to let her use it just so she'd shut up. I grabbed a piece of rope then returned to the cage. "Turn around."

"What are you going to do?"

When I released the breath I'd been holding, I flared my nostrils like a bull. "Do you want to use the bathroom or not?"

She stood up and brought her hands close to the bars.

I secured her wrists together so she couldn't grab something and try to stab me with it.

"How am I supposed to use the bathroom with no hands?"

"Figure it out." I unlocked the door and let her step out.

The second she was out of the cage, she swept her eyes across the room, looking for an escape. She looked at the stairs that led to the next floor, and then she looked around for some kind of object that could knock me out.

"Subtle…" I marched her in front of me to the bathroom and opened the door for her.

She turned back around. "I can't wash my hands or remove my clothes."

I blinked.

"Well…"

"You've got to be fucking kidding me."

"If you aren't going to cut my rope, what else am I gonna do?"

Yesterday, I was the Skull King, the most formidable guy in this country. Now, I was a babysitter to the most obnoxious woman ever. I think I'd rather watch her try to kill me than do this shit. I grabbed her shoulders and forced her to turn around before I removed the knot. "Make it quick. And if you give me any bullshit when you get out, I'll give you two black eyes."

"What a gentleman…" She closed the door behind her and did her business.

I waited outside the door and knew whenever she came out,

she would have some trick up her sleeve. Maybe she would put soap on her fingertips then rub them into my eyes so I wouldn't be able to see. With her, there was really no telling. She was totally unpredictable.

The toilet flushed, and the sink started to run. She did that for at least two minutes, presumably scrubbing her hands and arms to get my blood off. Then the faucet went quiet, and her footsteps were audible as she approached the door.

I sighed. "Here we go..."

She opened the door with force, making it swing out fast until it smacked into the concrete wall behind it. Then she charged me with a plunger.

A dirty, disgusting fucking plunger.

She swung at me, drops from its last use spraying into the air. "Ha!"

I dashed out of the way before an entire civilization of bacteria sprayed all over me.

She kept swinging frantically, looking ridiculous wielding the plunger like a goddamn sword. "Come here!" She swung again and again, getting shit all over the place.

I didn't want to come near her and get the stench on my clothes, so I continued to duck out of the way. "Woman." I dodged to the right then came up behind her and smacked the plunger down. "Give it a rest." I grabbed her arms and secured them behind her back and lifted her from the ground.

She kicked violently. "Put me down."

I carried her to the cage and pushed her inside. "You just proved you aren't allowed to come out of this thing." I shoved her inside and locked the door behind her.

She crashed against the wall and released a groan of disappointment.

I picked up the plunger and came to the door of the cage. "I could spray you good right now."

She grimaced and covered her face with her hands.

"Keep your mouth shut, or I will." I returned the plunger to the bathroom then came back. "Eat. I'm not bringing you anything else."

She pulled the bagel through the bars, along with a bottled water I'd left for her, and leaned against the wall to eat. She stared at me the whole time she enjoyed her breakfast, like she was trying to figure out a Plan B.

There would be no Plan B. "Did you really think that was going to work?"

She shrugged and kept eating. "The Trojan horse worked, didn't it?"

"The Trojan horse was a genius idea from a great civilization. Not at all comparable to a plunger tirade." Damien was one of my biggest enemies, someone stupid enough not to submit to my rule of law, but I couldn't believe I was now thinking he was preferable to this woman. She made him look like a genius.

She kept eating, clearly starving after not having eaten dinner last night. "Do you want to fuck me?" She asked the question so casually, still eating her bagel and cream cheese with blood on her clothes, resembling a vagrant.

I stared at her blankly, unable to believe what she'd just asked. "What?"

She took a large bite and talked with her mouth full. "Do you wanna have sex with me?" she mumbled between her obnoxious chewing. "Like, an exchange. We sleep together, and you let me go."

I stuck my arms through the cage and leaned against it for support because I couldn't believe the shit that had just flown out of her mouth. She was more attractive yesterday, but after sleeping in a cage all night, throwing toilet water at me, and talking all the time, I could honestly say sex was the last thing on my mind. "I'm good."

"A blow job?"

She seemed like someone who wouldn't resort to those tactics to escape. She had too much respect for herself. "You would really do that?"

She shrugged. "I'll do anything to survive, anything to save my family, so judge me all you want. I don't give a damn."

And just like that, so quickly, my opinion of her changed—for the better.

"Well?"

The offer wasn't the least bit appealing. "No thanks."

"I'm pretty good..."

Still not interested. "This conversation's over."

"You got a lady?"

I shook my head. "No. I just don't want a dirty prisoner to suck my cock."

She finished her bagel and chewed the last bites. "Fine. You're missing out, but whatever."

I found that unlikely. I pulled away from the cage and headed to the stairs.

"Where are you going?"

I turned back to her. "You're the prisoner here. I'm not."

"Well, do you want to play a game or something?"

She was locked in a cage, and if her brother didn't come for her, she would be dead. Did she not fully comprehend the situation? I walked back. "I don't think you understand how serious this is."

She stared at me with those eyes identical to Damien's and didn't show a hint of emotion. While they were clearly related, they really didn't look much alike. She was much more feminine, much softer. "There's nothing I can do inside these bars. Why worry about something you can't change?" She pulled her knees to her chest and crossed her arms over her body. "I just don't understand why this is happening. Damien is in love with Anna—like, real love—and you're trying to get in the way of that. And he really loves me, would do anything for me, and you're getting in the way of that too. I know my father favors me over Damien, not because I'm better, but because I look just like my mother, whom he lost. So, he's gonna lose me too. Do you understand what you're doing to an entire family? All for what?"

I listened to every word of her speech, watched her full lips move as she spoke the words. Her eyes were like a screen where a film projected, showing her emotions through every scene, every act. For a man who was unable to feel anything, I actually felt something...whatever it was. "Damien is the one who decided to interfere in a marriage. He has to pay the consequences."

"Marriages fall apart every day. The divorce rate is fifty percent for a reason. Get over it. Does that mean Liam is the one who took Anna? Is that what this is about?"

I didn't see the harm in answering. "Yes."

She shook her head slightly. "So, he thinks if he kills Damien,

Anna will somehow fall in love with him again? Why do you guys think keeping women as prisoners is the only way to get stuff done? She'll never love him, she'll never submit, and this is all an colossal waste of time. Killing Damien doesn't solve the problem."

I actually agreed with her, but I would never admit it. Liam was determined to win back the woman he was continually unfaithful to, which was idiotic and boring. I couldn't care less who he loved, who he fucked.

"So why are you involved in this? Unless you're getting a fat check?"

I debated telling her the truth, but then I remembered I had nothing to hide. I didn't owe this woman anything, and her opinion was irrelevant. "Revenge."

"And what did Damien do to you?"

"He didn't pay me, like everyone else. And then he turned my own brother against me, defied me in front of my crew."

She tilted her head slightly then rubbed her fingers across her bottom lip. "Let me get this straight. You're going to kill his sister, potentially let the woman he loves be raped by a crazy-ass guy, kill him when he turns himself in to save his family... over something like that? Seems petty to me."

Her response angered me, but I realized I shouldn't care what she thought. "You wouldn't understand."

"Did he owe you money?"

"Yes."

"Why? All you guys are so rich. Why would you need to borrow money from each other?"

I didn't give her the details. "Doesn't matter. I don't like your brother, and I want him to pay."

She shook her head in disappointment. "That's sad. To live your life that way, to hold on to the past like that...must be exhausting. I choose to let things go, to find happiness wherever I can, not look for opportunities to get back at people I don't like or even think about."

Even when she wasn't trying to kill me, she annoyed me.

"What's your name?"

"What does it matter?"

She shrugged. "I'm stuck in this house with you. Just seems weird I don't know your name."

My name wasn't important. It was my title that contained my identity. It may not mean anything to her, but it was still powerful. "I'm the Skull King."

Her expression remained blank, as if that didn't mean a damn thing to her. Then the corners of her lips rose toward the ceiling, and she did her best to suppress the smile that crept into her features. When she could no longer hide it, she cupped her face with her hand and suppressed the laugh she couldn't control. "I'm sorry..."

I was not amused. That was a title that made men shake, that made men kill themselves so they wouldn't have to face me when I hunted them down. It was the title that allowed me to run this town like I'd built it with my bare hands. It was the title of an executioner, an emperor.

She continued to laugh. "People actually call you that?"

I wouldn't justify anything she said with a response. I turned around and headed to the door.

"Okay, okay, I'm sorry." She took a deep breath and silenced her giggles. "The Skull King...got it."

I kept walking to the stairs.

"Wait, where are you going?"

"I'm gonna call your brother and get this shit over with." I reached the top of the stairs and slammed the door behind me.

LIAM CALLED. "WHAT'D DAMIEN SAY?"

I sat on the leather couch with my drink beside me. It was quiet in my apartment because I didn't have the TV on. I didn't listen to music either. I just sat in the dark...thinking. I hadn't called Damien like I was supposed to...and I wasn't sure why. "He didn't answer."

"Why the fuck would he not answer?"

"No idea," I said in a bored voice. "But he'll call back soon. He knows what I'll do to him if he ignores me."

"Call me when he does." He hung up.

I tossed the phone aside and closed my eyes, processing aggravation in my temples like it was a migraine. A prisoner had never gotten under my skin, let alone a person. This woman made me hate her but also pity her.

But I had to do what I had to do.

After I brought her dinner, potentially giving her a final meal, I'd call Damien and get this shit over with. I imagined he would come to his sister's aid immediately, but Catalina made a valid point. If Damien came for his sister, he could never save Anna. So, what would he choose? His family or his lover?

What if I had to kill the woman in my basement? Could I?

If I came down to it, yes. I'd done worse things before. I'd killed women before. She would be no different.

I went to the kitchen and made dinner. I ate my meal while it was hot then brought the rest to her. It was cold and no longer fresh, but since she'd attacked me with a goddamn plunger, I don't really care.

I opened the door and began to walk down the stairs.

Then I heard the sound of her tears.

I halted as I listened because I was so surprised by the sound. I'd only known her for a day, but she didn't strike me as the type of person to sit in her cage and feel sorry for herself. She didn't seem like a person capable of shedding tears because she was too headstrong, too optimistic. But I listened anyway, listened to her express her heartbreak.

She took a lot of deep breaths to stifle her tears, as if she were afraid I might hear her upstairs. Or maybe she didn't wanna listen to herself cry. Maybe it made her feel weak. Made her pity herself.

She snapped loudly. "Look, I know it's been a while since we talked and it's super annoying when I only come to you when I want something..." She paused to cry for a few seconds, to get her breathing under control again. "But I don't want something for me. I want something for my brother."

I could head back upstairs so I wouldn't have to listen to her pray. But I stayed.

"I know it's his fault I'm in this situation, so instead of asking for your help, I should ask you to punish him instead of me. If he lived an honorable life, none of this would be happening.

But I know he didn't mean for these things to happen. He would never want anything bad to happen to me. My father. Anna." She cried again and brought herself back to calm. "I know I don't show my feelings very well, never indicate how much I actually love him, respect him. I'm always saying stupid shit that really doesn't matter, but I really do think the world of him. He's going to be given a choice—to save me or save her. And I want you to save her. If Damien comes for me, I don't want that... I really don't want that."

She was quiet for a while as if she was finished, but the sound of her ongoing tears indicated she just needed time before she could go on. "Let me die instead of him. Let him find Anna and save her. Let them be happy together. I know my father will be devastated, so give him the strength he needs to carry on, to not suffer the way he suffers over my mom every day. I know I've done a lot of things I'm not proud of, all the drinking, partying, all the guys... I can't even count them all, so I hope you forgive me for everything. And I hope you let me go peacefully. Please protect my family. Please bless my family." She fell quiet as she continued to cry to herself. She had nothing left to say, but the pain of her suppressed sobs showed everything that was in her heart. "Thank you, God. Amen."

I stood halfway down the stairs with the tray in my hand. Motionless, I just stood there, thinking about everything she'd said, that she was so unbelievably selfless I could hardly believe it. I let out a deep sigh and closed my eyes. "Goddammit."

I PACED my living room as I called him.

He picked up on the first ring. "What happened?"

I wasn't the kind of man that lied. It didn't suit my self-interest because I simply had no reason to hide information from anyone. I was at the top of the food chain, having no enemies of consequence. But I lied now. "He hasn't called back."

He growled into the phone. "I want that fucker dead."

"I know. That's why I've come up with a better plan."

He remained quiet.

"Challenge him to a fight in the ring. We both know he has no chance."

Liam was still quiet, but when he didn't reject it right away, I knew he was interested. His beef with Damien was personal, intimate, and he wanted to destroy him with his bare hands. Whether Damien handed himself over or they met in the ring, the outcome would be exactly the same. "You think he'd go for it?"

"Absolutely." Damien was impulsive and stupid, and he would agree to this without thinking about the consequences. He would either believe he could actually win, or he wouldn't think that far and would do anything he could to get Anna back.

"I like that idea better. I can kill him in front of everyone...and Anna."

TWENTY-TWO

CATALINA

"Get up."

I stirred from my cot on the floor, my back aching from lying on the hard surface all night. Washing my hands had made me feel better, but now it'd been a few days since I'd showered and that was uncomfortable. I sat up and rubbed the sleep from my eyes and tried to make my vision cooperate.

"I said, get up." He came to the cage and stared down at me. Instead of holding a tray of food, he held handcuffs.

"What are you gonna do?" I leaned against the wall and watched the metal cuffs shift back and forth.

He tossed the cuffs on the ground. "Put these on."

"Why?"

His gaze darkened in irritation.

He was obviously going to move me from the cage, so it was probably in my best interest to comply. But I would never be able to get the restraints off because they were solid metal. My only chance was to run. I grabbed them from the floor and secured them in front of my body.

He unlocked the door. "Let's go."

I pushed my back against the wall as I rose to my feet without using my hands. "Are you gonna let me use the bathroom? Because this is still going to be hard."

He grabbed me by the arm and pulled me out of the cage. "No."

"No?" If he wasn't gonna let me use the restroom, then what was he going to do with me? Did he talk to Damien? Was he about to hand me over to my brother? Or did Damien say no, and now I was going to be executed?

Maybe this was the end.

Everyone died at some point, so I could be scared or brave. I chose to be brave. I went quiet and allowed him to guide me upstairs to the next level. It was an entryway that led to a much bigger staircase. There was a sitting room that seemed unused, and lots of paintings and sculptures.

Didn't seem like his style at all.

He guided me into another room that connected to his garage, and he put me in the passenger seat of his truck.

Maybe he was going to hand me over. Didn't make sense to execute me at another location, unless he'd already dug my grave and would shoot me once he threw me inside.

I felt anxiety and fear, but I forced myself to stay calm and not give in to my emotional response. Mind over matter. Courage over fear. Peace over despair.

The garage door opened, and he pulled out. He turned onto the street and drove away.

Not that it mattered, but I glanced at the street signs and

memorized the address. Just in case I managed to escape and wanted to know where I could find him again to finish the job. The fact that he let me see where we were and where we were going meant only one thing.

He was going to kill me.

As we drove down the street in silence, I tried to think of a way to survive. I could throw myself at him, make him lose control of the wheel, and put us in a bad crash. With any luck, the collision would kill him, and I could get out of there.

But it could also kill me.

Too risky. I'd have to wait until we reached our destination.

He made a few more turns then approached the building where my apartment was located. It was ironic, to pass the place where he'd originally grabbed me, the place I called home.

He drove right by it, but then he stopped. He pulled up to the curb and put the truck in park.

What the fuck was going on?

I turned to him, completely bewildered. Did he want me to go inside and grab a few things? Was he taking me somewhere else for a long time? Was there something in there that he wanted for himself? A keepsake of his victim?

He grabbed me by the wrist and pulled my cuffs closer to him. He dug out the key from his pocket, unlocked them, and then pulled the metal off my wrists. He left them on the seat between us and looked straight ahead.

Was this a test?

His deep voice shattered the silence. "You can go." I didn't look at him, watching the cars pass by until they disappeared in the distance.

"What?"

"I said you could go." He turned his gaze to me, his blue eyes devoid of any emotion.

"Why? I don't understand..."

"There's not much to understand. I said you can leave, so leave."

"Does that mean Damien took my place?" Did the thing I feared most come to pass? Was I going to lose my only brother? The man I looked up to? "I'd rather die than let anything happen to him." I pushed my wrists toward him. "Take me back. Please." I'd fought so hard to be free, was even willing to kill this guy for it, but now I asked for the exact opposite.

Without looking at my wrists, he pushed them away. "No. Damien isn't taking your place."

"Then why are you letting me go?"

He looked away. "Doesn't matter. Get the hell out of my truck and go home."

I looked toward my building and stared at the entryway before I turned back to him. "Is this a test? Are you going to come back for me later?"

"No test. No strings attached. And you'll never see me again... thank fucking god." He turned to look out the windshield, his arm resting along the windowsill. He was in a blue shirt and jeans, his tattoos stark against his fair skin. His short brown hair was unremarkable, and there was a shadow along his jawline that matched the darkness of his ink. I'd thought I understood this man, but now he was the biggest enigma I'd ever met.

"What's going to happen to Damien?"

He took a long time to respond. "Liam is dealing with him directly. That's all I'll say about that."

"So, you don't need me anymore?"

He nodded. "Yes."

God either answered my prayer, or I was just incredibly lucky. Or...he had something to do with it. I looked at my apartment again, but I didn't get out of the truck.

"You fought me the entire time, tried to kill me with a goddamn plunger, and now we are literally at your doorstep... and you just sit there."

"I just..." I turned back to him, staring at the side of his face. "I just don't understand why you're letting me go."

He leaned his head back against the headrest and sighed. "I just told you."

"No. I don't understand why *you* are letting me go."

After a few breaths, he turned back to me, his gaze dark and guarded. He probably hoped I wouldn't figure out he was the one who'd granted me freedom. It wasn't luck. It wasn't prayer. It was all him. "Good luck, Catalina."

Now that I knew this was real, that I really was free to go, I opened the door and got out. "My friends call me Cat..." This man could've been my executioner, but he'd decided to spare my life instead. I didn't think of him as an enemy anymore.

He was still as cold as ever to me. "I don't want to be your friend." He leaned forward and grabbed the door handle before he slammed it shut. He gave me one final look of irritation before he pulled away from the curb and headed down the street.

I watched him go before I turned around and looked at my apartment. I'd thought I would never see it again. I'd thought I would die in that cage, but that my death would give my brother life and happiness.

Instead, the Skull King gave me those things.

TWENTY-THREE

DAMIEN

I LOST MY FUCKING MIND.

My woman was being held hostage somewhere, and I didn't have a single lead, a single idea where she could be. What kind of man was I? How could I let this happen to her? I paced in my bedroom, needing to move constantly because sitting still made me feel worse.

Then I got a phone call...from the Skull King.

He'd refused to help me, to give me any clue, and he enjoyed making me suffer, enjoyed the taste of revenge. I almost didn't answer, but in the back of my mind, I knew I couldn't afford to reject any possibility. I answered. "Hope you've changed your mind."

"I'm the kind of man that never changes his mind."

"Then what the fuck do you want?"

He wasn't as argumentative as usual, as if he wanted to say as few words as possible. "Liam wants to challenge you."

I stopped pacing and went still. My breathing stopped altogether, but my body needed oxygen more than ever before. "Meaning?"

"Tonight. You and him. Fight to the death."

Liam had the upper hand because he was an experienced fighter, and he also had rage on his side because of everything I'd done to Annabella in bed. He was also familiar with the surroundings of the ring, with the shouts of the men in the stands. And the reason he only gave me twelve hours' notice was so I would have no time to prepare for the battle.

"One-time offer. Take it, or never see Anna again."

I wasn't stupid. I knew my odds of winning were slim, despite my knowledge of martial arts and my own experience street fighting. But I'd been searching for her for weeks and hadn't figured out a single detail. If this was my only chance, I was going to take it. Liam could disappear with Annabella and forget about me, but he was spiteful, vengeful, and angry.

He was willing to lose Annabella just to kill me.

I had to take advantage of that. "Yes."

"I figured you'd say that." He hung up.

HADES WATCHED me pace back and forth. "Are you sure you wanna do this?"

"Yes."

"I don't mean to doubt you, but Liam has the advantage. He has the size, experience, and training."

"I'm aware. But I don't have another choice. This is my one and only opportunity."

"But what kind of opportunity is it if you're likely to lose?"

I never did anything unless it was a sure thing, and this was definitely uncertain. I was quick on my feet, with strong reflexes, and I could anticipate things before they happened. But that might not be enough for a fight like this. "I'd rather die trying to get her back than give up altogether."

"You don't have to fight him. We'll find her."

"But how long will it take? What if it's a year? Two?"

He leaned back into the wooden chair and rubbed the back of his head. "If you're worried her feelings will change in that amount of time, don't. What you have is real. There's no way Anna would fall in love with a man who's committed these kinds of crimes."

"That's not what I'm worried about." I kept walking.

"Then what?"

I stopped and looked out the window. "She could get pregnant...have a kid."

"I was always under the impression that was unlikely."

"But not impossible." I turned to him. "If they have a kid, they would have what they've always wanted. She might not want to rip them apart. And even if she did, he would always be a problem. And as a father of her child, she would never let me kill him, then. That happens...it doesn't look good for us."

"This is all under the assumption she's sleeping with him."

I knew she wouldn't get into bed with him willingly. "She may not have that choice..." It hurt to say that out loud, to even think that way. It was why I had to do this, to put this to bed before it got worse. "I appreciate what you're saying, but I have to do this. You, of all people, should understand..."

He dropped his gaze. "Yeah...unfortunately."

Loud footsteps sounded outside the door before Catalina appeared. She stopped and stared at me, her eyes taking me in with a look I'd never seen on her face before. There was relief, love, so many other things. Then she ran to me and jumped into my arms.

I staggered back as I caught her, having no idea where this reaction had come from. I hadn't even told her Annabella was missing.

"I'm so happy to see you..."

I hugged her back but shot Hades a quizzical expression. "Everything okay, Cat?"

She kept her face buried in my chest and nodded, but she didn't release me or look me in the eye. She squeezed me like she never wanted to let go. "You're the best brother in the world. I'm sorry I never told you that before."

I cupped the back of her head and still didn't understand. "Did something happen?"

She pulled away and finally looked at me, her eyes filled with a hint of tears. She took a few deep breaths and touched my biceps and forearms, like she'd almost just lost me. She closed her eyes for a second. "I just had a bad dream...that I lost you."

I was touched by her affection, by the way she wore her heart on her sleeve for the first time. I always knew my sister loved me and I didn't need to hear her say it, but it was nice...once in a while. "Well, I'm fine. And I love you too." I kissed her on the forehead before I let her go.

"He's fine...for now." Hades sat in the chair with his chin propped on his knuckles.

Catalina stared at me, no longer comforted. "What's that supposed to mean?"

My initial annoyance with Hades faded away because this conversation was inevitable. I couldn't go down to the ring without telling her I might not come back. "This is going to be a lot to take in, just so you know."

"I know Anna is missing. And I know Liam took her." With her arms crossed over her chest, she stood in a white halter dress with a jean jacket.

I assumed Sofia had told her. "Well, a mutual friend just called me and invited me to fight Liam directly in the ring."

"Who is this mutual friend?" she asked. "The Skull King?"

I didn't realize she and Sofia talked that much. "Yes."

"Fight in the ring?" she asked. "What does that mean?"

"It means Liam and I will fight to the death. Winner gets Annabella." It was a lot of pressure on my shoulders, because if I lost, not only did I lose my life, but I lost my woman too. She would be a prisoner to him for the rest of her life. "I can't lose."

Catalina watched me as if she expected me to say something else, to elaborate on this insane plan. When I was quiet, she expressed her skepticism. "Fight to the death? That's barbaric. Are we in ancient times?"

"That's just how it is."

"Can you just show up and shoot him?" She turned to Hades, as if she expected him to agree with her. "Or I could shoot him. I have good aim."

"No," I answered. "That's dishonorable."

She rolled her eyes. "This whole thing is dishonorable. So, you're really going to do this?"

I expected her to be more difficult about it, to beg me to change my mind. She was oddly understanding of the whole thing, which was even weirder because she knew nothing about my world. "I don't have a choice."

She looked down at the floor for a few seconds before she lifted her gaze once again. "You have to win. Alright?"

"I know."

"He's never fought you before?"

I shook my head.

"Then you can catch him off guard. I kicked his ass in that restaurant because it took him so long to process what was happening. He's big and slow. Be unpredictable. Be fast. That's how you'll win."

Did my little sister just give me fight advice? "I appreciate your support in this. I figured you would beg me to walk away."

She shrugged and ran her fingers through her hair. "I know how much she means to you. I know you can't walk away and leave her."

"You're right. I can't."

"So, you need to win. You have to."

"I know."

TWENTY-FOUR

ANNABELLA

MY BRAIN WANTED TO DISASSOCIATE FROM REALITY because it was such a burden to think about Catalina locked away, to think about how worried Damien must be, to think about my own horrible fate.

It was too fucking much.

Tears were stained on my cheeks, and my eyes burned because they were completely dry. Every time I took a breath, my chest ached because I'd been hyperventilating on and off all day. He'd captured Catalina, my closest friend, and either she would die, or I would never be free.

I really wished Liam were dead.

Liam didn't knock before entering my bedroom.

I already hated him, but now my feelings were much more intense. The energy in the room was totally different, very much kidnapper and prisoner. Our past relationship no longer existed in my mind. He was just my tormentor now, the man ruining my life and the life of everyone else's I cared about.

He faced me in silence, waiting for me to look at him.

I refused. I sat on the bed with my knees to my chest, my gaze focused out the window.

Liam grew impatient and spoke. "I released Catalina."

I turned to him, my eyebrows raised. "You did?"

He nodded. "I released her yesterday."

"Why?" Did he have a change of heart? Did he realize his behavior would never get him what he wanted?

"Because I have a better idea."

Hope drained from my body again.

"I challenged Damien to a fight. Tonight. Winner takes all."

I didn't even process everything before I reacted. "What? Are you insane? We aren't animals, Liam. Why would he agree to that when you're the professional fighter?"

He shrugged. "Well, he did."

No. God, no. I crawled out of bed and got to my feet so I could face him. This was the closest I'd been to him, because I always stayed on the bed or kept an obstacle between us. "Please don't do this…"

"I'm not making him do anything."

"But you know it's not a fair fight. You know you'll win."

He smiled at my misfortune. "Yeah, I know."

"Please don't do this. Let's just move somewhere and start over. Forget about him."

He shook his head. "I've learned that neither one of us can live a full life while the other is still alive. He'll always come after me, always look for you, and as long as he's breathing, he'll remain in your heart. One of us needs to die, and it's not going to be me."

"Dead or alive, he'll always be the man in my heart. You don't become the winner by default. I'll never love you again. I'll never want to be with you again. Don't you see this is ludicrous? If you really kill him, I'll always hate you."

He stared into my eyes for a long time, as if he was searching for my sincerity.

"I mean it."

"Give it enough time. You'll change your mind."

My temper took over, and I shoved him in the chest. "Fuck you, Liam."

He faltered back into the wall because he hadn't expected me to hit him. He growled when his back hit the solid surface, closed his eyes as he gathered his patience. Then he turned back to me, his eyes filled with the same anger. "I'm going to kill him, Anna. That's it."

I was so angry, brand-new tears flooded my eyes and spilled down my cheeks. If only I were bigger, stronger, I'd figure out a way to kill him myself, to put an end to this madness. All our good memories were gone from my mind, all my affection dead in the ground. It was hard to believe I'd ever wanted a family with this man, that I'd ever vowed to love him forever. Now I wanted to murder him with my bare hands. "I hope he kills you first."

He came closer to me, bringing his face nearer to mine so he could whisper. "Just for that, I'm gonna make you watch."

IT'D BEEN a long time since I'd been here, to this underground room where the most brutal men fought to claim the lives of their opponents, to add another notch on their belts. It was a place where I once saw Liam betray me, agree to a fight to the death without even telling me about it.

I should've left him then.

A part of me was excited to see Damien, but there was another part that hoped he wouldn't show up, that he would realize his life wasn't worth the risk.

Liam kept me close to his side as he led me through the crowd. Just to make sure I wouldn't run away, he kept his other fighting cronies nearby, circling around me so I couldn't slip through the cracks and disappear. He obviously anticipated that Damien would try to extract me in some way, and he wasn't gonna let that happen.

Liam took me to the stands and put me in a chair. The other five men sat around me, giving me no avenue of escape. He pulled his shirt over his head and stood in his black running shorts. His physique was muscle on muscle, strength on top of strength, and he was so strong, he was like a wild animal. And in addition to that, he looked livid.

There was nothing he wanted more than to kill my lover.

A part of me wished I could have stayed at the house so I wouldn't have to watch this, but I also couldn't abandon Damien. If he won, I wanted to be with him as quickly as possible. I wanted to run into his arms and finally be with the man I loved.

But he had to win first.

I wasn't ignorant of the odds. Liam was a professional, a veteran, and, worst of all, undefeated. The odds weren't in Damien's favor.

The stands were packed with men who'd come to see the fight. Since this battle was the most anticipated, even though it had been posted on such short notice, Liam and Damien were going to fight first. My eyes looked across the room to the other side of the stands, where I knew Damien and Hades would be. My heart was racing with adrenaline, and my stomach was sick with unease. I just wanted this to be over.

And then I saw him.

He walked up the stairs and headed to the platform. Instead of wearing a suit or jeans and a shirt, he was in only a pair of shorts, dressed like the other fighters. His toned body was tanned and shiny because oil had already been rubbed across his skin. He had two distinct pectoral muscles, a tight waist with chiseled abs, and narrow hips. His body was the exact opposite of Liam's, toned and athletic rather than big and burly.

It'd been weeks since I'd seen him, and I forgot just how beautiful he was.

Hades was with him and also Catalina. I was surprised she'd made the trip, would approve of this barbaric match, support her brother, no matter what.

My breathing quickened the longer I stared at him, the longing overwhelming. I couldn't watch his man die; I just couldn't. He had to win.

Damien faced my direction, and it only took him a few moments to find me in the crowd. His gaze landed on mine, and he stared for several seconds, his face stoic but his eyes filled with layers of emotion, of longing, desire, and, most obvious of all, love.

Instinctively, my eyes watered.

He mouthed something to me. "I'll win. I promise."

When I inhaled a breath, it was painful to my lungs. There was nothing I wanted more than to go home with this man and for us to spend the rest of our lives together. Hearing a promise like that didn't make me feel better; it only made me more afraid.

Afraid to lose that dream.

The MC turned to Liam. "Ready?"

I faced Damien again and mouthed back, "This doesn't mean anything." I got out of my chair and walked up to Liam. I had to make sure he lost, make sure Damien would have the best chance possible. I grabbed Liam by the arm and tugged him toward me.

He looked down at me, hostile because he was pumped for the fight. He was focused, angry, ready to rip my lover to shreds.

That was exactly why I was going to do this. "I'm sorry about what I said earlier... I don't want you to die. I don't wanna watch you die."

His eyes were still guarded, impenetrable.

"Call the fight off. I don't want either one of you to die tonight...especially not you." I pressed my hands to his chest, right over his heart. "I'm sorry about what I said before. I was just mad, upset. I don't want you to go in there thinking I hate you, because I don't. I still love you..."

He began to soften.

It was working. I rose on my tiptoes and kissed him on the lips. It wasn't soft and smooth like it used to be. I felt like I was kissing the dirt in a rocky desert. It was disgusting, like kissing a cousin. It was hard to swallow my hatred and do something I despised, but I believed it would make a difference when he walked into the ring. I pulled away and lowered myself to my chair.

Now, his macho energy was gone, and he wanted to stay there with me. He was snapped out of his focus, no longer the angry animal that wanted to take another human life.

Good.

"Let's just go home. Let's call this off."

"You know I can't do that." He leaned down and kissed me again.

I had to suffer through it.

He gave me a firm hug before he turned away. "Wish me luck."

I took a deep breath and forced myself to say the words. "Good luck." And I watched him take the stairs and enter the ring. His shoulders weren't as tense, and his skin wasn't bright red because some of the rage was gone. His focus was disrupted now that he wasn't the bloodthirsty animal he'd been just moments ago.

I looked across the arena to where Damien stood.

His eyes were still locked on mine, and instead of being hurt by what he'd just watched, he understood exactly what I'd done. He gave a simple nod of appreciation.

Then he took the stairs and stepped into the ring.

TWENTY-FIVE

DAMIEN

I'D BE LYING IF I SAID I WASN'T WORRIED.

I stood in the ring, coated with oil, while the men in the stands cheered for us to begin the match. Liam was a large opponent, having more muscle density than I possessed, and coupled with the fact that he was undefeated, my odds weren't the best.

I could hold my own in a fight, but I'd never participated in a match like this. I always had other tools at my disposal—guns, knives, and different objects in any room I could turn on my opponent.

All I had now were my bare hands.

I saw the way Liam was worked up on the other side of stands. He threw his fists around to get his blood flowing, and the crazed look in his eyes showed how pumped he was. It hurt to watch Annabella touch him, kiss him, but I knew she might've just saved my life.

She said something significant to him, to think about his love for her rather than my death, I assumed. She'd successfully toned down his rage, and when he stepped into the ring, he wasn't behaving like an animal anymore.

I hadn't had much time to prepare for this, and I knew that was by design. I would have to focus on him, watch him, be quicker than him.

And then kill him.

Liam shook out his arms as he stared at me, waiting for the buzzer to go off so he could attack me. There would be no mercy from him. The second he got me on the floor, he would crush my skull with his fists or his feet.

Whenever I was in extreme circumstances like this, my heart-beat was suspiciously slow. Right now, it was calm. Maybe that was an asset, or maybe it was a flaw. It allowed me to be more pragmatic, not to give in to the spikes of adrenaline, anxiety, and all the other shit that dumped into my blood.

The buzzer blared, and the match began.

Just as I'd anticipated, Liam tried to run me down as quickly as possible, to get his hands on me so he could finish this match in record-breaking time, just so he could humiliate me further.

Since I knew it was coming, I dodged out of the way.

His momentum carried him forward, and he hit the side of the ring with the loud thud.

I came up behind him and slammed his face directly into the corner. I didn't linger because I knew I didn't have the time to stay, so I quickly jumped back before he spun around with his hand outstretched to grab me.

When he turned, his face was red and bruised, but he wasn't bleeding. He was still slightly confused since it had been a hard hit, but he was still too dangerous to overpower. He started to pace toward me, both of his hands tightened into fists.

I kept my fists close to my face and tuned out the noise around us. I got in sync with my opponent, studying him, watching him, trying to be him.

When he was close enough, he swung.

I ducked and slammed my fist into his stomach three times before I danced away.

He grunted when the air left his lungs, and he released a deep growl of pain. "Chickenshit, fight me."

Slow and steady wins the race.

I kept moving on my feet, knowing if I stayed put, it would just be a battle of strength, which I couldn't possibly win. I had to tire him out, make every hit count because I couldn't linger.

The fight went that way for a long time, bringing us together for short bursts that ended up with a few blows, before I bounced away again. It wasn't a traditional fight, much longer than the kind the men usually witnessed. I got a black eye, and Liam had a cut along his cheek.

"You know what I'm gonna do tonight after I kill you?" With his fists near his face like a boxer, he circled as he drew closer to me, looking for the right time to charge me. "I'm gonna take Anna to the courthouse, marry her, and then take her home and fuck her."

I resisted the urge to respond, told myself to stay focused and unemotional because losing my pragmatism could lead to dire mistakes, but it was a good trick because it pissed me off.

"I've enjoyed fucking her as my woman. But I want to fuck her as my wife."

The image made me sick to my stomach, to imagine Annabella sleeping with him, whether by choice or force. But I didn't allow him to make me drop my guard. I pretended I was about to sprint at him like he wanted, and he threw out his fist automatically to land several blows. But once his fists had been launched, I came at him and landed a series of hits, striking him in the temple, the face, pounding him in the stomach, and then I twisted him around so I could kick him in the back.

He tried to stop the fall, but he was too heavy. He landed hard against the concrete.

I didn't let the opportunity slip from my grasp, so I got on top of him and locked his neck in my arms. I squeezed his throat so he couldn't breathe as I started to turn his head to snap his neck.

The crowd was so loud, cheering because they were about to win their bets at unbelievable odds, while others booed because they were about to lose their money, having bet on the guy who wasn't supposed to lose.

Liam tried to get out of it, and the longer he didn't have air, the quicker his pulse thudded against my skin. He was strong, fighting with power, fighting for his life—which was about to be extinguished.

I'd thought I would feel good about what I was about to do, killing this guy. He didn't deserve to live. He didn't deserve to be spared after everything he'd done. But I didn't get pleasure out of my victory, out of taking his life.

And I knew why.

Annabella understood I had to do this. She wouldn't hold it against me; it had to be done.

But I knew she'd loved him for a long time, had been married to him, wanted a family with him. He needed to die, but it would still hurt her, still haunt her. So, I did something really stupid.

I pulled his neck tighter, so close to snapping his neck. "I'll make a deal with you."

He couldn't say anything because he couldn't breathe. All he could do was fight my twist, fight the pain in his neck before it turned into complete paralysis.

"I let you live, you disappear." Hades would be pissed that I'd offered this guy any mercy. Even my sister would think I was weak. I had no love for him, but I loved Annabella so fucking much that I would do this for her. "Do you accept those terms?" He might say yes but turn around and stab me in the back. He might say yes and change his mind later. I was willing to take that chance.

"Yes or no?"

He breathed hard to stay conscious.

"If you say yes, I don't wanna see you ever again. You can't contact Annabella again. You leave us in peace."

He tried to fight me again as if he might be able to get out of it.

But then I twisted him a little harder, making it clear he would lose. "You have to decide—do you want to live and lead a life without her? Or would you rather die?"

He stopped fighting. His body relaxed completely. Then he nodded.

I let him go and stood up.

The crowd was silent because they couldn't believe what had just happened. Death was the only way these matches ended, but a life had been spared rather than taken away. I walked away with my hands on my hips, regaining control of my breathing. I turned to look at Hades.

All he did was shake his head.

Liam slowly got to his feet, looking weak now that he'd been defeated. He turned to look at me, his face red because he hadn't had adequate oxygen for minutes. Living with everyone's disappointment was probably the worst part. He had been defeated by a man with no professional experience, a man who wasn't even in his weight class. He swallowed his shame and could barely look at me.

When I knew he wasn't going to pull a stunt, I turned to the MC. "This match is over."

ANNABELLA

I couldn't believe what had just happened.

Did that just happen?

Damien could've killed the man who had tortured us both... and he didn't.

I knew he'd done that for me, and I couldn't describe the way it made me feel. I knew he loved me to be able to do something like that, to spare the life of the man I used to love just because it would be hard for me to watch him die.

And he'd had my full blessing to kill him.

Liam took the stairs and returned to the platform where I was sitting. Some of his men came up to him and exchanged quiet words, either condolences or pity.

I got to my feet because I didn't know what to do. All I wanted to do was run across to the other side so I could be with Damien, but I felt like I had to speak to Liam first, to say goodbye.

Liam walked up to me with sadness in his eyes, either because he'd lost or because Damien was the bigger man...again. There was no doubt who I should be with; Damien was a better partner to have for a lifetime. Liam had to see it by now.

In silence, he stared, at a loss for words. "Did you mean anything you said before?"

I actually felt bad for lying to him. Instead of answering with words, all I could do was shake my head.

He didn't seem disappointed, as if he expected it.

"I'm sorry..."

He glanced at his surroundings for a few seconds before he looked at me again. "Deal's a deal. I'll leave you alone."

Had this been the solution the entire time? To gain Liam's respect on his own turf? Maybe fighting was the only language he could understand. Maybe it was the only way for him to feel like Damien deserved me more. "Glad he didn't kill you."

He shook his head slightly. "It's gonna be hard for me to bounce back from the humiliation. And also from that mercy."

"He didn't do it to be merciful. He did it for me."

He stared down at me with his blue eyes. "Yeah..."

I didn't know what else to say. We should have parted ways a long time ago. This heartbreak would have been spared if we'd let the relationship die out a long time ago. I never should've gone back to him in the first place. All of this could've been avoided. It was time for a goodbye—long overdue.

"I know this isn't going to be much, but I am sorry about everything."

I was speechless as he apologized.

"Not just about my infidelity, but losing my temper, trying to kill the man you want to be with, kidnapping you... All that shit. I just love you so much, and I don't know how to handle these feelings. That's no justification for what I did, but I'm sorry, nonetheless. It was just love that drove me to madness."

He didn't deserve my forgiveness, but I wanted to give it to him anyway. "I'm willing to forgive you if this is really the end. If you aren't going to show up and try to take me again. If you aren't going to try to kill Damien when he drops his guard. I'm willing to start over and give you a clean slate if this is genuine."

He sighed loudly. "Surprised you're willing to forgive me at all..."

"Love triumphs over hate. I'm not in love with you anymore, but I will always love you."

Guilt moved into his gaze. "I'll always love you too. I wish we could have more, but I know what I did was wrong."

"I hope you learn from those mistakes and can be better for the next person. Because you're a handsome man with a lot to offer. You could have any woman you want."

"You know you're the only woman I've ever loved. The others...they're just physical. I'm not sure I'll ever feel this way about someone again."

I'd thought the same thing until I'd walked into Damien's office. "You will...someday."

Damien reached our side of the stands, and when he came close to us, he was wearing a t-shirt with his shorts. His eyes moved back and forth as he watched our conversation. Instead of pushing his way through and grabbing me, he let us finish.

I glanced at him and turned back to Liam.

Liam noticed he was there. He sighed quietly to himself and looked at me one final time. "Take care, Anna."

His goodbye was so heartfelt and genuine, it almost made me want to cry. It was peaceful, just a little painful, exactly what it should've been a long time ago. "You too..."

Before Liam departed, he turned to Damien and stared at him for a while, gathering his thoughts as he looked at his former opponent. Liam wasn't the kind of man to lose, and accepting this defeat was probably harder than anyone could understand. But instead of lashing out, he extended his right hand.

Damien clearly hadn't expected that because he was slightly taken aback. It took him a few seconds to reciprocate, the place his palm in Liam's and give it a firm shake.

Liam pulled away and walked off.

Damien watched him go before he turned to me. I waited patiently for his demeanor to change, for him to look at me as the love of his life rather than as a trophy. He started to soften, started to turn into the man I knew. He released a painful sigh of relief as he came closer to me, his eyes growing more emotional the nearer he got. When he was in front of me, his hand slid into my hair, and he pulled my face to his to give me a soft kiss.

My arms wrapped around his neck, and I breathed a deep breath, blocking out the noise of the buzzer as the next fight began, the sounds of cheers and boos as men forgot about the fight that had just taken place. We'd been separated for weeks, and knowing this was finally the beginning of a real relationship was so beautiful. I breathed against his lips and felt my eyes water because I knew this was exactly where I was supposed to be, with the person I was supposed to be with.

I looked into his eyes and saw the expression that I was sure matched mine, so deep and so full of love that I felt safe. Damien would never hurt me, never betray me, and he would be everything I deserved. It'd been weeks since we'd talked, seen each other in the flesh, but no conversation was forthcoming. He only said one thing. "Let's go home."

RETURNING to his home felt so strange. I'd honestly feared I would never come back.

It'd only been a few weeks since the last time I was there, but it felt like forever, and the place also felt exactly the same. I moved to the couch and thought about everything that had happened. It was a lot to process.

Damien sat beside me and stared at my features as if he never wanted to stop, as if he wanted to look at me every day for the rest of his life. His fingers lightly caressed my hair, and he held me close like nothing else mattered.

I gently touched his discolored eyes, which were swollen and bruised. He had a few other injuries, but nothing serious. "Will you be okay?"

He grabbed my wrist and pulled my fingers away from his face. "I've been through worse. And it was totally worth it."

It was the first time I'd smiled in so long.

"Are you okay? That's what I'm more concerned about."

"What do you mean? I'm sitting here with you. I've never been happier..."

He squeezed my fingers. "I know." He locked our fingers together. "I'm just scared...of whatever you had to go through while you were there."

Now, I understood exactly what he feared. Liam had said things to him in the ring, but I couldn't make them out, probably things to get under Damien's skin. "I was upset Liam held me against my will, so I was in my bedroom the whole time. I refused to come out. He tried to talk to me. I wasn't interested. He brought me meals. That was it."

"He didn't..." He couldn't bring himself to finish the question.

"No. I was afraid that might happen too...but it didn't. Liam had more honor than I expected."

He closed his eyes and breathed a sigh of relief. "Thank god."

I hadn't thanked Damien for what he'd done, hadn't acknowledged it at all. It was so selfless, I didn't know where to begin. "You could've killed him...why didn't you?"

"Annabella, you know why."

"I would've understood. I even told him to his face I wanted him dead."

"But I knew it would haunt you down the road. And I gave him the power to make the decision. If I spared his life, he would leave us alone. He accepted. I took a leap of faith and trusted him to mean that. I hope that wasn't a mistake."

I didn't want to reveal the details of my final conversation with Liam because it was personal. It was a goodbye, bittersweet and painful. But I could tell Damien this. "It wasn't a mistake."

He caressed my knuckles with this and gave a slight nod, but didn't ask me to be more specific. "Now what?"

"Don't we live happily ever after?"

He gave a slight smile. "Is that what you want?"

I nodded. "My feelings haven't changed. Won't ever change. This is where I want to be...for the rest of my life."

❄

DAMIEN and I didn't leave the house for a long time.

We were in bed together for most of it, cuddling even if we weren't doing anything more serious. I loved to feel his hard body, smell his cologne, and just be with the person who made it so easy to breathe.

Everything felt like a bad dream, as if it never happened in the first place. Our lives had been like this without pause, gourmet dinners over candlelight, and passionate lovemaking like there had never been anyone else for either of us.

I never wanted it to end.

There was no one trying to keep us apart. We could go out to dinner whenever we wanted, but we never did. His bed was my bed. Half of the bathroom was filled with my stuff. My clothes were in his closet.

It was nice.

Now that there was no danger, I'd have to return to my apartment sometime, to live alone again so we could have a normal relationship. We'd never really dated, never really had time to get to know each other traditionally. Most of the time I'd known him, I'd been married to somebody else.

I kissed his shoulder then his chest, happy that the bruises had finally started to fade. His eyes weren't so dark anymore, almost normal. I kissed him again because I was so happy he was there. So happy he was in my life. I pulled away and dragged my fingers across his perfect body. "This has been the best week of my life."

His fingers glided into my hair, and he gave me that sexy look with his dark eyes, like he was happy without really showing it. His jawline was covered in hair because he hadn't shaved the entire week. If he allowed it to grow any longer, it would turn into a beard. "Me too."

"I want to stay here forever, but I should get back to my apartment. I haven't been there in...a long time." I knew he was happy to have me back, but I didn't want to overstay my welcome. I wanted us to continue to be happy, but we had lives to return to. Damien hadn't worked much, and I still hadn't gone back to the hotel.

His expression slowly deflated, like he didn't like being reminded of reality.

We'd been making love all day and night, and I had to remind myself that it wouldn't end just because I was returning to my apartment. We could still do those things, but at a normal pace. I kissed his stomach then got out of bed. I grabbed my clothes and started to get dressed.

He stayed in bed and watched me, moving his arm behind his head. Glorious and beautiful, his perfect body lay on top of the bed, so lean and toned.

I fixed my hair with my hands then came to his side of the bed. "Can you give me a ride?"

Without moving, he continued to stare.

I didn't know what I'd said to change his mood, but he was definitely different, far more different than he'd ever been before. He was a closed book, so I couldn't read his pages.

He sat up and stared at me. "Do you want to live in your apartment?"

I sat beside him, gently rubbing my arm. "That's my home..." I'd been bouncing around this last year, going from my husband's house to my own apartment, back to his place, and then to Damien's... I'd never been steady.

He dropped his gaze for a moment, rubbing his palms together.

"I thought this was your home." He lifted his gaze and looked at me, this time visibly disappointed.

I didn't know what I'd said to offend him. "*You* are home, Damien. But my apartment is where I live..."

"Why don't you live here?"

The puzzle pieces started to come together. "Are you asking me...?"

"No," he said coldly. "I'm telling you. I just assumed you'd move in. Doesn't make sense for you to go back to your apartment and live alone. I don't want you on your own, and I don't want to be in this bed alone. I've lived without you for so long." He shook his head and pressed his lips tightly together. "I don't want to do it anymore."

My heart was touched. "I want to stay with you too. But...do you think that's too soon? We've never really had the chance to date. We've never really...been together. Now we have a chance, the chance that was taken from us."

He continued to rub his hands together as he carefully phrased his response. "We can take things slow, but what's the point? We aren't strangers. We've been through something together, and we can't erase that. I don't want to start over. I don't want to see each other for a year before we take the next step. I don't want to follow some fictional guideline. I want you to live here with me. And I don't want you to leave."

"Really?"

He nodded. "I probably shouldn't say this, but I'd ask you to marry me if I thought you would say yes." He looked me straight in the eye, showing no hesitation or embarrassment, putting all his cards on the table without fear of losing the game.

I inhaled a deep breath.

"But I know that's too soon, not because it's too soon for us, but after everything you've been through...it's best to wait. So, if you wanna live with me...the offer's on the table."

My answer was quick. "Of course, I want to live with you, Damien. I want to sleep with you beside me every night. I want to wake up next to you every morning. I want to be with you as much as I can. But there's something we've never talked about..."

"What?"

"A long time ago, you said you didn't want to be with me because of your dangerous career. You didn't want me to get hurt, to get caught up in that. Have your feelings about that changed?" I'd never asked because I didn't want to give him a reason to leave, to doubt that this relationship could work.

He couldn't look me in the eye anymore, and he turned away. It was a question that would require a deep and complicated answer. After a long time, he responded. "I left you to protect you, and it didn't make a difference anyway. I don't want to leave my businesses because I enjoy them, but I suspect my retirement will be inevitable...someday. When we have children, that's when I'll hang up my coat."

"Damien, I've never asked you to give anything up. I'm just asking how you feel about it."

He was quiet again, considering his response. "I'm not ready to walk away right now. I have unfinished business. But I've learned from Hades, and at some point, it'll have to be over. When we start a family in a few years, that's when I'll leave. Gives me time to get things in order." He rested his forearms on his thighs and looked straight ahead. "I'll do everything I can to protect you, but I can't promise to always keep you safe. I can't promise that enemies won't try to use you against me.

There's one person in particular that I have to eliminate because he's never going to disappear. I can't sugarcoat that."

"Who?"

He turned back to me. "The Skull King."

"Why?"

"He was Liam's accomplice. He's been trying to ruin my life since I refused to pay him. A year ago, he would've killed my father if I hadn't stopped it. I have to kill him...at some point."

Staying with Damien would be dangerous, but I still didn't want to live any other way. "I'm okay with that."

"Another reason why you should live with me. I can take you to work in the morning and pick you up later. And when you're in my home, no one will get to you. It's the safest option, but I'm using it as an excuse, more than anything else." He watched me for a long time, his green eyes appreciating me with his deep gaze. He was a man who wasn't afraid to show how much he loved me, how much I meant to him.

"Then let's go to my apartment and get the rest of my things."

He seemed a little stunned by my response, surprised that I would give up everything and risk it all to be with him. He'd just told me he still had a battle to fight and I could even be a casualty, but I still wanted to be with him...forever. "Let's go."

TWENTY-SEVEN

DAMIEN

She opened the last box and gathered the clothes still hung up on hangers. She lifted them and carried them into the closet, taking the entire left wall, the place where I used to hang my t-shirts and jeans.

Now it was hers.

The box was empty, and she placed it in the corner so Patricia could recycle it later. "That's it. That's all my stuff."

I came up behind her and wrapped my arms around her shoulders. "Looks good in here."

Her hands grabbed my forearms. "I think so too." She slowly turned around and came face-to-face with me, deep affection in her eyes. "No going back now. You have a roommate."

"A hot roommate."

She grinned.

"Who's really good at sex."

Her cheeks started to blush.

"And even better at sucking my dick."

Now she slapped me with her hands. "Oh my god, shut up."

I wrapped my arms around her again and hugged her. "Come on, it's a compliment."

"I hope there are other reasons you like living with me."

I shrugged. "You have a nice body?"

She pushed me off again.

"Baby, I'm kidding." I pulled her back to me and buried my face in her hair, kissing her neck and the shell of her ear. "I want to live with you because you're the woman I'm madly in love with. You're my best friend." I turned her around and pressed my nose against hers. "Is that better?"

Her eyes looked like melted butter, so her answer was obvious. She grabbed the front of my t-shirt and pulled me close so she could kiss me, a deep and sultry embrace that showed how much she wanted me. She hated it when I teased her, but then she was all over me a couple seconds later.

I walked her backward out of the closet into our bedroom while getting her jeans undone. We'd packed up everything from her old apartment and brought it here. A lot of her extra things were in a guest bedroom because we don't know where to put them just yet. But I didn't tell her to throw anything away, because her stuff was my stuff. I pushed her jeans over her ass then got her panties off too. My hands gripped both of her cheeks, like I was squeezing a juicy nectarine. Then I got her top off, her bra falling to the floor along with the rest of her clothes.

When she was naked, she practically ripped my clothes off. She always wanted to me, anytime, any part of the day, even in the middle of the night, and she did everything with such urgency that it was sexy. She threw my clothes on the floor with hers and backed up onto the bed.

With her ass hanging over the edge, she grabbed my thighs and pulled me close to her.

My hands moved underneath her knees, and I positioned her beneath me, loving this angle of her tits. I grabbed her hips and pulled her down to me so I could slide inside her smoothly.

She moaned like she'd never taken such a good dick. Her head rolled back, and she dug her nails into my skin as her back arched. She released another moan, a louder one, and I hadn't even moved yet.

"Best roommate ever." I leaned over her and looked down to see a slightly amused expression in her gaze. She tried to suppress a smile, but it was obvious I got under her skin.

Her hands went to my chest, and she started to rock her hips against me, taking my dick over and over. "Make love to me, Damien."

My hips started to move automatically, and I lowered myself until my face was close to hers. I didn't kiss her, but I breathed with her, moved with her. My hand gripped the back of her neck and held her in place so I could rock into her easier. "Yes."

She looked into my eyes while barely blinking, connecting her soul to mine as well as her body. She wore her heart on her sleeve, showed me how much she loved me every time she made love to me. It wasn't just her enthusiasm, but the brightness in her eyes, the way her nails dug deep into my skin. "I love you."

I rocked into her harder because those words invigorated me, made me fall deeper into this woman. "I love you too..."

ANNABELLA HAD LIVED with me for two weeks, and

those two weeks had given me more joy than any other time of my life. The gypsy had never said Annabella was my soulmate, but maybe she was. Maybe the gypsy simply didn't mention it. Because I couldn't imagine ever loving anyone the way I loved her.

Liam never showed his face again, and I actually believed he would keep his word. He owed me his life. I easily could've killed him and not felt any guilt about it. The least he could do was bow out permanently.

Annabella and I had a long conversation before she moved in—about my professional ambitions and how they would affect her. I wanted to forget about my beef with the Skull King and just be happy.

But he was part of everything. He'd helped Liam get Annabella out of the hospital room. Helped him break in to my home. He was an accomplice, and in my eyes, he was just as responsible for what I could've lost. Not to mention, he would've killed my father if I hadn't stopped him.

I wouldn't let that go.

That would be like asking Hades to forget about Maddox, to forget what that man did to the woman he loved.

The Skull King had been my enemy since the beginning, and no amount of rational conversation could change his attitude. He would continue to pursue revenge until I was dead or I wished I were dead.

I had to kill him.

It was eleven at night when I got out of bed, and I tried not to wake Annabella. I put on my jeans and t-shirt and prepared to walk out the door.

But she seemed to know anytime I left the bed, even if it was just to go to the bathroom for a piss. She sat up in bed, her hair pulled over one shoulder. With squinting eyes, she asked, "Where are you going?"

"Work." I came back to the bed and kissed her forehead. "I'll be home in a few hours."

She was always devastated when I left, but she never pestered me to stay, never complained about my profession. "Be safe." She kissed me goodbye.

"I will." I kissed her forehead again. "Love you."

"Love you too."

I left her behind and headed to the lab. I knew exactly who would stop by my office, and when I walked inside, I realized he'd beaten me to the punch. He sat in the black chair in front of my desk, slicing an apple with a pocketknife.

"Who let you in?" I always locked the door.

He held up the knife. "This did." He sliced into the apple, the noise loud and full of crunch. "Want a slice?"

I ignored him and opened the safe to start packing his money. I stuffed the cash into the duffel bag and threw it at his feet. "Get the fuck out."

He took a long bite of his apple, chewing loudly just to be obnoxious. "Did you know apples have a significant portion of your daily value of vitamin C? You know what they say...an apple a day keeps the doctor away."

"I'm gonna shove that apple up your ass if you don't get the fuck out of here."

He rose to his feet and tossed the slices on my desk. "That's an odd way to treat your business partner."

"That's what you think you are? A business partner?"

"Unless you think of us as friends?" He topped off the insult with a smile.

It was hard for me to look at him, to keep up this goddamn charade. If I'd had a plan, I'd kill him right then and there. "Enjoy your money while you can. It's going to run out soon."

"Business not doing well?"

"My business with you isn't."

He grabbed the bag of money and hoisted it over his shoulder. "Yeah, I thought you might be upset with me."

I was tired of the sarcastic jokes, tired of this restrained diplomacy. "I'm gonna kill you."

With no reaction at all, he stared at me blankly, as if his face was the surface of a wall. He was unintimidated, practically looking bored. "Be careful, Damien."

"I could've lost her because of you. I have no reason to be careful."

"It worked out in the end. I suggest you let it go."

"Like you did?" I asked sarcastically. "You won't stop until your pettiness is fulfilled. And now, I won't stop until my vengeance is satisfied. Gravy train is about to stop. I don't care what it takes. I will hurt you for what you've done to my family."

He stood rigid in front of my desk, staring at me without blinking. He was a big guy with a lot of tattoos, and he was the most difficult person to read. He had unlimited resources and an endless scowl. It seemed like he might say something, but he never did.

"Leave."

He turned toward the door. "Don't make me kill you, Damien. I don't want that, and neither do you."

"No, I don't," I said. "But I do want to kill you. And I will."

I SAT with Hades and told him everything that had happened with Heath.

"You'll take care of him, Damien. Eventually."

I rubbed the back of my neck, so frustrated my skin burned. "I want to take care of him now."

"Be patient. You've got to do this right."

"Easier said than done..."

"You have something else to focus on right now." Despite the late hour, he'd admitted me into his home, both of us drinking coffee instead of booze. "You have Anna now. Be happy. Don't spend your time thinking about Heath."

"I know. But he's gonna keep collecting his money until he kills me...or I kill him."

"You know I'm here if you need help."

I wouldn't bring him into this.

He watched the fire for a while before he turned back to me. "Look at us, drinking coffee like a bunch of pussies."

I chuckled slightly. "Yeah. We used to spend our time at the bars and whorehouses. Now...we spend our time with our women."

"I guess we've grown up."

"And accepted our curses."

He was quiet for a while. "After we left that purple tent, I thought we were cursed. But now, I think we were blessed... both of us." He raised his mug in a toast. "To Sofia and Anna... our better halves."

We were two grown men who had settled down. But instead of being bitter about it, we were happy...really happy. I grabbed my mug and tapped it against his. "And to us, too. Been friends for over a decade now."

He smiled. "And we'll be friends forever."

ALSO BY PENELOPE SKY

Order Now

Printed in Great Britain
by Amazon